HONOR

Blackstone Series

J.L. Drake

HONOR

Limitless Publishing, LLC
Kailua, HI 96734
www.limitlesspublishing.com

Formatting: Limitless Publishing

ISBN-13: 978-1-64034-761-8
ISBN-10: 1-64034-761-5

DEDICATION

Dedicated to my street team, "The Blackstone Girls," who have fallen in love with Mark and have stood patiently by my side while I hibernated in my cave to finish his story. I thank you.

CAST OF CHARACTERS

Savannah: Held in Tijuana, Mexico for seven months. Saved by Blackstone, fell in love with Cole Logan. Now lives at Shadows.

Cole: Owner of the safe house in Montana called Shadows. Fell in love with a picture of a victim. Found, saved, and married her. Leader of the Blackstone special ops team.

Olivia: Savannah and Cole's daughter.

Mark: Best friend to Cole Logan, Blackstone member. Uses humor to escape the pain from his past.

Keith: Newest member of Blackstone. Savannah's "big brother."

Paul: Blackstone member.

John: Blackstone member.

Abigail: Mark's adopted mother, Cole's childhood nanny, and now house aide. Dating the house doctor.

Doctor Roberts: House doctor, kind soul, and in love with Abigail.

June: Abigail's younger sister.

Mike: Agent at Shadows. Scary-looking teddy bear, covered head to toe in tattoos.

Dell: Agent at Shadows.

Davie: Agent at Shadows.

Molly: Nurse at North Dakota Hospital. Signed NDA to work with the Blackstone men when they come in.

Mia: Nurse at North Dakota Hospital.

Scoot: Moody house cat. Has no shame.

PROLOGUE

Mark Lopez, 7 Years Old

Her body lay sprawled in the usual spot, sunk into the dirty yellow couch that smelled of pee. Her dress was covered in vomit, and her breaths were shallow. Most kids would have been scared to see their mother like that, but not me. I really preferred it this way; I couldn't hear her scream, couldn't feel her hateful stare, and most of all, I couldn't feel her fists when they landed on my slight, bony frame.

My belly hurt, though. It always did. We didn't bother to go into the kitchen in the mornings. There was no point, as Mom never got up before twelve. The truth was the world would be better without her in it. I stuck two fingers into the side pocket of my book bag, pulled out a small piece of Hubba Bubba, and popped it in my mouth, hoping I could trick my belly into thinking it was full.

This was the sad, sick, twisted reality of my childhood...my life.

I took one last look at her and closed the door

behind me. At least I had about five hours of peace before being subjected to my mother's usual hangover.

CHAPTER ONE

Location: Mexico
Coordinates: Classified

Mark

I ran as fast as I could. The bullets were getting closer, one whipping by my head. My feet pounded the dirt, making a small dust trail that gave up my location. I dove into a gully where I hastily reloaded and moved myself into a better position. The sun was blinding. I pulled out a tube of paint and ran a smudge under each of my eyes to relieve the glare.

"Raven One to Raven Two, what is your location?" Cole's voice commanded over the radio.

I pushed the tiny button on my neck. "Raven Two to Raven One, northwest, three yards from the barn."

"Copy that, Raven Two. Fox One is heading to you. Cover him."

"Copy that, Raven One, cover Fox One."

I scanned the horizon then clicked my radio to let

Paul know all was clear. Paul popped up seemingly out of nowhere and ran low across the field, weapon held to his eye in case of a threat.

Then I saw it—the flash from the barrel of a gun. I knew from its location it was not a Blackstone member. It was one of them. I licked my lips and pulled the trigger, spraying bullets in the direction of the flash. The man's body plowed backward then fell out of sight.

Paul dove to the ground, tucking into a ball as he rolled to my feet and smiled his thanks up at me.

"Nice. Raven Two, move to next location," Cole instructed.

"10-4, Raven One." I nodded for Paul to go first.

Paul checked his gun before he jumped up and ran the rest of the way to the barn. Once John sent a click over the radio indicating all was safe, I took a quick look around, then moved into position and started to run.

My mind cleared. Nothing mattered when you were in this situation. Live, or die tryin'.

I knew the moment it hit. Sadly, no amount of gear would stop these bullets. On the street, they're called "cop killers." They pierce through any armor, including the type I wore. I felt the bullet as it tore into my flesh, landing right around my kidney. It burrowed deep and lodged into the muscle.

There was nothing I could do but try to turn off the pain and run for cover. I heard Cole's gun fire in the direction of the shooter.

The buzz over the radio didn't register in my brain. I was almost there, but nowhere close to where the chopper was. *Run, just run.*

4

Paul was waiting, and he grabbed me when I got close enough. Cole must have told him what happened.

"Where you hit?" Paul helped me to the ground, rolling me onto my side. "Shit!"

I took a painful gasp of air. "Not what I want to hear, man."

A tiny smile broke over Paul's lips. "Well, then, don't get shot."

"I'll keep that in mind," I huffed.

Paul started to pull supplies out of his vest. "This is going to tickle."

"Fuck off." I laughed then grunted as he poured powder over the open wound. Paul started to tape my back, all the while muttering about what a pussy I was. He helped me to my feet, as we wasted enough time as it was.

"Can you run?"

"Yeah, man, it's just a scratch." Sweat pooled into my gear as we moved to the back of the barn. We exited and ran as fast as we could to the tree line.

Every step, every breath, every blink became an effort. My eyes watered with the deep burn that traveled up my spine. I vomited mid-stride but kept moving, though it caused me to slow my pace. Paul glanced back then nodded behind me. A moment later, I realized why. Keith grabbed my vest and hauled me along with him until we were deep enough into the forest that we could stop.

I dropped to my knees, unable to stand. I could normally block out pain, but this was too much. Something wasn't right.

"Stay with me, brother," Cole said.

Images flashed in front of me as I stared up at the darkening sky.

This is not good. Shit, where am I? One moment I'm in Tijuana the next I'm a kid crouching under the kitchen table.

"Mark!" His voice sent a chill to my fingertips. "Mark!" Cole slapped my cheek as he brought me back. His face said a lot; I was in trouble.

"He's here," I whispered, confused as to where I was.

Cole didn't have to ask. He could read my tone. "No," he shook his head, "no, he's not. Stay with me, brother."

"He is. I can hear him." My grip tightened on his arm. "Cole."

Cole lowered his head and whispered as I closed my eyes and gave in to the relief of letting go of the pain.

***

Mia

"Come on, Mia." Dr. Evans handed me a coffee as I filled out a patient's chart.

I didn't bother to look up. His puppy dog eyes wouldn't work on me. "Like I told you last week, yesterday, and today, I do not have time to date."

"You work, you go home, and you work, Mia." He sighed. "At some point, you're going to wake up and see you've wasted your life here in this hospital doing…what?"

My pen stopped mid-stroke, and I glanced up. "Saving lives."

"You're a nurse, not a doctor. Though you're smart enough to be one." Dr. Evans slid the chart out from under my hands and sat in its spot.

"Pardon me?" The nerve of this ass! I felt the vein on my neck twitch.

He waved off my anger. "Look, all I'm saying is have some fun. When was the last time you were out?"

I folded my arms to resist the urge to throw a punch and break his nose. "Last night, at the Thirsty Duck."

"I mean a date. I mean—"

The doors burst open, and in ran Truck 59 paramedics pushing a gurney with a gunshot victim. Three firemen followed, with two men who looked like they just came from a war.

"I need help here," Wyatt, the paramedic, shouted. When he saw me, he started in on a detailed report. "Male, age thirty, gunshot wound to the lower back."

I glanced around and wondered where he came from. Where were the police? They were normally here when there had been a shooting. Then I saw his dog tags as Molly, the other nurse, shifted the man onto his side. I reached for the tags and saw he was Special Forces. Major Mark Lopez.

Molly had mentioned a special unit of the Army came through here, if needed, before they headed to their safe house. I looked at her, and she nodded as if I had asked her, then she shook her head, reminding me not to ask any questions.

"All right," I said after a good look at his wound. "Bed four is open." I pointed then glanced at the other men, who were against the wall, out of the way.

I headed over, but took my time and tried to find the right words. These men looked like they'd been through hell and back already today.

One large man stepped forward and extended a hand. "Nurse?"

"Harper, Mia Harper." I returned the shake.

"Colonel Logan." He cleared his throat. "The shot happened over three hours ago. We got ambushed, and Lopez took one in the back. He didn't think it hit his kidney, but he mentioned his spine was burning. We packed it as best we could, but he lost a lot of blood."

"All right." The other man took a step toward me. His nametag said Agent Keith. "He'll be heading directly to the OR. I'll be in there with your Major Lopez, Colonel, and I'll give you an update as soon as I can."

"Thanks, Mia," Logan said with a sigh then he pulled out a cell phone and made a call.

"You're new?" Agent Keith drew my attention to him.

"I am," I confirmed. "I'll take good care of your friend. Join together, retire together, right?" Logan turned to look at me, as Agent Keith narrowed his gaze. I knew only a select few knew their unit's motto. I turned on my heel and hoped it would give them some comfort.

***

The door flew open, and I gulped a breath of fresh air. A laundry basket held my weight as I took a moment to gather myself. Good Lord, I'd never had a patient wake up like that during surgery.

"Mia, the sponge, please," Dr. Evans asked with a little gleam in his eye. "So, have you thought any more about what I asked?" The room was full of nurses concentrating on their jobs, but I knew they were listening to our conversation.

I shook my head and checked the patient's oxygen levels. Molly's eyes were little slits, and I knew she found the doctor's persistence funny. "No, Dr. Evans, I have been busy dealing with a gunshot victim."

"He's stable, he's got one of the best teams around him, so—"

The patient's hand shot forward and his fingers snapped around my wrist. I looked down and found his dark brown eyes latched solidly onto mine.

"Hi, there, Mark." My voice remained calm as I reached over and held onto his hand tightly. His body suddenly registered pain, and his neck muscles strained. "You're a fighter, big fella, that's for sure. Most people are out cold with this stuff." I smiled and glanced up at Molly, who was ready to give him another dose. Mark tried to speak, but the tube down his throat made him gag. "I know." I pulled a stool over so I could sit. "We're almost done, but Molly is going to put you back under so you don't hurt." He shook his head. I couldn't help it, and I brushed my hand through his messy hair. I had never been intimate with a patient before, but he

was such a big man and was so vulnerable. There was something about the situation that drew out my protective instincts.

His eyes softened, then closed, but not before he gave me a slight nod. "I'll be here the whole time," I whispered, looking over at Molly as she started to feed the medicine into the line. In a matter of seconds he was back out. His grip loosened, but I didn't pull away immediately, not until I was sure he was completely relaxed.

"Jesus," I huffed and let my shoulders sag. Dr. Evans had a strange look on his face.

Molly broke the silence. "Yikes. That was a tad scary."

After a few deep breaths, I pushed Mark's look out of my head and then stood. Letting go of the laundry basket, I moved on to complete my rounds.

After a hot shower and a clean set of scrubs, I removed a book from my bag and headed to the ER and sat in the corner. I enjoyed watching people as they came in. You could always tell who was really hurt and who wasn't. I rated them from one to ten. It was a good skill to have working in this field.

"Mia?" Molly handed me a coffee and took a seat next to me. "How *are* you?"

I shrugged and ran a finger through the hot steam above my cup. "Fine, I guess."

"You want to talk about anything?"

I nodded when I realized she was thinking about it too. "I've seen worse, Molly. The gunshot was nothing."

"I didn't mean that. I meant you did well when

he woke up. You were able to calm him. Mark's a big guy. I'm surprised he didn't take you out and run for the door."

"Hmm..." I thought for a moment. "So, does Blackstone come here often?"

"Blackstone?" Molly's face twisted. "How do you know their name?"

"I overheard Logan speaking."

"Oh." I could tell she didn't really believe me, but she let it go. "I once had such a crush on Logan, but he's married with a child. Shame." She laughed as she sipped her coffee. "Then there's Mark. Lord, that man sends sparks directly to my well." She gave a wink.

I leaned my head back and cracked up. Molly had a point.

"So," she settled into the chair next to me, "care to share something about yourself? You've been working here for two months, and I don't even know where you're from or where you worked last."

"Ah, let's see." I dug up something in a hurry that I could share from one side of the real story. The other was better left untold. "I was born and raised in Arizona, later moving to California because I wanted to be near the water, then went to college there, then I moved around some. My mother always said I was a bit of gypsy."

"Are you close with your parents?"

I glanced at the clock on the wall and realized I needed to get back to work. I held up my coffee as I got to my feet. "Thanks for the coffee, Molly. I'll get yours next time." I started to walk away, but she called out after me.

"Mia." I turned to see her squinting at me. "Just so you know, they never mention *anything* about themselves when they're here."

I shrugged. "Lucky guess, I suppose." I waved over my head as I disappeared down the long hallway.

***

Mark

"You're hungry?" She sneered as she chucked a piece of stale bread at my head. "You ungrateful piece of shit."

"But my tummy hurts, Momma." I cried as I reached for the bread that was now beneath the couch. Anything was better than the internal ache that consumed my every thought.

"Go, beg like a good little dog." She flicked her finger toward the door.

My chin quivered. I knew what she wanted me to do. I c-c-can't, I w-w-won't. It was embarrassing.

"Did I stutter, boy?" she screamed as she took another swig from the vodka bottle.

Shoot.

I grabbed my shoes, which were worn out to the point that I felt every rock and crack, then pulled on my hoodie. What was the point? It was pouring rain out. I'd be frozen in a few minutes anyway.

"Don't come back unless you have something to share."

I heard his footsteps, and it made me move

faster. I grabbed a plastic bag and hurried out into the dark night.

I knocked on my neighbor's door, only to get a smack to the head for begging for food. I trudged on. My shoes squeaked, and my feet were numb as the night dragged on. I decided to take a new direction and headed south into the wealthier neighborhood, knowing I was taking a bigger risk.

I walked for a long time. It was getting dark when I found someone's gate wide open. I looked ahead to a red door, and I remembered a story I heard from my teacher that a red door meant welcome. I slipped my body through and hurried down the driveway.

I raised my cold knuckles to the door and knocked as hard as I could, hoping it wasn't too late to ask for food.

The door opened, and there stood a sweetly smiling lady holding a teacup and saucer.

"Sweetheart." Her voice nearly brought me to tears. "What on earth are you doing out here so late?"

"I-I..." I couldn't even think. This lady just called me sweetheart. No one had ever called me anything but boy. "I was wondering if you could spare some food?"

Her eyes widened as my words sank in.

"Please, I'm so hungry, and if I go back without food, my momma will hit me."

She didn't miss a beat as she wrapped her warm arms around me and pulled me into the comfort of the big house. "Come in, and I'll warm up some soup for you."

"Really?" I nearly tripped over my own feet. Oh my, the house was huge and warm. They must have paid a lot for heat, because Momma always said it was too expensive to heat our small place.

"Sue!" she called as we passed by the staircase. "Could you please come down here?"

The kitchen had a fireplace! I could hardly believe my eyes, and I headed over to seek its warmth. My bones soon thawed, but I still shivered in my damp clothes.

"Here." The sweet lady handed me some clothes. She pointed to a restroom and urged me to go change.

The person in the mirror didn't look like me. I looked like everyone else. Just a kid in normal clean clothes. I loved how they felt. I rubbed the dirt from my face and ran my fingers through my soaked hair so it lay flat.

I headed back out to the kitchen where my growling tummy led me to a yummy smell. The lady was stirring a huge pot of soup.

"Come and sit, dear." She pointed to a stool at the island. I climbed up as she set a steaming bowl of soup next to me and then placed a roll with butter next to it. Oh my, even butter! Wow! I bowed my head and gave thanks. We never prayed at home, but this sure was something to pray over.

"What is your name?" she asked as she eased onto the stool across from me.

"Mark, ma'am," I muttered through a bite of the roll. Oh my, it was so good!

"Nice to meet you, Mark. My name is Abigail." She gave me a warm smile. "The clothes fit well, as

I thought they would. He's about your size."

"He?" I wondered who he was.

She refilled my milk glass. "Yes, the little boy who lives here is about your age. What are you, seven or eight?"

"Seven, ma'am."

"That's a good age." She handed me another roll. "Where do you live?"

I swallowed a large piece of bread and tried to remember my manners. "I live in the trailer park on Sixth Row."

Her face softened, and I knew she knew exactly where I lived.

"You're out late."

"Nah, Momma doesn't like me home when she's drinking. She sends me out lookin' for food when she doesn't want to take me to the soup kitchen." I placed my soup down and remembered I couldn't go home empty-handed or I'd get another beating.

"Thanks, miss, for the food and clothes. Do you think it would be okay to take a roll with me? Momma doesn't like me to come with nothin' for her."

She placed her warm hand over mine. "You eat, Mark. I'll make you something to take home to your momma."

Really? *"'Kay." I started to eat the soup as fast as I could just as someone came into the kitchen.*

"Sue," Abigail whispered, "we have a late night visitor."

"Oh," she eyed me and broke into a large smile, "are you a friend of my son's?"

"Umm, no, miss." I drank the entire glass of

milk, and as soon as I put it down, Abigail refilled it. *"Thank you."*

"Of course. Boys like you need lots of milk to grow big and strong. Do you drink much milk?" I shook my head. I thought I had milk once. It tasted really good.

After she packed me a box of food, she led me out to a garage.

Abigail drove me home, and the car started on the first try! The seats were warm as I sank into them. Wow, they had a lot of money. I wanted to know what it felt like to drive in a car, especially one that had the heat working.

"Umm, thank you for everything," I nervously said as we got close to our trailer. *"Momma might get mad…"* I didn't want to talk about how she beat me for no reason. I opened the door, and before I stepped out into the rain, I turned to her. *"Thank you for the food. I'll return the clothes tomorrow."*

Abigail placed her hand on my shoulder. *"Why don't you keep the clothes and come back for dinner tomorrow?"*

My stomach tightened at this. *"Really? Ah, okay, thank you."*

Little did I know those clean clothes would earn me the beating of a lifetime.

***

The warm sun beat against my sore eyelids. A shadow crossed over me and my senses kicked in. I reached for my gun, but it wasn't there. *Oh shit! Where am I?* My memory raced back, but it was fuzzy. Someone touched my arm and I grabbed the hand and pulled them down.

"Oh!" a female voice gasped.

I opened my tired eyes and saw a pair of deep green eyes staring back at me.

"It's okay," she whispered as her long brown hair moved about her midsection. "I'm a nurse, and you're at North Dakota Hospital. I was just going to check your temperature."

I recalled the few memories I had before I blacked out. I loosened my grip, but she didn't remove her hand right away.

"Can you answer a few questions?" Her voice was calm and soothing and seemed to ease the pounding headache behind my eyes. I gave a careful nod as the pain started to surface. "Do you know your name?"

I nodded.

She smiled.

"Do you know what year it is?"

I nodded.

She smiled wider, which made her face light up. Damn, she was pretty.

"What color are my eyes?"

I started to nod, but stopped when I saw her angle. She wanted an actual answer. I couldn't help but grin.

"Well, that was worth the wait." She laughed gently. *Wait?* "You've been out for a day and a half." She started to fiddle with my IV bag. "But that's normal, considering what you have been through. You know you were shot?"

Okay, she must have been under the same

contract as Molly.

She glanced at her bright red watch. "My shift ends in twenty, so Alvin will be your nurse for the next twelve hours." *Alvin?*

My stomach sank. She was a hot little thing. I watched her as she busied herself with her tasks and wrote on her clipboard. Sexy green eyes, tight ass, and long brown hair with a slight wave through it. The black scrubs showed off her Converse sneakers that made me smile, considering most nurses wore practical shoes. I thought of those horrible Crocs some people insisted on, even to the point of sticking decorations in the holes.

She continued to scribble on her chart, then flipped it closed. "Can I get you anything?"

I stared at her for a moment. She didn't shift like she was uncomfortable as some women did when they were around men like me. She just stared back with a faint smirk.

I cleared my throat and managed to grunt out, "Water."

"Sure thing." She opened a small fridge and returned with a yellow cup and straw. She held the straw to my mouth and waited for me to take it. I felt like a fool, so I raised my hand, but she batted it away. "I had to sponge bathe a sixty-year-old man earlier. You can handle me taking care of you for a few moments." I grinned, feeling sorry for her, and opened my lips and downed the inch and a half of water she gave me.

"More," I croaked through a sandpaper throat.

She shook her head with a sad face. "Sorry, that's all, Major."

I placed my hand on hers to make her stop. "Please."

"You could vomit and do damage to your stitches. You had *a lot* of medication—"

"I won't, I promise." My hand flexed. I needed water so badly. "Promise."

Her eyes closed and she let out a sigh. "Just a tiny bit more." Her laugh made me happy. I could see she was breaking her own rules, and I loved it.

Like before, I downed the entire thing in seconds but didn't push my luck.

"Not a word." She pointed her finger at me as she stepped back. "I know where you live." She laughed and moved her hands in the air to outline the room. "Room 2203." Her nose scrunched as she opened the door. "Get some sleep, Major Lopez."

I gave her a salute, and she moved out into the bright hallway. That chick was funny. With the pain clicker in hand, I soon dozed off to a heavy sleep.

***

Manuel

My fat lip made it hard to drink from the glass. I drooled as I popped three Advils. What a fucking night. I spat blood off to the side and ran my tongue along my back teeth. Shit. The molar was cracked, and half of it was gone.

"You look like shit," Billy muttered as he walked out of the locker room.

I waited for him to leave before I changed my shirt and tucked my gun in its holster. My cell vibrated, and I cursed when I read the text.

Noah: Five days before first payment.

I swiped my thumb to open the phone and scrolled the page down to refresh the email. Nothing. Motherfucker was going to get me killed.

I caught my reflection in the locker mirror that hung on the door. Rage burned from my gut right through to my skin. I hated that we even looked similar. I squeezed my eyes shut, trying to block out the memory I knew was coming.

"Hey there, big fella, what's your name?" His smile was sleazy, and I knew what this man wanted. I knew because this wasn't the first time it had happened. Mark's red jacket caught my attention through the window, and my anger grew as he ran to his freedom while I had to stay in this fucking hell.

Fuck it. I glanced around and saw I was alone. Spinning the top, I opened the Snapple bottle and downed half of it. The vodka was strong. I gave up measuring it long ago. These days it was just a splash of juice, and the rest was whatever liquor I could get my hands on.

With that, I slammed my locker and went to take what I needed.

CHAPTER TWO

Mark

The next forty-eight hours were rough. Nurse Alvin was a complete ass who couldn't even read my damn chart. Then there was Nurse Dawn. She thought she was at a fucking quilting class, sticking me with her flippin' needles. Where the hell did these people get their degrees?

My head hurt, my side hurt, and this goddamn place wouldn't give me any food.

The sheets needed to be burned, the walls were insanely bright, and they needed some fucking food! *I can't wait until they deliver my Jell-O. Really Jell-O?* That shouldn't ever be considered food. They brought it in, and they took it back out. *Get the fucking point! I hate Jell-O!*

"What-up, sunshine?" Cole smirked from the doorway, and by the look of it, he had been watching me.

"Go away."

"Still milking it?"

21

"Screw off."

"Aw, someone seems pissy. What, they not feeding you?" I flinched, but he saw it. His hand flew to his chest. "Ah, brother, I wish you were there last night. Abby made one huge rib eye, with this sauce that was—"

"You're dead to me."

He laughed as he jumped forward, moving out of the way for…there she was.

"Hey, guys." She beamed as she headed for my IV. "Now, you look much better." She gave me a wink.

Cole shot me a look as he checked her out.

"Savannah," I mouthed back, getting a middle finger.

She opened my chart before she asked, "How are you, Colonel?"

"Quite well, thanks," he glanced at me, "Mia."

Really, asshole, first name basis?

"Good." She looked at him, and I flipped him the finger back. "Glad to hear it."

Cole's phone went off, and he excused himself from the room.

Yes, leave.

Mia took a moment to finish the paperwork, swiping her long bangs out of her line of sight.

"Deep green." My voice was gruff.

She looked up. "Pardon?"

"The color of your eyes. They're deep green."

The corners of those green eyes crinkled as her cheeks pinked up, turning them a few shades darker.

"Good." There was a lightness to her voice. She slid the chart into the sleeve on the end of the bed.

"What day is today?"

"Wednesday."

"What's your name, Major?"

"Major Mark Lopez, with the United States Army."

"Good."

"My turn," I stated. "What's your name?"

"Huh." She chuckled as she crossed her arms and raised an eyebrow. "Mia Harper. I'm a nurse for North Dakota Hospital."

"How new are you?"

"How…?" she trailed off.

"The last two jackass nurses I had didn't know who you were."

"You were checking up on me?"

Shit. "No, I—"

"Why were you checking up on me?"

"Wait. How," I tossed my hands in the air, "how did I lose control here?"

She chuckled and poured me some water.

"Oww," I hissed, leaning way over to the side, "Shit that hurts."

"Oh, God." She rushed to my side, putting her hands on my shoulders to keep me from falling. "Easy, now."

"You smell nice." I gave her a devilish grin.

She closed her eyes then reached for a button to call for help. "You're going to be trouble for me, aren't you, Mark?"

"Me? Never."

She pushed the button and waited for someone to answer. "Alvin, could you please give patient Mark Lopez a sponge bath?" My face dropped. "He seems to be bouncing back rather quickly."

"Sure thing, Mia." Alvin sounded a little too eager for me.

"No one is going to wash me." I folded my arms with a wince. "I am a grown-ass man, been through worse than this. Give me the soap, and I'll gladly wash myself."

She leaned me back and tucked in my blanket. "Now, Mark, we have rules."

Alvin came in whistling a tune.

"Out!" I shouted, but Mia's face made me chuckle.

Alvin looked at her for help. "Mia?"

"Okay, Mr. Lopez." A doctor came in, but stopped when he saw my fucked up room party. "So this is where my staff is hanging out." He made a point to look at Mia, who shrugged, but winked at me when she patted Alvin on the shoulder.

Alvin walked out, but as Mia turned, the doctor called her back.

"Stay, I could use the company." He gave her a smile, and she returned it, but I couldn't tell if it was because he was her boss.

"My name is Dr. Evans." He didn't look up from his chart. I was a firm believer in eye contact, and it rubbed the wrong way he wouldn't give it to me, the patient. "Mark, how are you feeling today?"

"Well, Doc, I feel like I've been shot." Mia couldn't hide her amusement at my comment.

"So it's painful?"

"Yes, gunshots are normally pretty painful."

"One would think so." He nodded while he flipped through my chart. "I'm surprised I haven't run into you before, considering this has been your third gunshot in the past five years. Jesus." He stopped when he realized what he said.

"Well, it's not something I have *aimed* for," I muttered, feeling sore and cranky. He obviously didn't even get my intended pun. I didn't like how quiet Mia was now that the doctor arrived. It led me to believe they had a history.

Dr. Evans came to my side, pulled back the blanket, and felt around the exit wound. "You're either on a lot of pain medication, or you're not in that much pain."

"You learn quickly to internalize pain in my line of work, Doc," I answered, feeling tired. "Five," I sighed. "My pain on the scale."

He smiled with a nod. "You *have* been down this route before."

"Yup."

Mia handed me a glass of cold water. A page had her leaning her ear to her shoulder as she listened. "Excuse me."

Dr. Evans pushed the button on the intercom. "Alvin, you can come back in and give Mr. Lopez his bath now."

"I'll pass."

"Trust me, Mark, this is not for you." He snapped the chart closed. "You have a good day."

"Oh, yeah, you too, Doc." I snickered as he left.

Alvin came in with a grin. "You ready, Mark?"

"I hope you die a slow painful death for this."

***

Mia

Twelve hours, two surgeries, and a near death later, I was pretty damn tired. The week had gone by fast, and there was a lot of buzz about the upcoming Friday night down at The Grid. It sounded kind of fun. However, the weight of people's problems never left me when the shift ended. I needed time to process. Socializing with staff wasn't something that interested me.

"Lopez is asking for another dinner." One of the nurses shook her head. Mark was starting to grow on the staff this week. He was a terrible flirt with the older ladies, and he seemed to have caught the eye of Alvin too.

I held up a hand, grabbed my bag and book from behind the station, and hurried into his room.

"I knew if I complained enough they'd send you in." He flashed a sexy smirk. Christ, his eyes looked right into me. Sometimes he made me feel vulnerable.

"My shift is over, Major. Is there something I can get for you?"

"Please, something that wasn't made inside a sweat factory." He pushed his beef and gravy away. "I've eaten worse, but I can't handle it anymore. Not when I can see a Marie Callender's from my window. That's kind of mean, don't you think?"

I laughed before I opened my bag and pulled out my shepherd's pie. "Here." ~

His eyes lit up as he peeked under the lid. "Well, fuck me sideways." I had to look away when he grinned. The feeling he gave me was different than I was used to. "Did *you* make this?" I gave a quick nod before I closed my bag and headed for the door.

"Where are you going?"

"Home."

"Why?"

"I'm tired."

"But I'm bored." I saw his playful grin when I turned around and crossed my arms. "I have gossip. Girls like that, right?"

"I haven't been here long enough to know who most of the nurses even are."

His face scrunched, and I could see he was going to try another angle. "I heard you like to read."

This threw me. "How did you—" I closed my eyes. "Why are you and Molly talking about me?"

"I wanted to know what you liked."

"Why?"

He ignored my question as he tossed the lid of the shepherd's pie container on his lap then grabbed a plastic spoon from his tray and dug in.

"Mia." Dr. Evans stuck his head in the door, then stopped and looked at both of us. "You heading out?"

I wanted to sigh, but I held it back. I noticed Mark was watching me carefully.

"No, I think I'm going to go home."

"Case in point." He shrugged as he closed the door. *I know, I know, I'm a loner.*

With a fake smile, I turned to Mark. "I should get going. See you later." Just as I gripped the door handle, he spoke up.

"Thanks for the dinner. It's really delicious. A definite improvement on the beef."

"No problem."

I headed down the hallway and hoped no one would spot me. I just wanted to go home.

***

Knock knock. My fist met the door of my downstairs neighbor, who greeted me with his normal gummy smile.

"Shift?"

"Long, but good."

He leaned his shoulder into the doorway. "You look different." His eyes narrowed in on me. "You're not telling me something."

I held out my hand. He whistled, and a moment later Butters, our Siberian husky, came running toward me, jumped up on my chest, and nearly knocked me down. He was a massive dog and weighed just a little less than I did. A while back, our neighbor who had lived in the building for over twenty years passed away. Somehow the dog was left with all of us, so we took turns looking after him. Butters seemed to have a small attachment to me. His giant pink tongue licked the entire length of my face.

"I just need sleep." I called for Butters to follow. "See you later, Ed."

The heavy elevator door shut, and I soon stepped into my art-studio style apartment. Kyle, my best friend, and I rented this place. He finally convinced me to move here two months ago. He received word one month ago that he won a spot at a major art gallery to show off his work. To say I was heartbroken when he left was an understatement.

Now I had this massive apartment, floor to ceiling windows about thirty feet tall, and no one to share it with.

I grabbed last night's pizza, dropped it on a plate, hooked a bottle of water from the fridge, and headed to the couch. Butters followed and settled in next to me. Normally, I'd cook, but these shifts were getting to me. I didn't take a break when I was supposed to, and I also volunteered at the local medical center. Bad mistake. I dropped my Chucks to the floor, drew my knees up, and clicked on the TV.

I wasn't sure what time I headed to bed. It was dark, and the moon shone enough that I didn't need to use a light. Once I was tucked in between the blankets, I patted the bed, and Butters slammed himself to my front. My arm slid around his chest, and I buried my head next to his.

"Love you, boy." I kissed his head and closed my eyes.

***

Manuel

Four aces rested between my fingers, so my chances were pretty good. Big Joe, who had been cleaning up, sat next to me, looking like he might keel over at any time from a heart attack. I wished I had sat across from him so I could read his face, but no such luck. Instead, I needed to bluff my hand.

My neck was itchy with sweat that had been

steadily running down my back. I needed to win this hand or Noah was going to cave in my face again.

"Fold," the skinny guy across from me said and tossed his cards into the center of the table.

The light bulb that hung from the ceiling on a single wire flickered and made us all look up. The warehouse was a meat market and stunk of flesh, even here, way in the back where they held these tournaments.

My chair squeaked as I shifted, trying to wait out the next man's move.

"Fold." He sighed before he got up and headed for the bar.

The blonde woman who I'd seen around a few times flipped a red chip over and over between her fingers as she thought.

"I raise a thousand." She slid a black chip into the pile.

Without hesitating, I placed my chips. "I see your thousand and raise you two thousand."

"Call." Big Joe followed with his chips and waited to see what would happen next.

***

The ice felt good on my forehead, but bed sounded even better.

"What the hell happened to you?" One of the girls from the booking department stuck her head in my cubicle.

"Wrong place, wrong time," I lied and pushed the images of his fist smashing into my head as far away as I could. I could still conjure up the sound of the pipe cracking my skull. Memories of the card game were fuzzy.

"You may want to get that looked at. Jeez, are you going to press charges?"

I nearly laughed. My life was so fucked up right now that the last thing I needed was more people in my shit.

"Nah, not worth the paperwork."

I waited until she left before I opened my email. Nothing. *Are you fucking kidding me?*

***

Mark

It had been two days since I'd seen Mia. They stuck with me Nurse Alvin and some other lady who had the personality of a doorknob. Boredom was not something I did well. Cole and Abigail wanted to visit, but I told them to stay home. There was nothing they could do, and they were needed at the house.

With a quick jerk of the IV, I freed myself from the goddamn bed. I didn't like being told when to eat, when to sleep, when to take my meds. I was a grown-ass man, and I needed to get back to my routine.

"Ahh," I moaned as I swung my legs over the edge of the bed. With my feet planted on the ground, I eased myself to a standing position. Pushing back the dull ache, I moved toward the door. Right before I headed out, I caught sight of myself in the mirror. There was my bare ass

31

hanging out for the world to see. *Huh.*

The hallway was busy, lots going on. This was perfect. My feet felt like lead as I moved to an open chair across from my room. Tucking my ridiculous gown under my legs, I sat back and watched as people buzzed by me.

My freedom lasted an hour and a half before Nurse Vikki Taylor found me.

Her arms were folded over her large chest, her scrubs were a bright lime green, and her—yup—*Crocs* had little decals through the toes. *No comment.*

"Mr. Lopez," her eyes narrowed in on me, "what on earth are you doing out of bed?"

"I wanted to see you again." I flashed her a killer smile. "Do you feel that?"

"What?" she asked.

"That." I carefully reached for her hand and saw her blush as she glanced at the other ladies watching. "The connection we have." She rolled her eyes, but I could tell I had her. "Oh, Nurse Taylor, what is going on inside that beautiful head of yours?"

"Mr. Lopez." She scowled but didn't remove her hand from mine.

"Are you thinking inappropriate thoughts about me?"

"No!" Her voice went up, but she loved this.

"You are a dirty little nurse, aren't you?" I rose to my unsteady feet. "Look, now you're making the other ladies blush." I laughed, but then I saw Mia walking next to Dr. Evans, who waved goodbye before she spotted me.

"Mr. Lopez, bed, now!" Nurse Taylor flicked her wrist toward my door. "Move it along."

"Okay, okay." I raised my hand then turned and heard them gasp at my bare ass. "Just something to remember me by, ladies."

Someone laughed. "Oh, he's terrible!"

"I'd bite it!" someone else chimed in.

I waved over my shoulder and shut the door to the cell behind me.

Nurse Taylor came in and put my IV back in, and the whole time she laughed and blushed. She pushed a painkiller into the needle and warned me not to leave again.

Needless to say, I fell asleep pretty quickly after my journey out in the hallway. Plus, the medication didn't take long to kick in.

***

I hated school; I didn't fit in. Fighting was how I kept the bullies at bay. Kids were mean, and they picked on me for having a drunk for a mother, where I lived, what I wore. I didn't fit in anywhere, it seemed. Tears only made the situation worse, and fear seemed to be the only trick that worked with them.

"Oh, look, I wonder if there is some booze in that bag for his mom. No wonder he doesn't have a father. He probably killed himself to get away from his drunk old lady!" It was that little shit Tommy, who loved to make my life a living hell.

"Screw off." I had way too much of a mouth for a seven-year-old.

Four more boys appeared out of nowhere, and Tommy's smirk grew wider. I dropped my book bag and got into position to get my ass kicked.

"Let's just get this over with." My fists came up to protect my face.

The biggest kid stepped forward and tossed a punch, but I ducked and flew around him. I would never throw the first punch. I did have some morals.

Before I knew it, all the boys formed a circle around me, and they started chanting.

"Trailer trash, drunken trash...let's all kick him in the ass."

Someone turned one of the boys around and kicked him in the balls. Huh? A punch to my stomach brought me back to reality. I swung, kneed, and kicked blindly, doing whatever it took to get these jerks off my back.

Once the kids got their asses kicked, I leaned over to catch my breath. My bloody nose dripped onto my shirt. The kid who helped me came over and patted my shoulder.

"You okay?"

"Yeah, thanks."

"I'm Cole."

"Mark."

"I know." He nodded and wiped his bloody brow. "You met my nanny Abigail the other night."

I bit down on my lip and wished I could have beaten him up. I was so embarrassed that he knew I begged at his house.

"You hungry?" He handed me my backpack like he didn't care about it.

"Yeah, I could eat," I answered after some

hesitation. We started down the road. "Thanks for that."

"Sure, they're assholes."

I laughed. It seemed I wasn't the only one who cursed like a sailor.

We almost made it to Cole's road when I saw the green pickup truck plowing down the road toward us. I knew it was his *truck.*

Shit.

Cole sensed my mood change and suggested we take a shortcut. We made it a few yards into the woods before the truck slowed and its window rolled down. Cole pulled me behind a rock to hide ourselves.

"Who's that?"

***

I shot forward, gulping in a huge breath. I was drenched in sweat and felt as though I was about to burst if I didn't get out of there.

"Get out, get out!" I smacked the side of my temple.

With another yank, I freed myself and stumbled over to the closet. Dropping my bag at my feet, I bent and twisted as I pulled my clothes on, which hurt like hell, but I hardly noticed.

My jeans were on, and I fumbled with the buttons when the door opened and Mia stopped dead in her tracks. Her eyes dropped to my bare stomach, then my open jeans.

"What are you doing?" She tossed her chart on the table.

"I need to get out of here." I tried to raise my arms over my head, but it wasn't happening.

"No, Mark." She placed her hands on my shoulders to stop me. "What happened?"

My mind was spinning. "I need to leave."

"No, you can't leave." Her hand moved to my chest over my wild heartbeat. "You are going a mile a minute, here, Mark. Please take a moment and calm down."

Her green eyes held mine as if to challenge, and I tuned into the coolness that came from her palm. We were skin to skin. She twitched and began to remove it, but to my surprise, my hand landed on top of hers.

"Not yet," I whispered.

Her eyes never broke contact. "Okay."

There were two feet between us, but her fresh vanilla smell found me and helped calm the storm inside. I mentally lit a match to chase the memories away. If I wasn't aggressive with them, they'd return and haunt me again within the hour.

I stepped away and dropped my head. It had been a long time since that thought surfaced.

"No more pain meds, okay? It seems to kinda mess with my head some." I tried for a smile and got a small one back.

"A few more days and you'll be sprung from here and you can go home." She turned away and grabbed her chart. "I'll get the doctor to come in and see what we can change. Some people have different reactions to—"

"No, no more, please, Mia. I'd rather do my trippin' on my own two feet, not in my head."

"Okay." She smiled. "I get it, but put some clothes on before I get Alvin to wash that sweat off you. I have rounds to do." I reached to give her a swat, but she laughed and batted my hand away.

"Behave yourself." She left the room, chuckling.

I returned to the bed, reassured by Mia's visit.

I woke when something soft touched my face. I was too tired to care. I had spent most of the night staring at the wall, not wanting to go back to sleep. Again, it brushed over my cheek. My eyes fluttered open, and there was Keith grinning at me.

Great...

"Morning, sunshine."

"Who let you in here?" I pushed the button on the bed so I could sit upright.

He snorted. "Aww, someone is cranky. They not feeding you enough?"

"Speaking of which, tell me you came to bring me something—" Keith held up a Wendy's bag. "Wendy's?" I grunted. I usually hated fast food, but at this point I could eat the gum under his chair, I was so hungry. "Gimme!" I snatched the bag from his hand and pulled out two burgers and an extra-large fries.

"How's the tear to your muscle?" Keith kicked his feet up on my bed as he took a huge bite of his burger.

"Better than the knife to the knee."

"Or the glass in the ear."

"Ohhh, yeah!" I cringed. "That was a rough few weeks."

The door swung open, and in walked Dr. Evans and Mia.

37

"I see you have your appetite back." Dr. Evans made a face in disgust.

"It never left." I jammed more of the burger into my mouth. Keith laughed at my true statement.

"A greasy burger wouldn't be my first food of choice after I'd been shot." Dr. Evans thought for a moment, then looked purposefully at Mia. "I would want a filet mignon, rare, with asparagus and baked potato." Mia rolled her eyes when he turned away. *Huh.* That made me smirk.

"Tell ya what, Doc, when you get shot, we'll see if a burger sounds good to you or not." Dr. Evans gave me a strange look before he started writing on his chart. "Looks like you're cleared to go home tomorrow."

"Well, a certain little lady will be happy." Keith balled up his trash and started in on his second burger. "Livy is sure getting naughty."

"She *is* part Savi." I grinned. I missed my little sidekick. Savannah didn't get a whole lot of time with Cole, so Keith and I tried to help out wherever we could.

"When can I get cleared for work, Doc?"

"A few more weeks—"

"We're needed in the field." I cut him off and glanced at Keith.

"Gonna be an epic trip." Keith's level of excitement had my skin amped up.

"Mark, you were shot—"

"Where's Dr. Flynn?" I hated that I sounded like a dick, but knew he would clear me early. I healed quickly and dealt with pain better than the average person. I would not miss this trip.

The doctor's lips curled over his teeth; he didn't like me over-stepping him. However, I could see he was weighing his decision carefully.

"Fine, if this is how it works with you men. I guess I have no choice but to clear you."

Mia's gaze snapped up to his. "Dr. Evans, I don't think that's a—"

"Not looking for a second opinion, Mia." With a huff, he left the room while Mia stood there with a strange expression on her face.

Keith pulled out his phone and started to text. Probably Cole.

Mia sank into the open chair next to Keith. "Mark, if you tear your internal stitches, it can go really bad, really quick."

"I'll be fine. I've been through worse."

"It is really worth it?"

I pushed my trash away. "Worth it to take down someone who has kidnapped and tortured children for sport? Yeah, it is."

Keith's head snapped up, no doubt because I was just very open with her. Yes, they signed an NDA, but still.

She leaned over, grabbed a fry, and started to nibble on the end. Keith grinned at the both of us.

"The last girl who stole food from Mark had to bake him cookies."

I laughed at that. Savannah did have balls, and so, it seemed, did Mia.

"He ate my shepherd's pie, so we're even." She winked at me.

"So, Mia, what's your story?" Keith asked as he tucked his phone away.

39

"Don't have much of one." She stood as a page came over her radio.

"Mia, patient in room 334 is asking for you...we need your help," the woman on the radio said in a panic.

Her face fell, worry spreading across her features. "Tell Kenny I'm on my way. Don't touch his arm." She looked at us. "I gotta go."

"See you around," Keith called as she raced out the door. He took his time to turn his head back to me. "You let her eat your fry."

"Screw off."

He laughed while he reached for the remote.

"Oh, you're staying?" Sarcasm was there, but he knew I wanted him to.

***

Mia

"Noooo! Don't touch me!" Kenny screamed as Nurse Taylor tried to stick him with another needle. "I want to die!"

"Kenny! You need to calm down. We are here to make you better—"

"I will not be your guinea pig."

I pushed through the sea of nurses and made sure he could see I was there. I took his right hand and gave it a tight squeeze. His wild eyes found mine, and I could see they'd pushed him too far before they called me.

"I am here now. Look at me." I lowered my voice and cautiously moved to sit on the side of the bed I knew he would accept. "No one else but you and me."

His grip was tight as he brought himself off his ledge.

"Where were you? I lost you." I pushed back the tears that always threatened when he said that.

"Always here, Kenny, always here." I kissed the back of his hand.

"I'm scared," he confessed, then his lip started to quiver. "I just want to go home."

"I know," my throat contracted, "but we need to give you your meds. Okay?" He gave a jerky nod as I took the needle from Vikki Taylor.

Kenny's muscles soon went lax, and his eyes grew heavy. I fought the emotions clawing to the surface. Fate had a screwed up way of showing it was in control.

"Wow, okay, good job, everyone." Dr. Evans appeared at the door. "Let's get back to our rounds."

A few of the nurses patted my shoulder as they left. I tucked Kenny's blankets around his arms to keep him warm.

"Are you okay?" Dr. Evans asked as he came into the room.

"Yes." I kept my back to him as I stood.

"Mia, you can't get attached."

"I'm not," I shot back.

"I'm happy you have a bond with Kenny, but his time is almost up."

"Don't." I whirled around on my toes. "Don't you dare talk about someone as if they weren't here."

Evans leaned back against the wall with a confused expression. He would never understand how much my job meant to me.

"Kenny's brain is shutting down. He thinks you're his mother."

"He's fifteen years old. Is it so bad that I can bring him some degree of comfort?"

"No," he shrugged, "I'm just nervous you won't be able to come back after this. It can be any day now."

"I have to go." I brushed by him.

Ever since I came to this hospital, Kenny began to think I was his mother. He had no one who cared for him. Yes, I was attached, but for a good reason. Besides, he was a child.

I reached out for the counter as I took some deep breaths. All I wanted to do was kick and scream at the world.

Dr. Evans appeared and moved toward me, so I turned the opposite direction and hurried down a quiet hallway.

I let myself sink down onto the cool floor, leaning my head back. I couldn't hold back a few tears that slid down my cheeks.

My cell phone rang and I pulled it free. I hit ignore when I saw the caller ID.

With my eyes squeezed shut, I let some pain release from my chest. It ripped through me and my body jerked with a sob. Life was so unfair sometimes. I exhaled a controlled sigh so I wouldn't lose myself completely, a tool I'd used time and time again. No one wanted to see a nurse upset. It made people lose hope.

"Is this hallway taken?" Mark stood in front of me, wearing jeans and a t-shirt. I quickly dried my cheeks, but it was no use, as more tears fell.

"Why aren't you in bed?" My voice was off.

"Oh, you know, just wanted to get some of that fresh hospital air." He waved his hands over his face as if he took a deep breath. I chuckled. He was funny. "You look beat."

"Beat doesn't describe how I am feeling."

He moved carefully to sit next to me.

"Yikes, Mark, please be careful."

"Oh, please, I'm okay." He blew off my concern. "I only fake the pain so the ladies will visit me." He flashed me a playful look.

"You're terrible." With a sigh, I tried to push the ache away. "So you leave tomorrow?"

"Looks that way." He stretched out the leg closest to me.

"When is your next assignment?"

He glanced over at me as if to read my face. "Few days."

"A few days?" I shook my head at him. "Wow, do you think you're ready for that?"

He grinned, and I could see he *was*…mentally.

"Is it pretty dangerous?" I couldn't help but ask.

He gave a shrug; I guessed he got asked that a lot. "It always is."

"Doesn't it scare you?"

"Nah, it's more of a rush."

"Yeah, bullets flying by sounds like a rush." I raised my eyebrow, but I knew I was out of my element with this topic. Kenny's condition was really preying on me today.

43

He chuckled. "Not to mention the stabbings, hostages, drug lords, bombs, and land mines."

My head flopped back and I closed my eyes. "Jesus. Why do you do it?"

He didn't answer, and I opened my eyes and saw him staring at the wall.

"I'm sorry, I stepped over the line there."

"No, not really. It's all I know. It's been my life since I was seventeen."

"Do you have a family?" The words slipped off my tongue.

"I do." My stomach sank. What on earth was that?

Mark turned to look at me. "I have my brothers and my adopted mother. My life is different than most, and women soon find they don't like when I disappear without any explanation. It's a battle all of us guys fight. Pretty hard to have a relationship."

"That must be difficult." I stared into his eyes; they seemed to have a crazy hold on me. His features were strong and well-defined with a soft undertone. He exuded confidence.

"It can get lonely," he admitted. "When the girlfriend starts to ask too many questions, well, let's just say when we hit that point, you usually have to end it." *Once in a while it can work, though,* I told myself, thinking of Cole and Savi.

"Sorry to hear that."

"Mm," he grunted, his eyes searched for something, but I wasn't sure what.

"I should get you to your room."

"Are you working tomorrow?" His question threw me.

"Yes."

"Good."

He hobbled to his feet in one swift move and offered me a hand. I took it, and he nearly lifted me right off the floor. His brown eyes latched on to mine, and he caught a tear with the back of his finger. I had to fight the temptation not to turn into his touch.

"It hurts to see such a pretty girl cry," he whispered near my ear. His breath smelled like a red Starburst, and my mouth nearly watered with want.

His gaze held mine before his face slipped back into a playful mood. He offered to link arms with me. I gave him a smile.

"What?" he teased. "I might fall, Mia. You want me to fall?"

"Oh, right." I batted his hand but did link arms with him. Holy hell, his arms were huge and as hard as concrete. "Hey, you're pretty warm, Mark." I stopped him and moved my hand to feel his forehead.

"Really, here, Mia?" he joked. "You're openly flirting with me at your work?"

"Oh, stop." I rolled my eyes, but he did feel very warm. I noticed his eyes fought not to close at my touch.

"Nurse Taylor is not going to like this." His eyes lit up with a dramatic sigh. "Do what you must." His arms spread open as if to let me feel all around his body.

I had to laugh. "How do you feel? Really?"

"When I am around you? Or in general?"

My cheeks went warm. "Do you flirt with all the women in your life?"

"Most of the women in my life are my aunts or my sister-in–law, so no, not overly."

I tried not to smile, but something about being around Mark was infectious.

He started us toward his room. "However, there is Livy. That beauty has me wrapped around her little pinky. She's my baby niece who runs the ship back home."

"Livy is a sweet name." I loved that he spoke about her that way. It showed a lot about his character.

His arm muscle flexed when he stepped wrong, but he ignored it and started right back up again.

"Don't let her sweetness trick you. She has her mother's feistiness and her father's stubbornness. The three of them are a deadly combo."

"Sounds like you're all close." I helped him back into his bed.

"Well, we're family, so you know."

I gave a little nod and pushed away yet another painful feeling.

"What about you?"

"Me?"

"Yes, you." He smiled as I tucked the covers around him.

"Both of my parents are together, and no siblings."

"You close?"

"Close as I want to be," I answered truthfully. I took his temperature, but it was fine.

"Just naturally run hot when I'm near you, I

46

guess."

"I wish I did. I'm always cold." I placed my hand on his arm. "See?"

His hand fell on mine. "And I'm always warm. See, we're a great match."

I turned to leave, but he caught my hand like last time. "Will you say goodbye to me tomorrow?"

"Yes." I waited for the unexpected lump to slide down my windpipe before I finished answering. "Of course."

***

Home didn't feel so great until I hit my bed fully clothed and was soon out cold.

"I just don't understand why you only want to be a nurse, Mia," Mom complained from my doorway.

"I love what I do. Doesn't that count for something?"

"No, not when you're wasting your talent." The sound of my father coming in had me reaching for the handle.

"My life, my way." I closed the door in her face, gently so as to not be disrespectful, but to make my point. It was my life, and the last thing I needed was my father bringing his opinion too.

Hot, stinky breath filled my nose and woke me from my usual nightly loop. Two ice blue eyes stared back at me, then his tongue licked the entire length of my face. This seemed to be his new thing.

Gross.

"Morning, boy." I rubbed right behind his ear. "You must be hungry."

He barked and jumped off the bed, taking some of the blankets with him. I groaned and flipped over to see the time. *Oh shit!*

Thirty minutes later I ran through the front door of the hospital with a bagel stuck in my mouth. My Chucks were untied, and my jeans and a sweater were barely dry since I snagged them directly from the dryer.

"I know, I know." I waved at Dr. Evans, who pointed to his watch. My locker was by the door, and after two tries I freed the lock. I tossed my stuff inside and struggled into a pair of dark blue scrubs.

I checked in on Kenny first, but he seemed to be stable at the moment, though today he looked paler than normal. I wondered what kind of God would bring such a lovely boy to this planet, only to strip him of everything he loved then offer him a slow death.

I tucked the lollipop I picked up for him yesterday in his pocket like his mother used to, and gave him a quick kiss on the head.

"Mia." Nurse Taylor called out my name, but I held up a finger as I opened Mark's door. I stopped when I saw his room was completely cleared out.

What?

"I wanted to tell you he got cleared today and had to leave."

"How long ago?" I felt a heavy belt cinch around my chest.

"An hour and a half. Guess they got called out to work or something."

I sank onto the bed that had already been changed.

"I'm sorry. I know he was a friend of yours."

"Yeah, he was." I sighed as Vikki handed me an envelope. "He left this for you."

I waited for her to leave before I opened it. My finger ran along the seal and broke it open.

I wanted to say goodbye in person. So, we'll just have to put it on hold. For now, I'll say,

See you later, Mia.

Mark.

My stomach twisted. I'd known this man for two weeks. Did I really care that he left me a note? I tucked it inside my pocket and headed out to work the rest of my shift.

CHAPTER THREE

Mark

"Here." Cole handed me a coffee as he took a seat next to me. We were set to hit a house in ten, but I needed a moment to get my head on straight.

It had been three weeks since I left the hospital in North Dakota. I hated that I left without saying goodbye.

"What's going on with you? Are you sure you are up to this? I was afraid it might be too soon," he asked as he checked his gun clip.

"I'm good, it's nothing," I huffed, only to get a pointed look from him. "Just thinking about things."

"Like?"

"Like personal things."

"Yeah, and..." Cole popped a piece of his nasty-ass gum in his mouth. "It's the girl from the hospital, isn't it? Magg—"

"Mia," I corrected, but stopped when I realized he'd trapped me.

"Did you get her number?"

"No."

"Why?"

"Why? What's the point?" I finished my coffee while a wave of misery swept over me. "Always ends the same way."

"Well, she's hot, I'll give her that."

"She's more than that, though."

Cole took a moment to twist his absent wedding band around his finger before he answered. We weren't supposed to wear anything personal in case we were captured. "One thing I've learned from Savi is that our job isn't everything." He looked up. "You've been through enough shit in your life, Mark. If you really like this girl, then go for it. If it's just a physical thing, then get her out of your system. No one would fault you for falling in love. They'd fault you for not."

"Love is a strong word to use for only knowing the girl just over a month."

"Maybe, but look at Savi. I fell for a picture and was lucky enough to get the girl."

"Yeah," I laughed, "someone to keep you in line."

"Fuck off. Let's go get these assholes."

We all had a bad feeling when we entered the house. Something was off. The door creaked and shook as it opened. Sunlight shone through the black bars on the windows. Cigarette smoke was pungent, and I forced back the memory that raced up my spine.

We moved inside with caution, one behind the other. A leaky faucet and a sink full of half-washed dishes proved we were not alone. A moment later, we figured out why.

"Move!" Cole screamed when a grenade bounced then rolled at our feet. All I could hear was my heartbeat as we both ran around the corner and dove behind a couch.

There was a moment between when you actually registered the threat and felt the danger. It was a moment in time when you saw all the chips laid out in front of you, and you wondered if this would be the last time you would take a breath. *Will I live to see another day with all my limbs intact?*

The sound traveled through the air, hitting my ears right before I was lifted and slammed into a wall. I landed on my side hard, but was on my feet a moment later. Stumbling around like a disoriented drunk, I blinked to clear my vison. The house was filled with dust and debris, and the wooden mantel was blown to shit. With my gun raised, I retraced my steps to where I had last seen Cole.

I found him under a collapsed table, out cold. Shit.

With a shaky hand, I pressed the button on my neck. "Raven Two to Fox One."

"Fox One to Raven Two, what the hell is happening in there?" Paul barked over the radio.

"Raven One is down. Repeat, Raven One is down." Just as I heard someone behind me, a rifle butt was swung, going for my windpipe. Slamming my body weight forward, I managed to buck the fucker away from me. I pulled back fast and popped two into his chest. I was about to turn when something crashed into my head, and my body dropped like a rock, my brain seeing stars. I heard a shot.

Keith's face appeared as my attacker fell to the ground next to me. His wide-open eyes still carried a shocked expression.

"Good?" Keith helped me to my feet, holding me firmly. My head felt light and I had vertigo, but I nodded for him to let go. We both grabbed Cole and carried him out of the house. His feet left a trail in the dirt, so we had to take the long way around through the shrubs. No need to advertise our direction.

Paul and John raced to help us to the Rover. My vision was blurry and my head pounded, but nothing mattered with Cole lying unconscious on the seat.

The helicopter ride was painful, but Cole, strapped tight to a back brace, was starting to stir, and that was a good sign.

Like many times before, we were met with an EMT squad on the tarmac and raced to the hospital elevators. Keith and I stayed by his side the whole way, and John and Paul did damage control back at the house. Someone was going to need to tame Savannah to keep her from charging over here.

Molly was the first to greet us, and she started to bark out orders to the others as they paged Dr. Flynn.

"What happened?" Molly shouted over the chatter. I saw Mia race over.

"Grenade."

53

Mia nearly froze when she heard me. She shook her head, then ordered them to take Cole to bed six.

She hurried to stand in front of me. Her hands went to my face, then retracted when she realized what she did. "Are you okay?"

I looked down at my black gear, two guns strapped to my hip, a knife on my thigh, and I looked like I was…well, like I was nearly blown up by a grenade.

"Yeah, I'm okay."

She reached up and gently touched my head. Her cold fingers immediately comforted me. "You need a CT and stitches."

"Stitches," I countered, "but only if you are the seamstress," I joked.

Her chest fell as she huffed in frustration. "Fine, come on."

She led me to a quiet room where she told me to sit on the bed and carefully cleaned my cut. The feeling in the room changed. I sensed she was upset by the way her breathing had changed.

I tried to lighten the mood. "We have to stop meeting like this."

"I'm guessing that grenade wasn't friendly fire?"

"Friendly fire?" I laughed at her choice of words.

"I work in a place where I hear lots of terms. You would be surprised what comes through those double doors." Her head lowered and she let out a sigh.

"Hey," I tipped her chin so she'd look at me, "what's wrong?"

Her mouth tugged up on one side, but I could tell she wasn't her normal playful self. "Just been a long

HONOR

couple of weeks." With a shake of her head, she
forced a smile. "So did you catch the bad guys?"

I sat straighter, my body's natural reaction when
I thought of the men we'd killed. I wasn't proud of
the number of deaths I'd been part of, but I wasn't
bothered by them either. The men we killed had
done terrible things to good people.

"Yeah, you could say that."

She moved in front of me, between my legs, and
held my head so I looked down at her. "How's your
vision?"

She licked her bottom lip. I silently begged to
know how she tasted.

"No complaints here."

Her smile touched her eyes and made them
sparkle. Her nose had the perfect downward slope
that made her pink lips pop. Her long, shiny hair
smelled freshly washed, and a soft, sweet scent
lingered on her skin. She was quite possibly the
most beautiful woman I'd ever seen. It made me
want to touch her...

"I wish you'd let me book you a CT scan," she
said, interrupting my thoughts.

"I'm fine." I tried to decide which place I would
kiss first.

"What if you're not?" She let go and stepped
back.

"Would you care?"

"Yes," she blurted, then tried to fix her outburst.
"I mean, of course, you're my patient. And I care
about all those people."

"Those people?" I grinned, loving this moment.

"You know what, on second thought, I'm sure

55

you're fine." She moved, and so did I.

"Ahh…" Fuck, my side.

"That's it. Take off your scary-looking gear."

"Really, it's—"

"Mark, please," she nearly begged, "let me do my job."

I stood, my chest almost touching hers, and carefully started removing my vest. My t-shirt was soaked with sweat, and some blood soaked through over my shoulder. She helped me peel the fabric from my sore torso. Her long hair brushed by my stomach, and I swallowed down a moan. It felt so soft.

Again her eyes grazed over my body, and everywhere they went, I felt a slight pull toward her.

"Why am I always naked around you?"

"Perks of the job," she teased, and I could see she was coming around.

"That perk could go south real quick with that old guy across the hallway."

She laughed and felt around my stomach.

"So, am I gonna live?"

"Today, I think you are. Lift your arms above your head."

"Yes, ma'am."

She peeked up at me from below her long bangs. Her cool, soft hands slid all around. "Hurt anywhere?"

"Not while you're doing that." I gave a huff at her touch. I wanted to be doing the same to her.

"I think you have two fractured ribs, and…" her fingers walked along my side, "some pretty intense bruising along your side here. Let me go grab you some tape. I'll check on how your friend is doing, okay?"

"No pain meds."

She stopped to look back at me. "I remember."

After Mia left, Nurse Alvin came in and taped me up, under Dr. Evans' orders. I saw I had a little competition. After I got touched a tad more than I needed to, I dressed and headed back into the waiting room where the rest of the team waited.

Nurse Taylor came over and gave us an update.

"Mr. Logan had a pretty good hit to the head. He's stable and will be released within forty-eight hours." She glanced at me with a shy smile.

"Are you undressing me with your eyes again, Nurse Taylor?" She blushed and laughed as she walked away.

"Okay, I'm heading out." Keith rose and flicked his head toward the other guys. "Mark seems at home here, so he can babysit."

I waved as they headed for the truck. After an hour of staring at the wall, I decided to wander a bit. It didn't take long to find her, and I hung back and listened from the doorway.

She had her back turned to me as she held onto a kid's hand. They seemed close. She smiled and ran her hands through his hair a few times.

"You are so special, Kenny." She kissed their hands.

"I love you, Mom." My stomach sank. *What?*

"And I love you. Time for a nap, okay?"

He nodded and closed his eyes. Mia started to sing "Sittin' on the Dock of the Bay" by Otis

Redding. I couldn't help but lean in and listen to her voice. With Savannah's piano skills and Mia's voice, we could have a band soon.

I smirked at the thought, mainly because I had never thought about a woman like that. Melanie was great, but...I pushed aside that dark cloud. I loved my job, but it could be a bit depressing thinking about the future.

I was lost in her words when she suddenly stopped singing. I snapped out of my fog and saw her staring at me. Her face was pale and her eyes glazed over.

She stood, tucked in the boy, then whisked past me and out to the nurse's station.

"Hey, Mia." I ran after her. "Who is that?"

"A patient."

"Is he your son?"

"What?"

"I heard what he said to you."

"That was private." Tears rimmed her eyes.

"Mia!" Dr. Evans' voice sliced through the tension. "I could use your help, if you could *spare* a moment." He looked over at me. "Your friend is in room 346." I got the point.

"Excuse me," Mia made her way over, her head down and her shoulders slumped forward.

"Be careful, Mark." Nurse Taylor pretended to organize her paperwork. "That's a touchy subject for her."

"Is he her son?"

"No." She turned away when another doctor came up and handed her a stack of charts.

"Mr. Lopez," Dr. Evans appeared at my side, "I

58

understand you are here for your friend, but he's in room 346."

"So you've mentioned." I could tell he was annoyed with me.

"I need you to leave my staff alone."

"You mean Mia?" I squared my shoulders. We were about the same height, but I had approximately a hundred pounds on him.

Nurse Taylor rolled her eyes at him. I took it they'd dealt with him before.

"I mean everyone."

With a wink, I slapped his shoulder. "You know the Logans invest a lot of funds in this hospital. We spend a great deal of time here."

"Your point, Mr. Lopez?"

"My point is you will be seeing a lot of me and my men." I gave him a grin. "And it's Major Lopez."

Moving past him, I made my way toward Cole's room.

"There's my sunshine."

"Die." Cole stared at the green Jell-O that wiggled as I propped my feet up on his bed.

"Done faking it yet?" I pulled out a protein bar, knowing Cole loved them.

"I want some."

"Nah," my eyes rolled back in my head, "not enough to share."

"Fuck you."

"Aw, is someone cranky? They not feeding you enough?" I enjoyed myself as I tossed his words back at him.

He pushed the Jell-O out of his sight. "When can

I get out of this place?"

"Forty-eight."

"Fuck me." His head fell back.

"It's fuck me sideways," I mumbled through a mouthful of food. Cole gave me an annoyed look.

"Please tell me you didn't call—"

"The Mrs." I interrupted. "Yeah, I kind of like to keep my balls where they are, thanks."

Cole laughed, then squinted when the pain kicked up. "God, I love that woman."

"And we are all thankful for that, but if you two could stop acting like rabbits in your office, that would be nice too."

He shrugged shamelessly. Cole didn't care he and Savannah were always starved for one another.

"Speaking of hot and heavy, you find your sexy nurse? Maya?"

"Mia?"

"Yeah," he smirked when I corrected her name again, "Mia."

"I seem to have some competition in Dr. Evans."

"The pretty doctor?" Cole laughed. "I think he gets his eyebrows waxed."

I made a face at his comment. "The day you catch me in a spa is the day I die."

"Amen to that, brother."

I entertained Cole until he passed out around six, then I watched *The Killing* until I followed him in sleep.

The nasty green vinyl chair nearly killed me around four a.m. I was entirely too big for such a tiny seat. My attempt at being quiet failed miserably as I knocked into the table and the glass Snapple bottle tipped and crashed to the floor.

"Door, now!" Cole pointed without opening his eyes.

"I'm fine, thanks for asking. You can pay for my therapy when I tell you what that armrest did to me earlier." I sauntered out of the room with a grin.

The hallway was dim, and only two nurses were at the station. I decided to wander around in search of some coffee or maybe an open bed.

I'd watched enough TV to know there was an on-call room the nurses used when they were on break.

Three hallways and twelve doors later, I found an open room for the staff. With a glance over my shoulder, I slipped inside.

"Oh, yes," I cooed and curled up on the rather large cot and passed out in a matter of seconds.

***

Mia

The last surgery went horribly. I watched a ten-year-old girl fight for her life, only to have it slip away when we were closing. She had been in the front seat when she and her mother were hit by an empty school bus. Her mother died on impact, but the daughter had a sixty percent chance. I'd lost four kids—well, now five—since I started working as a nurse, and nine adults. It didn't matter how detached you were from them. To lose a child patient left you feeling like nothing anyone could explain.

I flicked on the light and jumped. Mark was in my on-call bed. With a quick peek down the hallway, I moved to close the door behind me. I was so tired, and this bed was so comfy with its pillow-top mattress.

I sat on the edge of the bed and carefully shook his shoulder.

"Mark," I whispered. "Mark?"

His eyes opened and he squinted at me. "Oh, shit, I'm sorry." He started to move, but I stopped him. "Hey," his hand came up and touched my cheek, "you've been crying?"

My chin dipped and I looked away. "Rough night. Some nurse I am, crying over every patient."

"Sounds like you need this more than me."

"No," I tried to smile, "it's okay. I don't think I can sleep anyway."

He moved to lean his back against the wall and patted next to his leg. "Why don't you just sit with me for a bit?"

It had been a long time since I'd allowed myself some company. I guessed it wouldn't hurt.

With a twist, I settled in next to him. His body was much larger than mine, and the heat that radiated off him was comforting.

"You're freezing." He pulled the blanket over my lap in a caring way. I wasn't sure why I let him do that, but something about how much he seemed to like to take care of me was…nice.

"I can never seem to get warm." I yawned and covered my mouth when I realized I might have come off rude. "Sorry."

He granted me a sexy smile. "For what?"

"For yawning. It's been a day."

"So you mentioned."

I nodded as my eyes grew intensely heavy. "Lost a little girl today."

"I'm sorry, Mia." He wrapped an arm around my shoulders and gave me a hug. "If it helps any, I do know how that feels." He removed his arm, and I felt a sudden chill.

"It does, thanks." I shivered and moved closer. He moved his arm so it covered more of me.

I didn't remember much more than that, but I did know that was the first time in a long time I went to bed warm.

I opened my eyes at the sound of the door clicking open. It was the cleaning crew, who backed out when they saw the room wasn't empty. I was very comfortable, and it took my brain about thirty seconds to realize I wasn't alone. I scrambled to a sitting position and looked over at Mark propped up in the corner, and I apparently was using his shoulder as a pillow.

Oh my God! I wondered who else saw us this way. This was not okay. People could get fired for sleeping with a patient. The fleeting thought that he wasn't actually a patient, per se, was brushed aside as I slipped quickly off the bed. What was I thinking? With a glance over my shoulder, I saw he was still passed out. There was a part of me that wanted to snuggle back down and sleep for another twelve hours. I straightened my hair as best I could and glanced at my watch.

Shit! I was late to prepare for my next surgery. Dr. Evans wanted me on every one of his operations. He said we were a good team, but I thought he just wanted to get in my pants. He was nice enough, but like most doctors, pretty full of himself, and he was simply not my type.

As much as I didn't really want to, I shook Mark's shoulder until his eyes fluttered opened. A lazy grin appeared, and my knees nearly failed me.

"You need to leave. The other staff will be in here soon."

"Okay." He sprang up and rubbed his face. "Did you sleep?"

"Like a rock. However, I could use another twenty-four."

"When do you get off?"

I stopped fixing my scrubs. "Umm, five hours." He nodded. "I gotta go. I have surgery." Right before I opened the door, I turned to him. "When do you go back?"

"Tomorrow, I think." He caught my expression, but I recovered quickly.

"I guess I'll see you around." I left because I didn't like the knot that formed in my stomach when I thought about him leaving.

***

"Great job in there." Dr. Evans came up behind me as I hurried toward the nurse's station. "We make a great team."

"Yeah," was all I could think of to say back. Four surgeries in one shift, and I was about done.

"Mia." Nurse Taylor—Vikki—popped out from behind the station. "This was left for you." She gave me a smile, then scowled at Dr. Evans' shadow behind me.

"What is it?" I peeked in the bag just as she set a steamy cup of coffee in front of me. My mouth watered as she handed me a note.

Eat something, you'll feel better. Mark.

I grinned as I pulled out a breakfast sandwich and took a huge bite.

"Ohh, so good," I moaned, forgetting people were there. Normally, I only ate once, sometimes twice throughout my shift. I never seemed to stop.

"Who's this from?" Dr. Evans asked as he peered over my shoulder to see the note.

"A friend." I snatched my coffee and hurried down the hallway to Cole's room, where I hoped to find Mark.

By time I hit the room, my body was already recovering with the protein. The coffee was the icing on the cake. I opened the door and caught sight of a gorgeous woman leaning over Cole's bed.

"Good morning." I pulled Cole's chart to see how his night went.

"Oh, Mia," Cole pulled my attention, "this is my wife, Savannah."

"Nice to meet you." Savannah offered her hand for a shake, and I returned it, but not before she gave a funny look.

"Nice to meet you too."

She smiled at Cole, who shook his head. What was going on?

"So, Mia…" Savannah came over to my side.

She was stunning in a pair of black leggings, a swoop neck sweater, gold earrings, and bangles. My feet were envious when I took in her black heels. "Tell me something, Mia. Are you single?"

I nearly choked on my coffee. "I don't do threesomes. No offense."

"Oh, shit." Cole sputtered as he laughed into his pillow.

"None taken." Savannah dismissed my last comment cheerfully. "No, I was just asking for curiosity's sake."

The door flew open. "Nurse Taylor is one dirty—" Mark stopped when he saw me. "I see you got my gift."

"I did, thank you." I smiled but had to look away when I felt my cheeks heat. "I feel a lot better."

"Good to hear. How was your surgery?"

"Better than yesterday's." I caught his grin, and his teeth looked sparkling white against his dark complexion.

"I'm happy to hear that."

"So, Mia, when can I get this guy home? We have some catching up to do." Savannah held onto Cole's hand as she sat next to him. The love pouring off of them was palpable.

"Ahh…" I had to force my gaze away. "I will go grab Dr. Evans, but I think he'll release you late today or tomorrow morning."

"Okay." Savannah leaned down and gave Cole a long kiss.

Mark was watching me.

"I'll leave you three be."

"Yeah, thanks." Mark snickered. "Wait." He

opened the door for me and closed it behind him. He had changed into green army pants and a black t-shirt. Jesus, he was solid everywhere.

"Can I take you to dinner tonight?" I paused when I saw Dr. Evans round the corner. "Just so you know, I don't take rejection well."

This made me laugh. "That, I can see."

"So?"

"Mia," Dr. Evans called out and started walking our way.

"Did he chip you?" Mark asked, annoyed.

"Huh? Um, what time?"

He grinned and thought for a moment. "Six. Here," he handed me a card, "text me your address, and I'll pick you up."

"Okay."

"Mia!" Dr. Evans shouted my name, and a few of the nurses stopped and stared. "I have been paging you."

"I'm sorry. I didn't get any..." I checked my pager, and there wasn't one from him.

Dr. Evans looked at Mark then back at me. "You need to remember, Mia that you work here. It's not a hangout."

"Wow," Mark hissed.

"Sorry, it won't happen again." I tried to calm the storm that might touch down here soon. "I should get going." I turned to Mark and held up his card so he knew I was still in for tonight.

***

My entire closet was piled on my bed while I

picked something to wear. Butters watched, unimpressed, while sprawled on top of my pillows. He sensed there wasn't going to be any shared pizza tonight.

I finally broke down and took out my phone from under the heap of clothes.

Mia: Hi, at the risk of sounding like a chick, what do I wear tonight?

A moment later my phone buzzed.

Mark: We have reservations at The Toasty Ties. My apologies. Savi is now giving me shit for not telling you earlier.

I burst out laughing. Something told me Savannah and I would get along really well.

Mia: Not a problem. (I say that because Savannah is giving you shit, and I don't have to.) Thanks. ☺

After I Googled the restaurant and tried on three more outfits, I decided on a black wrap-around dress that hit just above the knee. I was going for sexy, but not trying too hard. With my red-bottom heels and my hair long and in waves, I stared at myself in the mirror. His face appeared, and I closed my eyes. I couldn't go there yet.

I tidied up, gave Butters water, and took a moment to breathe. Wow, I was really nervous. It had been a long time since I'd been on a date-date.

Bzzzzzzz Bzzzzzz. My intercom went off. I hurried over and pushed the little square button.

"Hello?"

"Hey, there, pretty lady." His voice had a small rasp to it, which made him even sexier.

Shit, it hit me—did I ask him up? Or did I just go down? Shit, shit, shit! I glanced at the clock and saw the reservations where in thirty. I went with my gut.

"I'll be right down." I closed my eyes and hoped he was okay with that. I pressed the button to say something when I heard him talking to someone. Screw it. I gave Butters a kiss, ignored his pathetic expression, and hurried to the elevator.

I stopped in the entryway when I caught sight of him. My stomach twisted as my gaze dropped down the length of the man. His dark blue dress shirt was tucked neatly into a black pair of dress pants. His hair was styled a little in the front, and his skin looked flawless. Oh, my God, was I going to be able to do this? Only two scrapes were visible from his encounter with the grenade, right at his hairline.

I almost chickened out when he turned and saw me. That amazing, deep, sexy grin of his spread across his lips, and his hand slapped his chest as if I made his heart jump. He stood straighter as he reached for the handle.

"Hey," he held the door for me, "you look…amazing."

"Thank you."

He led me over to his rental car and opened the door, and I eased myself onto the leather seats, going for graceful. I noticed he had turned on the

69

heated seat for me. Light music flowed from the speakers as he pulled onto the road.

"Pretty neat place you have there."

"Thanks," was all I could come up with. *Idiot.* "How's Cole?"

He chuckled. "Savannah made him be honest, and now they are for sure keeping him overnight."

"I like her."

He eyed me from the side. "Yeah, she's a pistol, that one."

I wanted to ask about the safe house, but that would only lead to more questions, so I left that topic alone.

"How was the rest of your shift?"

"Well," I gave half a grin, "except for another ass-chewing from Dr. Evans, it could have been worse."

"What his deal, anyway?"

"I don't know." And I really couldn't care less.

Once we were seated out on the restaurant's patio, I began to relax. We ordered wine and fish tacos. The place was neat, fancy but casual. Conversation flowed even easier after the second glass of wine. I really did enjoy his company; he had a great sense of humor. The way he looked at me made me feel like we were the only ones there.

"What are you thinking?" he asked, and I realized I had been staring at him. He leaned forward. "I can tell when you're lying." He winked. "Perks of *my* job."

"Well, that's a bit unfair, don't you think?"

"Hardly."

"But I'm at a disadvantage, here."

He leaned back. "No, you're really not."

I stopped and thought about what he was telling me. I cleared my throat. "I haven't dated a lot. It's just surprising me how much I'm enjoying your company."

"Why?"

I shrugged and took a sip of wine. "You're so easy to be around."

"No," he chuckled, "I meant, why haven't you dated much?"

Oh, yeah. My cheeks heated to the point of pain. He grinned but didn't point it out.

"Just haven't had the time."

"That's a cop-out."

My mouth twisted, and I knew he could see I was lying. "My last relationship was rough. I think he liked my parents more than me."

"And?" he asked boldly, but there was a sincerity to his question.

"And when I found him in bed with our neighbor, I ended it."

"Ouch, I'm sorry."

"Thanks, but in some ways I was almost relieved. I wasn't happy. He knew that, but didn't care."

"Why were you relieved?"

In spite of how personal the questions were, it actually felt good to talk about it. "I wasn't in love, and I didn't know how to deal with it all. His cheating did hurt me, but in some ways I understood why it happened. I work a lot, and he was still in school. He worked days, I worked a lot of nights. Square peg in a round hole kinda thing." I stopped when I realized we really *were* the only ones left in the restaurant. "I'm sorry, this can't be very fun for you."

"But I asked."

"And I rambled."

"I liked that."

"Why?" It was his turn to share.

"Because I like you, Mia." I smiled at him as he studied me.

Insert big old knot in my throat.

This is a bad move, Mia. Either be honest, or let him go. My internal warning meant nothing, apparently, as I started to speak.

"I like you too, Mark."

He stood and offered me a hand. Once I was on my feet, he threaded his fingers through mine. I couldn't help but notice how nice it felt.

"Walk with me?"

"Sure."

My feet were sore after my busy week, but I pushed past it. We walked down the main road, and as the sun disappeared, so did all its warmth. Mark stopped at the car and wrapped his suit jacket around my shoulders.

"Thank you."

He smiled down at me as he took my hand again. It felt so natural walking next to him. He was still a stranger to me, but I found myself wanting to put myself entirely in his hands.

Music poured out of a small pub, its tin roof amplifying the sound. Mark looked down at me, and I nodded, knowing what he was about to ask. We headed in.

***

Manuel

My nose looked two sizes bigger and bled like a sieve. The ice in my glass made the ring on the table grow as I stared at it. Pain danced around inside my nasal cavity, reminding me of what went down an hour ago. I leaned back, rested the bag of peas over my face, and cleared a space on the table for my feet. My gun sat, loaded, on my thigh in case anyone had followed me.

I flicked my eyes open to make sure the money was still there. Nineteen thousand in five stacks on my living room table. It was dirty money, taken from a pimp in Manhattan. It sat in the locker for three months until I was sure it was documented. I logged into the evidence locker to check a weapon for a case. I knew the rookie cop's schedule. He was predictable, took a smoke break every two hours on the dot. I waited for him to leave before I stole his key and opened the back cage. It wasn't the first time I'd been back there, and I knew the risks, but what choice did I have?

I tucked the bag between my chest and vest, but it was really thick and noticeable. I leaned back to see if the coast was clear. Tearing the evidence seal, I dumped the money on the table and started tucking stacks of bills into my dress shirt. The whole time, my ears were tuned for any echo of sound.

As I shoved the last stack of bills in and buttoned my shirt, I realized the stacks were short. The sum of currency was noticeably different than what we actually busted the pimp for.

What the fuck?

The buzz of the rookie's pass card made my heart pound as I jammed the bag into my pocket. I forced myself to move at a normal pace and closed the door behind me. As I began to turn, I heard him.

"What are you doing?"

I pulled out my pen-sized flashlight as I circled the counter to be where I was supposed to. "Sorry." I nodded at the flashlight. "Dropped it on my way out, and it rolled back there."

He gave me a strange look as he nodded and moved behind the desk. The key to the locker burned into my hand. *Fuck, I need to return it.*

"You playing hoops tonight?" I leaned my body over the counter in a lazy manner.

"Nah, the sergeant has me on a double shift down here. Don't know what I did to burn his ass." He checked his phone, but didn't turn around.

"Shitty deal." That's when I saw his bottle of Coke. "Oh, what's that?" I purposely reached over and knocked his drink with my arm. It tipped and drained onto his paperwork.

"Damn it!" He jumped for a paper towel, and the moment he did, I hooked the key back under the lip of the desk.

"Sorry, man." I left in a hurry.

Once outside, I texted Noah and got the address for the next game. My hands nearly shook with excitement.

***

Mia

I was positively gloating.

"Oh! Major, you really missed that shot?" I laughed over the music that blared "Old Time Rock and Roll" by Bob Seger and the Silver Bullet Band.

We had been playing pool for the past hour, and I was kicking his ass.

"You're a little distracting." He pointed to my chest.

I purposely leaned over a teeny bit more as I went to take my next shot. "Left pocket." I tapped the cue ball and gingerly placed my second to last ball in the pocket. I rose and gave him a playful smirk. "You're up."

He raised an eyebrow in a way that made my last comment into a dirty one. I rolled my eyes and laughed.

"Quit stalling. It's your loss."

"Mmm." He leaned down, and I mirrored him across the way. "You're a dirty player."

"Why, Mark, are you scared I might actually win this game?"

"Why don't we make this more fun?" He chalked the end of his pool cue. "If you win, I will carry you back to the car." He pointed to my heels, knowing they were killing me.

"And if *you* win?"

He moved in front of me. "You let me kiss you goodnight."

Deal.

"I don't know, Mark." I grinned playfully and held my composure together somehow. "Can you kiss as well as you play? 'Cause if that's any indication—"

He leaned off to the side and sank two balls into two different pockets. He continued to sink every single ball in a matter of minutes. When he went for the eight ball, he stared right into my eyes and sank it without hesitation.

I felt an invisible tug in his direction. I had never wanted to rip my clothes off and take someone in public more than I did right then and there.

He strolled in my direction until we were chest to chest. I couldn't help but press into him a little more.

"I win." His eyes flashed something else that nearly left me speechless.

"Shame."

His smile returned as he removed the pool cue from my hand. "I think we should go."

I couldn't agree more.

He slipped his jacket off the chair, took my hand, and hurried us to the front of the bar.

It was pouring rain when we stepped outside. Mark covered me with his jacket and rushed us down the walkway. We hopped, skipped, and jumped around puddles. When we waited for the light, a truck came by and soaked us.

I threw my head back and laughed into the rain. Mark looked at me like I was nuts, but then joined in. There was no use; we were soaked head to foot. We might as well embrace it.

We crossed the street and hurried under a small bistro awning for a break.

Mark's shirt clung to his solid body, which made

it hard to focus.

"Cold?" he asked as he came closer. He moved my damp hair off my face. "You're freezing."

"I'm all right."

He leaned down and scooped me up.

"What are you doing?"

"Carrying you."

"I can see that, but why?"

The rain beat down on us as he made it to his car. "You have been on your feet all day."

"Really, Mark, I'm fine."

"Maybe I wanted to hold you."

That shut me up. He could be so bold and sweet at the same time. I pressed my cold cheek to his warm shoulder and let his heat warm my face.

I felt like ice on the way home. Mark turned up the heat, but it was no use. His hand held mine, but when I rested it on my thigh, he almost jumped at how cold I was. He shook his hand and placed it on my bare skin.

"Jesus, Mia." He moved his hand back and forth, trying to make friction.

Sweet mother of lust, he felt amazing. My southern regions were begging me to do the same to him.

He pulled up in front of my building in record time. Thank God, because I was a mess.

Once inside the elevator, the sexual vibe heightened. My hands shook as I tried to unlock my door. It was a lovely mix of lust and cold.

"Wow," Mark said as he stepped into my apartment. "The view is amazing." He moved to look over the city as the rain beat the windows,

.sending a drum sound throughout my place.

"Can I offer you a drink?" I opened my fridge. Thankfully, my neighbor had dropped off some groceries like he normally did.

"No, not a drink," he said from behind me. His front pushed into my back. He closed the fridge and spun me around, and his hands cupped my face as he stared into my eyes.

"I want to kiss you." I nodded as he took his time to lower his mouth to mine. As soon as our lips made contact, I was lost.

His body pressed against me, making the containers on top of the fridge rattle together. He lifted me off the ground and gently placed me on top of the counter. Staring into my eyes, he pushed my wet dress up and moved between my bare legs.

He pulled away with a pant. "Sorry, I can't seem to control myself around you."

I pulled at the tie and opened my dress. "Seems we're both on the same page."

"I don't have sex on the first date, Mia." His words were strained. "I don't do one night stands either."

My arm hooked around his neck, and I wrapped my legs around his waist. "Me either, but it's either you or my vibrator." *Yeah, that was blunt.*

"Damn." His breath flowed across my face. "I knew kissing you would be a dangerous slope."

I was sure he meant that as a compliment, but I felt like I was begging, and that was gross. I released his waist and covered myself up.

"Maybe you should go."

What the hell am I doing?

He pulled me off the counter, walked me across the room, and placed me in front of the window. The night made the city sparkle below us.

"Look at yourself." He stood behind me, his arms wrapped around my middle. "You're soaking wet, your dress is clinging to your skin, and your hair smells like vanilla." He leaned down and softly kissed my neck. "You're beautiful, Mia." His fingers ran down my jaw. "Not just here," he pointed to our reflection, "but here." His strong hand covered my heart. "If I slept with you tonight and then left, how would that make you feel?"

My stomach sank. He was right. It wouldn't feel right, not with him.

"Don't you think we deserve better than that? Better than a one night stand?" His teeth nipped at my ear. "When we make love, I want to wake up with you in my arms, and kiss you right here." His lips dragged down the slope of my neck and stopped where it joined the shoulder then pressed with more pressure.

I swallowed hard and fought the urge to moan.

"I like that," he whispered.

Everything was jumbled. "What?"

"That I can make that look appear in your eyes." I glanced in the window. "Like hunger mixed with heat." He sucked a spot on my shoulder and drew my skin inward. "I like you."

I started to speak, but his finger hooked my chin and urged me to look at him.

"I like you, Mia. That's the third time I've said it tonight. I'm old school. Abigail raised me right, and I don't want to ruin the great thing we have here."

His eyes narrowed in on mine. "But don't be mistaken. I want this as much as you do, if not more."

His lips dove down and smothered mine. I couldn't think; I could barely stand. I hadn't had anyone speak to me like that before. So many emotions were surfacing. All I could do was hold on until my legs grew weak and I began to sink. He scooped me up and placed me in bed. He carefully helped remove my dress, leaving me in my bra and panties.

He removed his clothes, everything but his black briefs, and crawled in next to me. His hot body was heaven next to mine.

"I want to feel you against me."

His smooth chest moved to my back, and he wrapped me in his strong arms and breathed me in.

"Perfect," he muttered before his lips touched the nape of my neck. "Just perfect."

That was all I remembered before I passed out in a web of wonderful warmth.

***

Mark

What? The hell? What the hell is that smell? I was exhausted but somehow found the will to open my eyes and found a set of bright blue ones staring back at me.

Oh shit!

My mind raced back to last night. Nope, no dogs were present.

One moment he was staring at me, and the next his big pink tongue licked from my chin to my hair.

"Morning…" His green tag dangled in my face. I smirked at the South Park reference. "Butters."

Butters had somehow jammed himself in between me and Mia. Great, a fuzzy cock blocker. His face tipped to one side like he was wondering why the hell I was in his bed. I rubbed his soft fur.

"Nice to meet you. I'm Mark." He licked my hand and groaned as he settled back down.

My phone buzzed in my pants, and I mimicked his groan.

"Butters," I whispered, "go get my phone."

He yawned and laid his head on Mia's shoulder.

"I don't blame you." I tossed the covers aside and scrambled around until I freed the phone.

Really?

"This better be good, Cole," I hissed as I moved toward the kitchen.

"You need to come home."

"Why?"

Silence.

"Cole?"

"He wants to talk to you."

"Who?"

Then it hit me. Anger burned through my veins, which in turn made me hurt to be in my own skin. *Not again.* I glanced at Mia, who was now wearing a Butters fur scarf.

"How much time do I have?"

"None. I'm downstairs." Cole hung up.

Fuck!

I hurried back to the bedroom and dropped to the

floor to be eye level with her.

"Mia?" I shook her shoulder. Her eyes opened, but I could tell she wasn't there. "I need to go."

"Ah-huh," she groaned.

I grabbed my clothes and wrote her a quick note.

Welcome to my life. Mark.

With that, I left.

No one said a word as we drove to the helipad, flew to Shadows, and hurried down to the house.

Cole motioned for me to follow him into his office as Savannah raced to go find Olivia.

"Here's the email." He handed it to me. "I guess it came through the day before yesterday."

Quickly scanning the words, I felt that familiar rock land right in the center of my stomach. I used to have it lodged in my gut all the time when I was a child.

Mark,

I am in trouble. If you don't respond soon, I will have to find you myself.

Manuel.

"Okay." I shrugged. I didn't want to deal with this in the least. "I say we ignore it."

"He's already contacted Frank."

"What?" I shot out of my chair. "How?"

"He's got connections. You know that."

"Damn!" My fist pounded his desk. "I can't deal. I won't fall into this pit again, Cole."

Cole leaned back in his chair and let out a long sigh. "I'll get Frank here, and we'll discuss this further."

"Every goddamn time!" I clawed at the roots of my hair. I hated this. "I need to run or something, work out this shit." I left the room. Halfway down the hall, I ran into Savannah.

"Hey, Uncle Mark." She held Olivia up to see me. "She missed you. So did you ever find out who Keith's date was at my wedding?"

In one swoop, that little spitfire was in my arms for a snuggle. She smiled and blew me a spit bubble. "Nope, Uncle Keith doesn't do personal stuff." I puffed my cheeks out and made my eyes wide—a face she loved to bat at. "You are one lucky little girl, Livy." Savannah's face fell.

"What's wrong? Are you okay?"

"No," I said through a smile. I rubbed my nose over Livy's as she open-mouth drooled onto my chest.

"You know, I really hate it when you guys keep things from me." Her chin rose, and I knew she had her back up.

"Same old crap, different day." I gave her a wink, but I could tell she was upset.

"Is that so?" She brushed by me and swung open the office door.

"Hey, babe."

"Don't babe me. What is going on with Mark?" She planted her hands on her hips. I came up behind her. Livy started to wiggle when she saw her daddy.

Cole took two pills before he stood. "Manuel is looking for him."

J.L. DRAKE

Savannah whirled around to look at me, and her hands covered her mouth.

"There's my girl." Cole took Livy and kissed her tuft of hair. "Daddy missed you."

"Mark," Savannah touched my shoulder, "what do you think he wants?"

I shook my head. "My guess is he got himself in trouble again."

"But he's a police officer. Can't he get someone else to fix his messes?"

"Why would he risk his job, when he has me?" I smiled at her. "Look, don't worry, Savi. I can handle him." I ran my tongue along my teeth. My mouth felt dry. "I do need to go burn off some steam, though."

"Mario is here." Savanah made a face when she realized what she just said.

"And how would you know that?" Cole's tone didn't match his expression. We all tried to keep the stress out of Livy's life the best we could.

"In passing." She made a guilty face.

"Mark, take the afternoon off," Cole ordered, then turned to Savannah. "I think Mommy and I need to talk, little one. Uncle Mark will take you to Abigail for a bit."

Livy and I hurried out of the room before their fight and make-up session got in full swing. "Who knows, Livy, they might give you a little brother if Mommy keeps getting caught in that boxing ring." She gave me a gummy smile and laughed when she pulled at the collar of my sweater.

"You're home!" Abigail wrapped me in her arms and gave me one of her loving hugs. Livy pulled at her hair and screamed in delight. *Little crap.* "I have dinner on, but there is a quiche in the fridge, and Savannah made cookies before she joined you at the hospital."

Placing Livy in her bouncy chair, I sank onto the stool and leaned over the island.

"Problem, honey?"

"*He* wants to see me," I whispered.

She started to pour me some milk. "Who?"

When I didn't answer, she froze, and the milk poured over the rim of the glass and flowed across the counter top. I reached out and took the carton from her.

"Waa..." She cleared her throat. "Why does he want to see you?"

"Not sure."

She sank onto the seat next to me. "Okay, okay, we will deal with this. Just like last time."

My head hit the counter and I squeezed my eyes shut.

"Why don't you go get some sleep?"

"Yeah." I peeled my tired body off the stool and headed upstairs, where I passed out until morning.

I threw myself into early morning training, working harder than normal. If my muscles weren't screaming at me, Manuel was. That's how I spent the next twelve days.

Work out.

Eat a ton of carbs.

Sleep.

Repeat.

***

Manuel

The man in front of me at the bank had the worst smell. I tried to occupy myself by identifying the stench. It was like a homeless man covered in tomato sauce after being sprayed by a skunk. I wasn't the only one affected by his odor. The lady behind me kept clearing her throat and looking pointedly at him.

I glanced down at the paper in my hand. We just arrested an idiot for filing a false complaint against a customer who pissed him off at the corner market. I decided to help myself to his checkbook since I was in need of some fast cash, and because he had pissed *me* off.

"Next," the clerk said from behind the glass. The piece of human trash moved away, and I was finally able to take a deep breath of fresh air.

I watched as the tellers counted, gave out, and received different amounts of money. It made me giddy seeing all that cash transferring hands. Maybe I needed to think about robbing a bank.

I cashed the check I had made out for five hundred and followed the offensively stinking man to the parking lot. I waited until he was behind a truck before I pulled out my badge.

"Money, now," I demanded with my hand resting on my weapon.

"What?"

"Give me your money." I said it slower so he wouldn't question me again. I hated stupid people. Don't allow time to think; that's how you get yourself killed.

He carefully reached for his wallet, but then he leaped forward and charged at me. I elbowed him in the head, and he fell at my feet.

"Really?" I shook my head. "For Christ's sake, take a damn bath. You smell like a fucking trash bin!" I spat at him as I plucked the cash from his wallet. I dropped it by his head and hurried off, thinking he damn well deserved to be robbed.

***

Mark

Frank had been away the past few days, so I kept busy. Cole checked in often. I knew the house was worried about me, but I was fine as long as I stuck to my schedule. I craved another assignment to Mexico where I could let off some steam without getting into trouble.

My morning run up the mountain felt great, but nothing could shake the dread that stemmed from my past. We all had secrets, and mine were rooted deep. It didn't help that Manuel was the only one there that day.

"Stop," I muttered. "Don't go there right now."

I took a seat on a cool rock and looked over the lake and tried to clear my head. I munched on a protein bar and sipped my water. I thought about my life and how good it had been. Why did he have to show up again and ruin it? I needed a distraction.

Mark: Hi, things have been a bit rough around here. Just wanted to check in.

A few moments went by before it vibrated in my hand.

Mia: Crazy here too. Sorry I missed your last two calls. I've been thinking about you.

I felt the corner of my mouth tug upward.

Mark: So you miss me?

Mia: Kinda. Though I think I forget what you look like.

I smirked, then pulled a twelve-year-old girl move and took a selfie. I attached it to the text.

Mark: I want this mounted above your bed, in a brown frame to match my eyes.

Mia: Damn, you've bulked up. I may not recognize you the next time I see you.

A moment later, a picture came through of her in her blue scrubs in the nurse's lounge. Her hair was swept up into a messy bun, and her smile made me beam…I was glad I was alone.

My phone alerted me to another text. I opened it to see what she had to say when my stomach dropped.

Cole: Frank, thirty minutes, conference room.

Mark: 10-4.

I switched back to Mia's contact information.

Mark: Sorry, have to run. I'll try to call you later.

Mia: No problem, be safe.

I tipped my water and let it flow down the back of my throat before I raced back down the hill with Mia on my mind. I really missed her.

"Wow, Lopez, you've been working out extra hard." Frank took in my size. I had bulked up a bit, but I didn't think it was that noticeable.

"Ha! Someone has to keep in shape around here. How are you, Frank?"

We all took our seats at the long wooden table while Savannah placed coffee and cookies in front of us. She gave my shoulder a squeeze before she left.

"Okay," Frank opened a file and cut right to it like normal, "Manuel got hold of me two weeks ago looking for your number, Mark." I shifted in my seat. "No worries, I didn't give it to him, but I did pass along your email since I knew he already had it. When he didn't hear back from you, he tried me again. Said it was a huge emergency." He tossed a Post-It across the table. "Let's give Officer Lopez a call and see what he wants."

Cole gave me a nod, then brushed his finger over his lips—our code that he had my back, no matter what.

With a swipe to my jeans to clear the sweat from my hands, I dialed on the speakerphone. Three rings later, his voice barked over the line.

"Manuel!" he offered as a greeting.

"Been a while."

A door shut on his end, and his footsteps echoed loudly.

"Took you long enough."

"Been busy, Manuel."

"How have you been?"

"Heard you've been harassing my commander. You have my attention now. What do you want?"

"Typical Marine, aren't you? Nothing friendly, all business. Can't take some time for me?"

My temper was about to show itself. "Three minutes."

"Look, I—ah, got myself into a little trouble."

"Shocking…"

"I've had to skim out of the evidence locker. A deal that went wrong."

"Poker?"

"Yeah."

Frank reached for a pen and started to write on a pad of paper.

How much?

"How much?"

"Fifty-five thousand."

Fuck me!

I prepared to speak, but he cut me off.

"That was just the first time." My eyes shut. "It became a bit of a problem. Anyway, I didn't know the sergeant suspected something, and now they have me on tape."

"And how am I supposed to help?"

"Mark," his voice changed to the one I

remembered from our dark days, "remember I saw everything. I helped you get out of there—you owe me."

"It's been twenty-four years, Manuel. You can't just fuck up and expect me to clean up your messes. That cloud you hold over me covers you too."

Manuel cleared his throat. "I have you on video."

"All that could show is a traumatized little kid totally out of his mind. Not like they're going to try me for it now."

"Perhaps, but do you really want the truth getting out? Besides, you're not the only one who has connections."

"Then use yours."

Frank warned me to relax.

"You making any more trips to North Dakota?"

Cole lunged forward and muted the line in time as I jumped out of my seat, yelling.

"I'll fucking kill you if you touch her!"

"Okay," Cole held up his hands, "this is a game changer, Mark." He looked at Frank. "What do you suggest?"

"I don't want to know who is in North Dakota. Tell him you'll see what you can do just to buy us some time."

I unmuted the line and took a deep breath. "Give me some time, and I'll see what I can do."

"There he is." Manuel laughed, and my hand curled into a ball. "She's very pretty."

I lowered my head to the speaker and leveled out my voice. "If you touch her, kiss our arrangement goodbye."

***

Mia

"Why don't you plan a trip to visit, dear?"

"I don't have the time to take off right now, Mom." I paced a quiet room in the hospital.

"You always say that."

"Because it's true. I have patients who need me."

"Sweetheart, you're a nurse, not a doctor. You can take a weekend off and visit your family. We miss you." I pressed my head to the wall. "Ever since you moved to Minnesota, you haven't visited us once. Maybe we should come there."

"No." I cut her off, hating that I lied to my parents about which job I actually took. "Look, I'll see about getting a ticket to come out this weekend."

"Splendid."

Will Dad be there this weekend?

"Is Dad there?"

"No, sweetie, Dad is away right now. Some hunting thing. Lord knows with him. But if he knows you're coming, you know he'll work his time around you."

My pager started to vibrate. "Hey, hold on a second, Mom." I hit the button on my radio and spoke into the mic. "Go ahead."

"Mia, we need your help with Kenny."

"I'll be right there." I spoke back into the phone. "Mom—"

"I know, you *have* to go. Love you, Mia."

"Love you too, Mom." I raced down the hallway.

"Kenny!" Dr. Evans nearly shouted. "You need to calm down, and you need to take your medication."

"Get out!" Kenny screamed through his tears. *"Don't fucking touch me!"*

I wanted to run in the opposite direction. Kenny was getting worse. I hated that everyone was right. I was blinded by my love for the kid.

"Where's Mia?" Nurse Taylor called out.

"We paged her!" another voice said.

My tears were already on the surface. How much longer could I do this?

"No, you have poison on your hands." Kenny kicked the tray on the table, and I heard everything go flying. "Where's my mom?"

Shit. I stepped around the corner and rushed to his side.

"Kenny," I grabbed his head, "look at me. I'm here, right here by your side."

His eyes darted as he searched his brain until he made our connection.

"Mom?" His chest heaved while he looked around. "They tried to kill me."

"No," I kept my eyes locked on his, "they need to give you your medicine so you can get better. Don't you want to go outside soon and play lacrosse?" I pointed outside to where the sun was hovering over the mountains. "The only way you can get out of here is if you listen to Dr. Evans and do as the nurses say."

His grip on my arms soon relaxed and he leaned back to stare at the ceiling like he normally did when he knew I was right.

Dr. Evans gave me an annoyed look as he pushed the needle into the IV. I didn't stick around to find out why.

I burst through the rooftop doors in need of fresh air. When my hands landed on the cool metal railing, I let out the loudest scream I could muster. It just wasn't fair! I didn't know how much longer I could handle this. I closed my eyes and thought of her sweet face.

"I miss you so much, Kiley."

***

I was pleased I was able to get a window seat. My earphones were on immediately so I could tune the world out. Hozier found my stress and helped calm me.

My phone vibrated on my lap.

Mom: What is your flight number?

Mia: I had to fly into ND. AA768

Mom: Travel safe. Xo

Once we touched down, I grabbed my luggage and hurried to the doors.

"Mia!" Mom shouted with arms wide open. I raced toward her and nearly knocked her over. "Oh, sweetie, you look so good!"

"Hi, Mom." I buried my head into her hair and smelled the comfort I longed for.

She pulled back to look at me. "Are you all

right?"

No, but I wasn't about to dampen our mood.

I linked my arm through hers. "Yes, just tired. Let's get out of here."

Home was exactly how I remembered it, wide open with a sea salt breeze. The last time we all met up, we were at our cottage in New York, and before that, it was Arizona.

I opened the patio doors and leaned over the rail. The ocean sparkled, reminding me how much I missed it.

"Mia," Mom called from my doorway, "you want to go for a walk or grab something to eat?"

"Where's Dad?"

Her face fell slightly. "He hopes to be back Sunday."

Of course. Probably for the best anyway.

"A walk sounds nice."

Following our footprints back to the house a while later, we decided to sit for a bit. We caught up on everyone, and I learned my cousin Gab married one of my best friends in high school. That wasn't surprising, considering he had a lifelong crush on the girl.

"So," Mom's shoulder bumped mine, "when were you going to tell us that you took the job in North Dakota?"

I ducked my head. "How long have you known?"

"I wanted to send you flowers, and when I called the hospital's flower shop, they said no one by that name worked there. So, after some more calls, I heard my only daughter failed to mention she took the other offer."

"I'm sorry for lying, Mom, but I had to take that job."

She shrugged. "I guess. I'm just worried. Either way, it's not going to end well."

"I know that." My toes buried further into the sand. "It's just something I need to do."

"You're not his mother, Mia."

"But I'm all he's got. I might as well be. Mom, you're like his grandmother. You could visit him sometime."

Mom cleared her throat. "He doesn't know me anymore."

I dismissed her comment. I knew Kenny's condition hurt everyone, but that didn't mean we should give up on him.

"Maybe not, but I bring him comfort." I blinked the tears back. "Besides, it looks like it may only be a matter of weeks."

Mom reached out and took my hand. "Life can be unfair a lot of the time."

"Does Dad know I took the job?"

"No, I figured you would tell us when you were ready."

I leaned my head on her shoulder. "Thanks."

We spent the rest of the day relaxing and catching up. I used to be very close to my parents, but once I decided to go to nursing school, my father didn't understand why I didn't want to become a doctor. There were a few things my father and I didn't see eye to eye on.

"You've been checking your phone a lot," Mom observed as she set the salmon on the table. I dove into her famous garden salad from her greenhouse.

"You waiting on a call?" I poured some wine, which made her laugh. "Oh, a boy?"

My grin grew bigger. "Boy?"

"Sorry…man."

"No. I mean, I did meet someone, but it's nothing."

"Ha!" She raised an eyebrow. "You think you're going to get away with that? Spill it, lady."

"Okay, okay. He's nice, sweet, his smile makes me blush on the spot." My hair fell forward as I shook my head. "He almost let me win at pool." Mom laughed. "He just makes me feel good, you know? Like I don't have to try, and everything just comes naturally."

"Wow, sweetie, that's pretty special."

"Yeah, it kinda is, but his job makes him come and go a lot. So I'm not sure how easy it will be, if there is even a *will* left."

"Why do you say that? Did something happen?"

"It's been a month since I've seen him."

"A month? What does he do?"

Umm…

I reached for the ranch dressing, but she moved it out of my reach.

"Mia?"

"Military." Her face didn't fall, but it didn't light up either. "I know, Mom, please spare me the military life advice. But…"

"No, sweetie," she touched my hand, "you're misreading my reaction. I think I'm more processing the fact that you let someone in. After what you went through with—"

"I know. I didn't think I would ever be interested

in someone like that again. It's just Mark, is—"

"Ohhh, one syllable." She winked.

"Oh, God, no, not the bedroom talk again." I smacked my head, laughing. My mother could give a bit too much detail when it came to her sex life. I hated that my father had a one syllable name.

"I'm only saying it's easy to scream—"

"La-la-la…" I covered my ears like a child. "Mom, please, we have a delicious meal here. Let me keep it down, okay?"

"Fine." She sipped her wine. "So what does he look like?"

I hated that my face gave so much away. "He's tall, brown hair, perfect teeth, a body that could put any trainer to shame."

Mom started to fan herself. "Sweet Lord in heaven, my lady bits are on high alert."

"Yeah, mine too," I muttered into my glass.

"So," Mom said, changing the subject, "have you spoken to your brother much?"

I set my fork down. My brother and I were like oil and water. "Nope."

"Mia, he's been back for three weeks. You should give him a call."

"Phone works both ways, Mom." Nice to know he survived Afghanistan.

"He hurt his back, so they sent him home early."

I poked at a peppercorn. "Lucky break." My brother Ray was ten times worse than my father with his views on things. We hadn't gotten along since we were ten.

The trip was amazing. I really needed more one on one with my mother. It bothered me that she was there so often on her own. Dad worked entirely too much, but in fairness to him, he did warn her before they got married.

My return flight was on time and landed in North Dakota at four thirty a.m., which gave me exactly two and half hours before I started my shift.

Bed called my name, but I had to trudge on back, shower, change, and head to the hospital before I could even think of letting my mind turn off.

***

"Mia." My head bounced off something hard. "Mia, you need to wake up." My eyes opened to Molly. "Dr. Evans is looking for you."

My surroundings kicked in, and I swiftly moved to my feet off the bench in the ER.

"Okay." My head pleaded with me to go back to sleep, but I declined, not wanting to lose my job. I switched to autopilot, knowing I had to get to work.

"He's been paging you for, like, ten minutes." She looked annoyed.

She moved when I did and stayed close as I headed to the station.

"You're getting a bit of a reputation around here, Mia."

"What?" I mumbled over my shoulder. "For what?"

"For flirting with the patients."

I shook my head, not even sure I heard her right. She continued on my heels, huffing at every corner.

"And…that you screw in the on call room…" My heels drove into the squeaky floor, and I spun

99

around. As soon as she saw my face, her hand slapped over her mouth. "Oh, Mia," she squeaked, "I'm sorry."

"Wow." I threaded my fingers through the top of my hair and balled it in my palm. I was way beyond pissed, but I kept my composure. With a step toward her, I whispered, "Mark and I never slept together." Nice to know the staff thought we did. I swore I heard her sigh with relief. "Not that it's anyone's business who I sleep with."

She gave a slight nod, but I didn't trust her, which felt pretty shitty. I liked Molly.

I thought I should leave in case she had anything else to say, and if that was the case, I might toss a punch, and there went my career. Wow, that would be two times in one day. Evans and Molly. Fate was testing me big time.

Avoiding a pissed off doctor in a hospital was like avoiding an elephant in a tiny room. It ain't going to last long.

I felt like a complete fool in front of the staff, and every time I saw a white coat, I ducked to avoid meeting Dr. Evans. Once when I thought I heard his voice in the cafeteria, I ran out into the hall like an idiot.

It wasn't until I was walking out the door that I came face to face with the doctor.

"Mia. Where have you been?"

I shifted my bag over my shoulder. "Rounds, and helping out at the ER."

"We had a heart transplant, and I wanted you to be there."

So…you weren't upset that I fell asleep at work?

"Oh, wow."

"Yeah," he shrugged, "I know how much you wanted to be a part of one and...anyway."

"I'm sorry, I just..."

He checked his phone. "Well, Mia, I have to go. My sister and I have dinner plans."

"Yeah, yes, of course." I stepped back, not sure what to do with myself. That was so unlike his usual behavior. "Ahh," I decided to go for his first name, "Francis." He turned to look at me. "Thanks."

With tight smile, he nodded and hurried on his way. I contemplated his behavior the whole way home. Dr. Evans had always been flirty and seemed to have no boundaries when it came to my personal life choices. However, this was an odd side of him; this was different. I wouldn't go any further.

I felt a lot better after a ten-hour nap, a hot shower, and a decent meal. I curled up on my couch with Butters, and we watched *Homeland* until my phone vibrated next to me.

Dr. Evans: Will I see you today? Or will you hide away in the ER again?

"I didn't know we texted each other," I grumbled, not sure what to think.

Mia: I think you'll see me.

Dr. Evans: Good.

"Good," I repeated confidently. "What the hell

does that mean?"

CHAPTER FOUR

My coffee warmed my hand as I walked up the hospital steps. The bite in the air was the first sign of fall. It was my favorite time because it meant holidays, and that meant wine, meals, and pie. No matter what moron didn't bring the mashed potatoes or carrots, there was always pie.

"Someone brought bagels." Vikki Taylor pointed to the room. Before I could nab one, Dr. Evans stepped in my way.

"Good morning. You almost missed out." He held up an extra bagel. I started to reach for it, but he pulled it back. "Will you answer your pages?"

I crossed my arms. "Yes."

"Okay." He handed it to me.

"Okay?"

"Yeah, okay."

"Okay…"

"You already said that."

I rolled my eyes but raised the warm pastry in the air in thanks.

***

That was how the next two days went—he was friendly and always around.

I pushed open the door and plastered a warm smile on my face.

"Hey, Kenny." I rubbed his wrist gently. "How do you feel?"

"Hurt." His tongue ran along his pale lips. "I saw Dad today. He said he missed you."

"Yeah? That's nice."

His gaze darted around the room. "Mom?"

"Yes, Kenny?"

"I need to close my eyes."

"Of course." I tugged the blanket up to his chin and slipped outside. I pushed away the heavy cloud that hung low over that room.

"You okay?" Dr. Evans asked from the opposite wall, his hands in his pockets and a worried expression on his face.

"Yeah."

"Okay, do you want to assist with a fractured patella at two-thirty?"

"Count me in."

"OR Four, don't be late."

Nurse Alvin raced to my side with his palm up and his other fist in the center.

"On three, for room 33."

"Clever." I glanced over his shoulder.

"Stats?"

"Hot, eyes for days, huge boobs, and one of them burst. It's like *American Horror Story* up in there."

"I'm picking scissors." Sarcasm dripped from

104

my tongue.

He grinned. "I thought you'd be my favorite. I guess I was right."

And I thought you were gay, so we'll call it even.

I turned around and came to a halt. There was Mark on his phone. He looked over and found me instantly. I gave a wave, then I felt strange. What happened if he didn't like me anymore? I hadn't heard from him much.

Removing the first chart I could get my hands on, I moved into that room.

"What is going on today?" I quickly scanned his chart, and just as I saw the little red dot that indicated who he was, the door opened behind me.

"Paul is fine," Mark announced behind me.

"All right."

"Mia, can we—?"

Paul looked at me, then at Mark. "Fell out of the Land Rover, dislocated my shoulder, and I fucked up my spine."

"All right, let me get your vitals before we start anything else."

Threading the cuff up over his huge arm, I secured it in place. "Lord, sweetheart, your hands are freezing," Paul said with a laugh.

"Sorry, I can hardly ever get warm."

"Lucky."

"Not when you live where there's snow. I seem to be a lost cause."

I listened and recorded his blood pressure. "What's your pain level on a scale of one to ten?"

"One point five."

"He's fine," Mark huffed again as he went to

Paul's side and grabbed his shoulder and arm. "Take a deep breath."

"Mark!" I gasped, panicked.

Jerking Paul's elbow up with a twist, he snapped his shoulder back into place. I cupped my mouth and waited for his reaction.

"Thanks, man." Paul leaned back and sighed before looking at me. "I'm better now."

"Um…" I was lost for words. "You could have damaged his spine further, Mark!"

"No, that was a fib." Paul grinned. "My boy, here, has been trying to get us hurt so he had an excuse to see you."

Oh? Don't grin, don't grin.

"Thanks, man," Mark muttered.

"Sure thing." Paul settled into the bed. "Can I get some of that green Jell-O? You know, in the little cup with the mini spoon." He mimed eating. "It's my favorite."

I was still stunned. "I'm going to go find the doctor."

***

Mark

Paul pointed after Mia, and I ran out after her.

"Hey," I caught her arm, "what's wrong?" She started to say something but stopped herself. "What?"

"How have you been?" Her voice didn't match her face.

"Busy, stressed. You?"

She looked around as if she didn't want to be seen talking with me. "Same."

"Will you have dinner with me tonight?"

Her gaze shot to mine. "Umm, I have plans."

"Oh." My stomach dropped. "Can you cancel them?"

"Mark, I didn't know when I'd see you next, so no, I can't."

"I guess I deserved that."

"Did you get my text?"

Shit, she did text me a few days ago, but I forgot to respond. "Yeah, but I've been dealing with something kinda—"

She stepped back a pace. "I get it. Secret op stuff. Anyway, I need to grab the doctor."

Molly walked by. "Hey, Mark." She beamed up at me. "You're looking bigger than the last time I saw you."

Mia turned and started walking away.

"Wait." I brushed by Molly. "Wait, are you mad at me for not calling?"

Mia let out a deep sigh while she flipped her long, shiny hair out of her face.

"Look, Mark, trust me when I tell you I understand your job needs to be hush-hush. I can't even imagine what your life must be like." She lowered her voice so Molly couldn't hear. "You tell me you like me, but I barely heard from you. I guess I thought maybe you moved on."

"No, God, no." I started to take a step toward her, but she moved back with a glance at Molly watching us from the nurse's station. "I'm sorry. I'm dealing with something personal."

"Mia?" Dr. Evans came up holding a chart. When he caught sight of me, his eyebrows pinched together. "Mark, I wasn't aware you were back at the hospital."

"Buddy got hurt."

He ignored me and looked at Mia. "We still on for tonight?"

You have got to be shitting me! She swallowed hard then gave him a nod.

"Great, see you at eight."

Once he left, she was about to leave, but I stopped her. "Really? The doctor?"

"He's a friend."

"Does he know that's what he is to you?" The look on her face told me I stepped over a line. "I'm sorry."

"No." She shook her head. "People seem to have a lot to say to me today."

"When can I see you next?"

"I don't know." She turned and left.

Fuck.

"You fucked up," Paul mumbled around a mouthful of nasty green Jell-O. "So fix it."

"How?"

He laughed. "You're asking me?"

"You have a sister."

"We don't discuss those things. Ask June or Abby."

I pulled out my phone and made a quick call to June.

"Hello, Marcus. How are you, dear?" Within ten minutes, a plan was born, and I had the *dirty* little Nurse Vikki Taylor on board. I hurried down to the lobby to see what I could find.

I waited out of sight of the nurse's station and watched as Vikki called Mia over.

"Hey, sweetie, these came for you."

Mia smiled. "Really?" She touched the petal of one of the roses. "Who sent them?"

"Not sure, but there's a card."

She pulled the card free and read my note. "Where is he?" Her eyes narrowed as she scanned the hallways.

"Who?" Nurse Taylor shook her head at Mia, who made a face. "It's sweet, though."

"Mmmhmm." She tucked the note in her pocket and touched the flowers one more time before she left.

Nurse Taylor turned to me and shrugged.

***

Manuel

My leg bounced wildly under the table as I waited impatiently for the sergeant to call me in. I wanted a smoke, but I wasn't about to leave and have him hunt me down. Instead, I twirled the long Marlboro between my fingers like a drummer with his stick.

My partner was told to wait in another room. Why we were separated was beyond me. Finally, the door opened, and in walked the sergeant and two people I didn't recognize. If I were to guess, I'd say they were corporate.

"Mr. Lopez, my name is Connie Wilson. I'm

with Internal Affairs." A tall, broad-shouldered woman took a seat across from me. Her pantsuit looked as if it were tailored for a man. "Do you know why we called you in today?"

I shook my head. "Nope."

"Do you live locally, Mr. Lopez?" I didn't respond. I knew she would have read my file. She pulled out a pair of square framed glasses and placed them on the bridge of her nose while she read a document. "You've been on the force for how long?" I held my ground and stayed silent. "Would you say your partner and you are close?" With a sigh, she unbuttoned her jacket and leaned back to study me. "Okay."

She glanced at the man next to her, and he gave her a terse nod. She opened the file and handed me a photo.

Fuck me upright, this was not happening.

"You care to comment?"

I handed her back the photo and scratched at the two-day-old beard I was sporting. "I want a lawyer."

A grin almost slipped as she pushed to her feet. "That might be a wise idea."

***

Mark

I waited in the same spot and watched, ready for attempt number two. My morning effort was a bit of a failure, but this afternoon I was ready.

Mia came around the corner, looking tired. She

spotted the red box and eyed it carefully.

"Nurse Taylor?" she called out.

"It arrived ten minutes ago."

She opened the card with a sigh. The firm line of her lips softened into the beginning of a smile. Her finger ran under the cover and opened the box of Godiva chocolates.

"Where is he?" she asked again. This time I stepped around the corner and she saw me. "You need to stop sending me gifts."

"Why?"

She glanced around before she tucked a loose strand of hair behind her ear.

"Because people think we slept together."

"Okay?" I didn't get the big deal.

She took my hand and led me around the corner to an empty hallway. "Mark, we went on one date."

"I remember."

"We didn't even sleep together—"

"No." I stepped closer so her back pressed flat against the wall. "Seems to me, my lips were busy doing other things." She blinked a few times as if she were remembering. I stood straighter. She needed to know I wasn't playing around. "I'm sorry, Mia, I really am. Will you please give me another chance?"

She placed her hand on my chest to keep me back. "You're going to get me into trouble, Mark."

"Then have dinner with me tonight." My fingers moved to play with a piece of her silky hair. "Come on, Mia, you know there's something between us."

"Honestly, I don't want to be just someone you play with while you're here."

My head snapped back at her accusation. "You think that's what I'm doing?"

"Yeah, I do."

"Oh, Mia." I tilted my head, a little thrown off by the thought I would treat her that way. "That's so, so far from the truth."

"Look, I have to show up tonight. It's a staff thing." She sighed. "But I'll call you when I'm done."

"Thank you." I leaned down and kissed her cheek softly. My phone rang in my pocket, so I stepped back to let her go. She gave me a tentative smile before she hurried around the corner.

"Lopez," I muttered into my phone while I watched her walk away. She had a gorgeous sway to her hips.

"He is now on suspension. They got a tip from another cop that he was up to something, which made them check the tapes. Sure enough…" Frank rambled in his normal manner. "You know what that means."

My throat grew thick. "Yeah." I hung up and pressed number one on my speed dial.

"Cole, I need to get a tail on Manuel."

"Considerate it done. When will you be back?"

"Not sure yet."

"Do what you gotta do."

"Thanks, man."

Molly was visiting Paul when I came back into the room. I shook my head at Paul not to mention Mia.

"Hey, Mark." Molly smiled around a plastic spoon. "You want?" She held up some Jell-O.

"No, God, no." I made a face and tried not to watch it jiggle in her hand.

"The man doesn't stop eating, ever, but you show him Jell-O and he wants nothing to do with it."

"That's because it isn't even in the food groups." I sank into the chair. My stress was high, and I wasn't sure how to deal with it.

"You have plans tonight?" Molly popped the last spoonful of Jell-O in her mouth.

"Not until later."

"We're all meeting up at The Blue Room at eight thirty. You should come."

A grin broke across my face. "You know what, that might be fun."

She beamed. "Really?"

"Yeah." I glanced at Paul meaningfully. "You wanna go out tonight?"

"I just got cleared, so yeah, I could use a drink."

Paul and I met in the hotel lobby at nine. We took a cab to The Blue Room and walked through the doors around 9:15.

Mia was next to Dr. Evans, and they seemed to be hitting it off. She was laughing, and his arm was behind her chair.

"Hey, boys!" Molly yelled, waving as she jumped to her feet.

Mia turned, and her jaw nearly hit the table.

"You may have to run interference," I muttered to Paul, who knew Molly had a crush on both of us. Really, she wasn't particularly picky. She just wanted any one of the Blackstone members. She was great, but far from my type.

113

"Hey, I'm Mark." I introduced myself to a few people I didn't recognize. I gave Nurse Taylor a wink. "Now, are you going to behave tonight?"

"Oh, Mark," she said, blushing, "you're so bad."

"Molly, I didn't know you invited guests," Dr. Evans muttered into his beer.

"They were in town and had nothing to do, so I invited them along."

Mia glanced at me, and her gaze dropped down my front. I did the same to her, letting my focus run down her red halter, stopping at her cleavage. Oh, how I missed that cleavage.

"Mia, you look nice tonight." I smiled, not caring that the pretty doctor glared at me.

"So do you."

"I heard what you did today," Dr. Evans said, interrupting our little moment. "It was extremely dangerous. If that patient had a spinal injury, you could have done some real damage."

"But he didn't."

His eyes went wide. I took it not many talked back to him. "And you know that how, exactly?"

Paul smirked.

"Where did you go to school?" I asked.

Dr. Evans glanced at Mia before he answered. "Boston."

"Ever have to determine whether or not to remove someone's leg, while being fired at from three different directions? Or tuck in your buddy's organs and hope the stitch job you did will last until you hit the chopper?"

He didn't answer.

"I may not have gone to Boston, but I've done

my share of patching up. Paul's spine was in line, no swelling, no slipped discs, just a dislocated shoulder."

"You could have been wrong," he challenged pathetically.

"Not likely," Paul added, "because he was the one who popped it out."

"What?" Mia looked confused. "On purpose?" Paul smiled as he took a drink from his beer. "Why would you do such a thing?"

I looked directly at her. "You know why."

"That's insane!" Dr. Evans blurted out.

"Nah," Paul chuckled, "we're actually even."

I leaned over and clicked his bottle to mine.

"I don't think I want to know the rest of that story." She held up her hands, and a small smile played with the corners of her mouth. "Come on, Francis, why don't you buy me a drink?" Mia walked toward the bar with the doctor, not missing the smirk that passed between me and Paul.

Francis!

Nurse Taylor started to share a few ER stories, so I decided to mingle with some of the other staff. They all seemed pretty friendly.

After a bit of time, I could see the girls were tuning into the music. It was only a matter of time before...

"Who wants to dance?" Nurse Taylor clapped her hands together.

"I want to!" Molly chimed in.

Dr. Evans whispered in Mia's ear, and she shook her head as he stood and headed for the bar once again.

"Oh, I love this song," Molly squealed. "Come on, Mia, dance with me."

Mia's face fell. "Oh, I don't really—"

"Now, that's a flat-out lie." Nurse Taylor nearly lifted her out of her chair. "We all know you can shake it."

I twisted in my seat so I could see the dance floor better. Justin Timberlake's "Rock Your Body" boomed through the speakers.

She started to move to the beat. Nurse Taylor pointed to the screen where the video was streaming. Just as I wondered why, Mia started to mimic JT's dance moves. Paul laughed and slapped my shoulder as she moved her hips in a way you'd only see on the video. I couldn't hide my amusement.

"Where is everyone?" Dr. Evans asked one of the other girls.

"Dancing."

"Oh, shoot me now," he muttered before taking a shot of tequila.

Paul looked less than impressed himself.

"What's the matter, *Francis*, you don't dance?" I asked. He didn't answer, and I threw back my drink and stood.

The crowd was thick, but I moved easily across the floor. Molly spotted me first and yelled.

My body was right up behind Mia's when the song changed to "Imma Be" by The Black Eyed Peas. I watched to see what speed her hips would go and matched it before I slid my hand around her stomach.

"Mark," Molly mouthed to her with a strange

116

expression.

She reached back and grabbed my thigh as she ground her behind into my nearly painful erection. I couldn't help but watch the skin that peeked out on her lower back when she leaned forward. My hand roamed around her stomach, occasionally dipping low. Her head leaned against my shoulder, but as soon as the song picked up, she moved away and started dancing, then pointed at me to show my moves.

Oh, Mia, I always loved a challenge.

I pulled out the best moves I had and popped my body to the music. I spun on my toes and dropped to the floor, all my weight balanced on my wrist, then bounced to my feet. When I bent back down, I sent a wave through my body. I came up directly in front of Mia. She had on a sexy smile as she looked at up at me.

"I'm impressed," she said, laughing.

My arm hooked her waist, my knee wedged between her legs, and we started to dirty dance.

The music morphed into Tove Lo, "Talking Body." When the chorus came on, I gripped her tighter.

It wasn't until the song ended that we realized everyone else had gone back to the table.

"Drink?" I pointed to the bar. She nodded, and I took her hand and led her to the counter. I had to move her in front of me since there was only enough room for one. I locked my arms on either side of her and pressed my sweaty front to her back.

"Beer?" She looked over her shoulder. I leaned down and nearly brushed my lips over hers.

"Long Board." I handed the bartender my credit card.

She looked away. "Long Board," she called out, but the guy couldn't hear. She hopped up and leaned her body over the counter.

I had to blink back the dirty thoughts and force my hands to stay down. When she went to move, I helped her to her feet, spun her around, and leaned into her ear.

"I want to get out of here. I don't know how much longer I can behave in public."

The excitement in her eyes told me she felt the same.

"Let's finish our drinks, then we'll leave separately."

I shook my head. "Together."

"Mark," her hands went to her hips, "I work with these people. They already know too much about me. I don't want to be on Francis's shit list."

"That might be too late." I flicked my head toward where the man in question stared at us.

"Shit." Her eyes closed.

This was ridiculous. I ran my hands through her hair and lowered my lips to hers. I waited for her to meet me halfway. I would never force myself on her.

"Kiss me, Mia," I muttered across her lips. My heart beat like a drum. I wanted to feel the way I did before.

Her hands braced on my stomach as she stepped up on her toes and met me with the same intensity that was coursing through me.

I felt her moan travel over her tongue and vibrate

against mine. Jesus Christ, this girl was going to kill me. My hand moved under her shirt and swiped along her smooth skin. She pulled away. "We should go."

I paid the bill, and we hurried over to the table.

"Where were you?" Paul grinned. I gave him the finger but made sure Mia didn't see it.

"I'm going to go." Mia grabbed her jacket from her chair next to Dr. Evans.

He put his hand over hers. "Can I speak with you for a moment?" She glanced at me before she gave a quick nod.

***

Mia

I was so incredibly pumped up on lust that I could barely walk. My thighs practically screamed to be spread open, but instead I had to try to act normal and in control while I spoke with one of my superiors.

We stepped outside the building and into the chilly night air.

Dr. Evans stopped in front of me and turned with a strange expression.

"Call me crazy, Mia, but I thought we had something going on here."

"Oh! I…" I felt my face heat up. Why was it, when a woman found a male to be friends with, one of them had to screw it up with emotion? When would we learn? I guessed we could never be friends now.

"Maybe I need to be blunt." His lips twisted to one side. "I like you, Mia. I think you're funny and smart. I *do* think you're wasting your skills just being a nurse—"

...and there it was...

I stopped his chatter. "Dr. Evans, ah, Francis. For lack of a better expression, I'm flattered, and if we rewound to a few months ago, maybe some more could have happened. But where our biggest problem lies is that I love being *just* a nurse."

"But—"

"Please let me finish." He nodded and closed his mouth. "And I also met Mark, and we are really hitting it off."

He waited a beat before he spoke. "What kind of a future are you going to have with someone who disappears days—no, months—on end with no explanation? How do you know he doesn't have lots of you in different countries?"

Ouch. I hate doubt.

"I don't," I shrugged, "but that's something we're going to have to work out if this continues into something."

"Well," he sighed, "I guess there's nothing else to talk about."

"I'm sorry, Francis, I really am."

"Me too. I really hope you don't get hurt, Mia." He leaned down, kissed my cheek, then left.

I sagged against the window and whispered, "Me too."

"Hey," Mark called out softly. I looked over and saw he had his hands in his pockets. "You okay?"

"Yeah." I pushed off the glass. "Let's go."

Through the whole cab trip and elevator ride, we remained quiet. Dr. Evans' words bounced around in my head, making me questions things I didn't want to.

Mark had my hand, and a few times I caught him studying me.

I locked the door behind us and tossed my purse on the table. "You want anything?"

"Water, please." He sat on the stool and rested his elbows on the counter, watching as I moved about. "You know, I can speak five languages fluently, read lips, and I can bring a grown man to his knees just by tapping him hard on the side of the neck." He paused for a moment. "But for the life of me, I can't figure out why you've shut down on me tonight." He took the bottle of water from my hand.

"Sorry, I—"

"I'm not looking for an apology."

I cleared my head. Truth or lie? "I guess Dr. Evans just pointed out a few things that might make this hard for me...or us."

"Such as?"

"You leaving with no word for months."

He unscrewed his bottle of water and took a long sip. Now I wish I could read *his* mind.

"I won't disappear for months on end, but maybe a week here and there. I am sorry for being so quiet last time. There are some things going on that need my attention. I won't lie, Mia, being with me wouldn't be easy. I haven't figured it all out yet either, but I know I like being with you. Can't we at least try?"

Try? I analyzed my feelings to see if that was

something I could do.

"I think—" A knock sounded at my door, and I held up a finger.

"Sorry, Mia." My neighbor Ed had his security uniform on. "I wouldn't have come by, but I heard you come in. I got called to cover a shift."

Butters shoved past his legs, and his huge, furry paws landed on my chest. I had to take a step back to absorb his weight. "Hey, boy."

"He's been clawing at my door since you got home."

"No problem. I don't work tomorrow, so we can hang out. Oh, and thanks for the groceries. Let me know what I owe you."

"Okay." He looked over my shoulder. "Hey, I'm sorry." He gave Mark a wave. "I'll call you later."

"Sure thing." I took the leash from him. "Come on in."

The leash was yanked out of my hand as Butters ran to Mark, who opened his arms to greet him.

"Hey, Butters." He scratched his ears.

"You two know each other?" I picked up his bottle cap and fiddled with it between my fingers.

"Yes," Mark bent down and kissed his head, "I woke to hot breath in my face and a rather long lick last time I was here. It almost made me decide to stay!" He raised his eyebrows at me.

"Oh, really." I laughed as I leaned over the counter. "He's the building's dog. We all take turns looking after him. Though I seem to get him the most."

"That's because he's sweet on you. I can see I will have competition."

His comment made me smile. He could be so sweet without even trying. After another ear scratch, he glanced over at me, then reached for my hand to pull me around the counter and in front of him.

"You were saying something."

I slid my hands over his strong shoulders as he closed his eyes. My fingers dipped and rose over his muscles.

"I'd like to try," I whispered, and his eyes popped open, but instead of a smile, his eyes almost darkened.

He stood, and his gaze held mine as his hands slid around my neck. He dipped down and gave me a closed lip kiss. It was soft but had a lot behind it, almost as if he was sealing my decision to his.

My chest heaved against his, and the friction gave me temporary relief. His fingers inched around before my straps to my halter fell forward. I stepped back and removed my shirt and tossed it on the floor.

"Wow." His gaze roamed over me, but in a way that made me feel cherished. Mark had an incredible way of making me feel that I belonged to him, and I was all right with this.

He deliberately removed his shirt and dropped it on top of mine. With a step forward, I raised my hand and hovered it over one of his scars. I flicked my eyes up to see if it was all right. He gave a quick nod then flinched at my cold fingertip, but he soon relaxed. The raised skin was mostly smooth, but a few bumps were visible.

"Did they hurt?" I whispered, studying his body

further. It was like a human canvas of his life; every mark carried a story.

"Some did, yes."

My fingers slid around his side and stopped at a deep groove. His hand slapped on top of mine, and I caught his expression before he gave me a grin.

"Ticklish," he muttered, but I could see it was more than that. He raised my fingers and kissed them gently. "Come on." He nodded toward my bed.

Once at the foot of my bed, he brushed my hair up off my bare chest so it was exposed. He ran his fingers along the curve of my breasts, stopping to feel the weight of one. His pace was intoxicating. His slow movements nearly drove me mad, but I managed to remain still. I couldn't recall ever being touched like this. He tenderly rolled my nipple between his thumb and knuckle.

His free hand slid down the front of my belly and freed the button on my jeans. With a light tug they pooled around my feet and were kicked off to the side as I stepped away from them.

I felt his chest heave, but I was too excited to see what was waiting for me under his jeans. With quick work, I did the same to him.

Then there we were, both naked, standing in the darkness with only a little light peeking through from the city below.

Normally I'd be covering myself up, wanting to crawl under the covers to hide from my insecurities, but not with him. Mark made me feel…sexy and confident.

He stepped into me, wrapped his hands around

my face, and kissed me so hard I forgot who I was.

One hand slipped under my legs as he lifted me and carefully placed me on the bed. He slipped a condom on all the while he kept his eyes on me. His body hovered over me, and he smiled. His eyes sparkled in the little light we had.

"How?" His words were barely a whisper.

My eyebrows knit together.

He brushed my hair off my neck, then continued to travel along my collarbone.

"How have I gone this long without knowing you?" He kissed the corner of my eye. "Without knowing your touch?" He threaded his fingers through mine. "Without knowing your heartbeat?" His lips skimmed my chest. He positioned his hips before he pushed forward. "Without knowing what you feel like inside?" My back arched as he eased his way inside me, and he let out a puff of air once he was fully in.

With his jaw strained, he forced his eyes open. "Are you all right?"

I nodded but had to bite my bottom lip in fear I'd burst. His words still looped in my head. How could someone make you so warm inside?

He leaned his weight on one arm before he started to move. He watched himself slip in and out. I was lost in his body; the way his muscles moved was mesmerizing. I closed my eyes and let the euphoria spread right down to my toes. The coil inside started to tighten, and instead of overthinking the way I normally did, I gave myself over to him.

Mark nuzzled right behind my ear. "You make me forget when I'm with you." I wanted to ask what he meant, but he held me still and kissed me as he picked up the pace. He had taken over all of me, mind, body, and heart. I pushed all fear away, opened my arms, and let the rush take me over.

Colors—all I saw was a spectacular sea of colors floating by me.

His body flopped down next to me, and we both fought to catch our breath. His arm curled around my middle and pulled me to his chest. He kissed my hair with a deep sigh.

"Mia." He kissed down my shoulder.

I kissed his arm and felt my eyes grow heavy. I vaguely remembered him going into the washroom before I drifted off to a very pleasant sleep.

CHAPTER FIVE

Sunlight burst through my windows, and I rolled over to an empty bed. My eyes fluttered open as last night came racing back to me. I swiftly changed into a pair of panties and a shirt before stepping around the partition and stopping with a grin.

Mark and Butters were on the couch watching the news. Mark was talking to him about something while he ate a bowl of cereal.

I grabbed my camera and snapped a quick picture. The two of them turned around at the sound of the shutter.

Mark's expression was enough to send me running back to bed for round two.

"Morning." His voice had a slight rasp to it. "Hope you don't mind. We were hungry." He held up the bowl.

"Not at all." I was pleased he felt comfortable enough to help himself. "Come on, Butters, let's go outside."

Butters didn't move.

"We already went out." Mark rubbed the big

dog's head.

"Oh," I grinned, "thank you."

"Sure." He watched me pour some coffee, then his warm arms were around me. "You know, you're quite responsive when you're sleeping."

"Am I?" I leaned back and kissed him.

"Yes, it was almost torture."

I turned in his hold. "Well, you have my permission to wake me if that feeling comes back."

He bent down, lifted me over his shoulder, and headed back to the bed.

"Mark!" I shrieked, but all it gained me was a slap to the butt.

His phone rang, bringing us back to reality with news that he needed to leave around four.

He showered and changed while I watched from the bed. I didn't want to show I was disappointed he had to go. I knew this was how it was going to be.

I crawled to the edge of the mattress when he slipped his shoes on. I wrapped my arms around his neck and kissed his cheek. My hair fell around me and in his face.

"Call me when you can."

He twisted, took hold of me, and brought me onto his lap so I straddled him. His hand cupped my butt and gave it a squeeze.

"I can honestly say this is the hardest time I've ever had leaving someone." He rubbed the back of his fingers across my cheek. "I want to take you with me."

I smiled. "Do you have any idea when you'll be back?"

That's when I saw it, the flinch in his face. *Why*

didn't I keep my mouth shut? Before he could answer, I moved off his lap and tried to think of something else to say. I opened a small silver box on my dresser.

"Well, whenever it is," I held up two keys before I tossed them at him, "you know where to find me."

"Keys?" He smiled as he examined them. "Lucky me."

I got dressed since Butters started to whine by the door. Mark held my hand while we were in the elevator and outside.

"Well." I sighed inwardly. "See ya later."

He studied my face briefly before he pulled me in for a kiss.

"I'll call when I get there. Try to keep warm without me." Then he reconsidered his words and smiled an evil smile. "Cancel that, you'll just have to be chilly!" He kissed me one last time before he got in his car and left.

I was a left with an empty feeling, but I pushed it aside. I did agree to this.

Butters pulled on the lead. I opened the gate to the private yard for our building and let him run.

"Hi." A man waved from a bench behind me. "Beautiful afternoon, isn't it?" His heavy knit sweater stretched over his chest when he leaned back, and his well-worn boots were stuck way out as he straightened his knees.

I smiled back and looked up at the sky and saw the dark grey clouds that threatened to roll in. "It is now, but it looks like we might get a storm."

"Then I guess you could say it's the calm before the storm." He smiled, but somehow it made me uneasy. Plus he stared too long for my liking.

"Perhaps." I glanced at Butters, who had found a puddle to drink from.

"I'm Chris." The man offered a hand, and I noticed an upside down cross tattoo that bled into his fingers. "I just moved in."

"Nice to meet you," I said over my shoulder, pretending I didn't notice his gesture for a handshake.

"I'm taking over Larry's job for a bit."

What? I turned to him. "Larry, as in the manger?"

"Yup, some family thing." He scratched above his ear quickly. "What's your name?"

With a sigh, I turned to face my new neighbor. "Mia."

"Nice to meet you, Mia. 3D, right?"

I gave a short nod before I called Butters over. This man had a strange way of looking at someone, like he was searching for something. Butters was at my side in a flash.

"Pretty dog." Chris dropped his hand for Butters to come smell him, but he didn't go. I didn't blame him.

A raindrop hit my cheek with a splat, then another, and another.

"I should go. Come on, Butters."

"See you around." Chris stayed put as I ran inside.

***

Mark

I'd been home four days, and I kept missing Mia's calls. Between our hectic schedules, it had been hard to stay in touch.

When I actually did stop, my body hummed to be with her. When I closed my eyes at night, I could see her under me. The look on her face right before she gave herself over to me made my stomach tighten.

"Hey, man." Cole came into my room and jumped up on my desk. "You ready?"

"Yeah." I folded a pair of camo pants into my bag and zipped it closed.

"How's Mia?"

"Good." Her name made my insides twitch.

"Is your head in this?"

I turned around to find him with an odd expression. "Of course."

"All right." He hopped down and left. I stopped and thought if Cole was sensing something, I must not be right.

Get your shit together.

The trip to New York gave me time to clear my head and focus on what I had ahead.

The minute we landed, I texted Mia.

Mark: *Be out of reach for a bit, call you later.*

I waited a moment, then went with what was really on my mind.

Mark: *I need to see you.*

131

.   It was just after six where she was. She was probably in the middle of her rounds.

"Ready?" Keith unclipped his seatbelt and reached for his duffle bag.

Keith and Cole decided to come along to New York to help Frank and me deal with this situation. Manuel wanted to meet up, and we needed to handle it carefully.

We took a cab to the hotel where we met up with Frank and used his room as an office.

Frank greeted us at the door. "Men." He was always a man of few words. "Come in."

We sat at a table, and to my surprise, he offered us a beer. Even Cole shot me a confused look. This was not Frank behavior.

"So, tell me what you found." He looked around at us.

I stopped Cole from talking; this was my issue. "After Manuel joined the police force, he started gambling here in New York at the Dark Horse Casino until he was banned for counting cards." I opened a file with all his information. Others might have found this strange, but not me. I was used to it. "Two years later, he started playing at an underground group. That's when he started skimming money out of the evidence locker."

"How much?" Frank turned his pen to extend the tip.

"At first it was small amounts, five hundred to a thousand. Then he got in deeper, and it changed to fifty to a hundred thousand a couple of times a month." I scanned the paper and flipped the page. "Guess his partner suspected something, mentioned it to their sergeant, and they set up some cameras. Sure enough, there he was, stuffing it into the waistband of his pants."

Frank sighed then glanced out at the window while he thought about something.

"Okay," he cleared his throat, "Lopez, have you ever spoken to anyone about what happened back then?"

My stomach churned. "No."

"What about during the investigation?"

"No." I snapped my neck to relieve some tension. This wasn't a topic I spoke about often. "Not much evidence was found."

"Right." Frank scribbled on his yellow pad, and I appreciated that he didn't question my answers. "Good."

Keith's phone rang, and when he pulled it free, his face dropped. "Shit. I gotta take this." He glanced at Cole then left the room.

I squinted at Cole, wondering what was up, but he just gave a quick shake of the head to stay on task. Keith and I had become closer now that he was with Blackstone, but there seemed to be another side of him that he kept from us...well, maybe just from me. Cole knew everything. My throat contracted at that thought. Cole did know everything—even my secret—and he never judged. Ever.

"All right," Frank looked at me, "you're meeting Manuel in thirty in Central Park. Will you wear a wire?"

"No, he'll check."

Frank gave me a curt nod. "Leave your phone

on, then."

"I'd really prefer to go in clean," I admitted. Wires and bugs were not something I wanted on me when I hadn't seen him in almost five years. He was a loose cannon, and I didn't trust what could come out of his mouth.

Cole spoke up. "I'm fine with that." He always had my back. "We'll maintain a visual. I agree with Lopez. Manuel will suspect it. I know him well enough to say he'll be waiting for this."

"Fine," Frank assented, but I could tell he'd rather listen in. "Ask the questions we prompted you on, and if you need help, pull out your cell and bring it to your right ear."

"Mark." Cole pulled me out onto the balcony where he produced a shiny black box. "Ah, I got these for the team for Christmas, but I want you to wear yours now." He held the box up like he was about to propose.

"I'm kinda into chicks, man." I laughed as he shoved the box in my hand.

"You're not my type."

"That hurts real deep."

He rolled his eyes. "You'll get over it."

I popped open the lid with my thumb, my curiosity piqued.

"Damn, dude." I pulled the black watch free to study it better.

"It's made by a couple I met a few years back in L.A. It's the first watch line they've ever designed. I thought it would work well for Blackstone."

I read the name of the watch. "Joogii." The black leather strap flowed right into the black face. The hands reminded me of a tuxedo with its black arms and white tips, but the long, skinny second hand was what drew my eye. It was a bright yellow. Everything about this watch was crisp, clean, and attractive.

"Check this out." Cole turned the watch over and pointed to a tiny pin stuck in the stitching. "Army approved tracking device. Frank got me enough for all our field agents. After what happened to me…" He cleared his throat. I knew so much of what happened last year still preyed on him. "Well, at least these are undetectable."

"Thanks." I wrapped it around my wrist and fastened in place. "I really should wear watches more."

Cole shook his head before he went back into the hotel room. "Let's get moving."

I entered the park at 85th Street and Museum Mile and headed down to the water. Right under a huge oak tree was a red bench, with children's handprints all over it. I sat and waited; I knew he'd be late. He was most likely watching me to see if I would signal to my team. I made sure not to do anything but sit very still.

A twig snapped behind me, and I could almost feel the wind change. I knew it was him.

"You're late."

"Is that any way to greet your brother?" He opened his arms for a hug, but I just waited for him to sit. "Damn, boy, you've been working out."

"Yeah, you might want to try it." I took in the haggard look on his face.

"Hey," he lit a cigarette and took a long drag,

"I'm seven years older and didn't have the luxuries the U.S. Army gave you."

"That was your choice."

His dull green eyes squinted as he sucked back some more smoke. There it was. That was the look that haunted me when I was at my worst. "Hardly." His voice dropped low and was laced with a sharp edge. However, this time I wouldn't let it get to me—not when he included Mia in his threat. "So, are you gonna help me or not?"

"What do you expect me to do, here, Manuel? You were caught on tape."

He leaned forward, elbows on his knees, before he looked back. "I *want* you to tell them I did it for you."

"Are you fucking kidding me?"

He threw his cigarette onto the ground and stomped on it. "No." He lit another cigarette and got himself under control. "Remember what I did for *you*, Mark."

"How can I forget? Every time I think you're probably dead in a ditch somewhere, you pop your goddamn head up from the grave to remind me."

He flinched before he took a long drag. "Army grew you some balls."

"Yeah, and what a set I have." I held his stare. "You got yourself in this shit, get yourself out of it."

"You're not going to help me?"

"Fuck you, Manuel!" I stood and tucked my hands into the pockets of my long jacket.

"The girl. She's pretty." He smirked, his cigarette dangling from his lip.

I figured he'd go there, so I was ready.

"Yeah, she is." I turned on my heel and walked back toward the parking lot. Each step took effort. I wasn't sure if I had made the right decision yet. Only time would tell.

Frank's black Escalade pulled up and the door swung open. I hopped inside, and Cole let out a long breath.

"Good?" He held up his fist, and I bumped.

"Yeah."

When we finally got back to our hotel, I skipped drinks at the bar and headed to my room. I wanted to be alone. No, what I wanted was to be with Mia.

I plugged in my phone, as it had died on the way home, and headed for a shower.

My body hit the mattress with a heavy thud. I was too tired to change, so I just wrapped myself in a towel. I reached for my phone, wondering when the Penguins were playing tonight.

I jerked up on my elbow when I saw a bunch of missed texts from Mia.

Mia: *Hey you, I want you to be here too.*

Mia: *Something to help ;)*

There were three pictures. I tapped to download the text, since the Wi-Fi sucked here. My heart nearly froze when I saw she had taken a selfie of herself in the rain. The next one was her at the hospital, making an unhappy face at all the work she had to do. However, the third one had me smiling into my pillow like I was seventeen and in love. She was in bed, lying down, looking at the camera with a sleepy smile. There was a text attached to that one.

Mia: Good night, sweet dreams.

I turned my camera at my face and did my version of her last picture.

Mark: Good night, Mia. Sweet dreams.

I flicked on the TV and started to flip. My phone rang, and I dreaded to see who it was. I just closed my eyes and answered.

"Lopez," I muttered, figuring it was probably Frank.

"Hey." Her voice was low and went right to my chest.

"Wow," I laughed lightly, "I really did need to hear your voice."

I heard her move about. "Is everything all right?"

"Yeah, just work stuff."

"Oh." She yawned.

"How is work going?"

"Interesting."

"Is the manicured Doc *Francis* bothering you?" Strange. I didn't get jealous, but with her I was a bit. It bothered me that he got to see her every day, and I couldn't. She paused somewhat too long for my liking. "Mia?"

"No, he's been pretty good."

"Did something happen?"

"No! God, no, Mark." She cleared her throat. "I would never."

"I mean, it would make sense. He is there every day."

"Mark!"

I felt like a dick. "Sorry." I needed to pull it together. "It's been a day."

There was silence.

"Mia, I am sorry. I was just being a dick."

"Can I ask you something, without you getting upset?"

My stomach twisted; I wasn't sure I wanted to hear this. "Sure."

She sighed into the phone. "When am I going to see you next?"

My heart lightened, happy to know she wanted me like I wanted her.

"I'm not sure yet. Soon, I hope."

"Me too." She yawned again.

"Look, you go get some sleep, and I'll talk to you later." I heard Butters groan into the phone. "You take care of her while I'm gone, boy."

"He does, don't you, boy? Okay, call me later if you can."

"I will. Bye, hon."

"Bye."

***

The next week, I ran my drills with the team. I worked out, played with Livy, and waited. Two more days went by, and still no word from Manuel.

"Hey," Keith dropped his bag at my door, "you ready?"

"Yeah." I grabbed my jacket and did one last

check before we left.

Keith looked at his phone right before it rang. "Carlos." His voice was completely different. He turned to look at me, and he held his finger to his mouth to keep me quiet. "Oh, shit, this weekend? No, man, I can't, but I'll try to make the next meeting." He waited for a minute. "Yeah, brother, I'll be there." He hung up and kept his fast pace down the stairs.

"Good luck, guys." Savannah smiled from the doorway. "Be safe." She stopped Keith. "What?"

"He has other friends, besides us," I joked and hurried up the path to the chopper. We needed to be across the border soon if we were going to nab our next houseguest.

"All good." I heard Keith kiss her cheek before he followed behind me. "Hey, Lopez," he called out. "You heard nothing, okay?"

"Heard what?"

He gave me a slight nod. "Thanks."

I waited for the moment the chopper left the ground. It always made my adrenaline kick up a few notches.

***

Location: Mexico
Coordinates: Classified

"I'd never live here." Cole ran his finger along the inside of his shirt. "Too fucking hot."

"Yup." We'd been in this dugout for four and half hours, with no movement from the house

140

below.

"Why aren't you entertaining me?" Cole opened his water. "Hello."

"Thinking."

"'Bout?"

"Manuel."

"And?"

I rolled my eyes. "And Mia."

He shifted to lean on his other shoulder. "You seem different with this girl."

"Yeah." He waited for me to go on. "She doesn't mind me disappearing. I mean, she doesn't like it, but she seems to understand how it works. I guess since she signed the NDA, she would have had an idea."

"Okay."

"Okay." I knew there was more coming.

"I guess I want to know where your head is, if you two are getting serious."

There was that heavy feeling that crawled across my chest whenever this came up.

"Honestly, I have no idea, but I'd welcome any suggestions."

Cole rubbed his head as he thought. "Well, I can't lose you, so leave it with me, and I'll see what I can come up with."

"Sounds good." We went back to silence, then I smirked. "You can tell Savannah I'm okay."

He laughed softly and shook his head. Savannah was always looking out for us, and now used Cole to do her work. It was sweet she cared.

"Hey, what's up with Keith, anyway?"

Cole flopped his head back against the dirt.

"Personal stuff."

"Well, since Keith told us nothing about himself, that isn't helpful. Everything okay?"

"He needs to make some big decisions. His past is catching up."

"I hear that!"

"Yeah." I knew better than to push Cole. He kept everyone's secrets. Everything was on a need to know basis with him. Which, Lord knew, I appreciated.

Gunshots sounded in the distance, and we got on our knees and into position.

"Visual?" I asked Cole as I rested the side of my cheek on the hot steel and lined up my sights with the front door. With my breathing steady, I scanned the front of the house.

"Negative."

My finger flexed against the trigger; I loved this part. The unknown. Which way would this situation go?

"East gate," Cole muttered as he cocked his weapon.

I spat out the details to the rest of the team before Cole started to fire. In nine seconds, five cartel were down.

Let's move." He scrambled to his feet.

We ran down the hill, across a field, where we hunched behind a small wall. Cole got the team in place before we stormed the house.

With my back against the house, I took a quick peek inside the window, but something blocked my view.

I joined Cole as he prepared to clear the front

door. Paul rolled a smoke bomb inside before we entered. After the pop, we formed a line and moved forward.

Smoke, heat, and a horrible smell found us in a matter of seconds.

"Everyone get down!" I shouted through the blinding haze. I tripped over something heavy and bounced off something rubbery. My hands went out and landed against...

"Shit!" I shouted just as Keith ripped the blind off the window.

Piles and piles of dead bodies lay in all directions on the floor. My hand was on top of a woman's lifeless face. I jerked back as if I'd been burned.

"What the fuck?" John was almost green but managed to hold it together. Keith offered me an arm up so I wouldn't have to touch any more of them.

Cole stepped out to call it in.

"How many?" John covered his mouth.

"Must be eighty," Keith shook his head, "just in this room."

"There's more?" John coughed at the smell, waving his arm around to shoo the flies away.

Keith pointed up the stairs, where more bodies littered the floor.

"Let's get this over with." I wiped my hand over my pants before I pulled on rubber gloves.

We started at one end and shifted through body after body to see if our target was included in the massacre.

John struggled, so I told him to do lookout. We

all had our strengths. This wasn't his, and that was fine.

It became just a job after about the twelfth body. I turned off my emotions and did my thing. It wasn't until I came across the body of a young boy who had been shot in the stomach and the eye that I needed a moment.

Fuck it.

I pulled the boy free, cradled him in my arms, and carried him outside, where I laid him by some shrubs. His remaining eye stared up at the sky.

I bent down and fixed his t-shirt, and when I tugged it down, a tiny tin car fell from his pocket.

"Fuck," I grunted, a knot in my chest. I scooped it up and examined it. Yellow doors with a black stripe across the top. It was homemade, with the name Felipe on the bumper. I curled it in my fist and held it to my mouth to keep the sob back. This wasn't right. We fought every goddamn day in an endless war. Sadly, at this rate, by the time we found peace, what would be left? Nothing but destruction. "For what it's worth, little guy," I whispered, "I'm really sorry." I immediately stood and checked myself. Detached. I turned and found the guys watching me.

Cole shifted into my path. "You good?"

I brushed by him. "No."

That was how it went. Whenever one of us found a child this way, we would remove the small body from the site, place it outside under the sky, and then they were given a moment of our time. We didn't say much to whoever found the body. Mostly, we just touched their arm and let them continue with that small gesture of comfort. This was the worst trip I'd had yet.

Three hours later, we counted and checked sixty-three adults and seventeen children. The Mexican police arrived and started to take over.

"Logan." Keith stood at the top of the stairs. "Found our target."

"And?"

"Dead."

"How?"

"Hung from the ceiling, cut to the stomach. Bled to death."

"Fuck!"

***

Mia

"Oh, here, let me help." Chris, the new manager, opened the apartment door for me.

I tried to balance my groceries in my arms. "Thanks."

He raced forward and hit the call button for the elevator. "You need some help?"

"Ah, no, I think I got it."

"Okay." He actually gave me a friendly smile before he stepped back to let the door close between us.

Christ, he was an odd guy. I shook off the bad vibe. I couldn't wait to open my vodka and sip on a strong cosmo.

My keys were stuck between my fingers as I jammed them into the little hole and opened the door to my apartment. Then my heart jumped.

Mark was slumped forward, head in his hands, on my comfy chair.

"Hey." I wanted to be excited, but his body language made me nervous. I set my bags on the island. I didn't think he heard me, but when I started to speak, he abruptly stood and walked right over to me. He crushed his body to mine with a huge sigh. "Oh!"

He leaned back, took my face in his hands, and stared into my eyes before he leaned down and kissed me. I could tell this was what he needed, so I went along and kept my questions to myself.

I stepped back and removed my shirt. He did the same, and then his hands were all over my body. Cupping, kneading, rubbing—he was so much more intense than normal.

We barely made it to the bed before he rolled a condom on.

"I need you now." He laid me back before he crawled on top. His eyes showed his internal struggle, and when I cupped his cheek, he turned into it. "Mia," he nearly whimpered, "I need you to help me forget."

I knew his head was somewhere else, and I knew he needed me to bring him back. Even though his mind wasn't all in the present, he was still so sweet and careful. I dragged my nails down his back, but stopped at the now familiar deep groove on his side. Slowly but firmly, he removed my hand.

I took his face in my hands so he would look at me. "I'm here, Mark." He squeezed his eyes shut and his neck muscles strained. "Hey," I ran my fingertips down his cheeks, "let me help."

After a beat, he let me push him to the bed, where I climbed up and sank down over his length. His hands landed on my hips and set the pace. As my body moved, I leaned forward and kissed the scars on his chest, across his collarbone, and up along his neck.

"I'm here." My lips vibrated against his ribs.

His threaded his fingers into my hair and gently raised me to his lips. The moment we touched, he growled. The kiss was wild, but not a race—more like a hunger that consumed the entire body. I clenched around him.

Once he let go, I leaned back, took his hands in mine, and gently rocked to a pace that seemed to relax him. Neither of us spoke; we didn't need to.

At one point, when I saw him slip, I stopped and cupped his cheek again. "Hey." He closed his eyes, and I realized that was what he did when he tried to sort his thoughts. His hands moved to my hips before his eyes opened. "I saw some things." His jaw flexed. There weren't any tears, but the rawness in his voice was enough to make me feel his pain. "I need you to bring me back—to *me* again."

"Oh, Mark." I wrapped my arms around his neck and held him the best I could. After a bit, he moved me so I lay with my body wrapped around him from the side. His hand rubbed lightly from my shoulder to my elbow. It was soothing, but I was too worried to relax.

"Tell me something about you." I really wanted to know him. No boundaries, just who he was.

"Like what?"

I thought for a moment and started to laugh.

"What?" His tone was curious.

"Please don't take this the wrong way, but why do you smell like a fifteen-year-old girl sometimes?"

He moved to sit up, and his hands went to his chest very dramatically. "Pardon me?"

"It's like I keep having this deja vu of when I was seven riding my pink sparkly bike." I stood and picked up his jeans.

"Oh, that's not weird. Sure, smell my pants." His sarcasm made me smile, and then I felt a long, hard thing. "Okay, you don't need to—"

"Ohhhh." I laughed at the half-empty pack of Hubba Bubba. "Oh, thank God." I laughed harder. "I had a lot of things flash in front of me, there."

Mark smiled, then he started to laugh too. "Guess it's kind of a comfort thing."

"I think it's cute." I grinned as I returned the gum to his pants pocket. "Will you tell me something else?"

He inched down so he was lying flat on the bed and turned toward me. I did the same and we watched the glow of the city below from the massive windows behind us. I loved this apartment.

"Something personal that's about who you are. Something real."

His lips pressed into a straight line as he thought before answering. "I've been alone for so long that I will actually mess up the opposite side of the bed. So when I wake the next morning, disappointment isn't the first thought that pops in my head." He grinned at me.

It took me a moment to process what he said. "That's..." I scrambled for the right words.

"Sad, I know," he shrugged, "but true." He leaned forward and gave me a gentle kiss before he lay back down. "I've shared a lot, so now it's your turn."

His face popped up in front of me, but I couldn't. Not yet. That would change everything.

"Umm," my mind raced to think, "I promised myself I would wait three years before I'd date again after what went down with my ex."

"How long has it been?"

"Thirteen months."

He squinted at me. "Are you sure you're ready for another relationship?"

"At first, I wasn't sure—"

"And now?" he interrupted.

I stared at him for a moment. "What if I wasn't?"

He hooked his arm around my waist, pulled me to him, and hovered above me.

"I guess I'd have to find new and inventive ways to convince you." His lips caught mine and he took over. I forgot my own name when we were like this.

When we came up for air, I wiggled free and headed to the bathroom.

I was brushing my teeth when he came up behind me. He leaned against the doorframe and watched.

When I leaned down to rinse my mouth, I felt him remove the brush from my hand. I came back up, and he was using my toothbrush. I smirked at how comfortable he already was with me.

Bed felt good, but knowing he was going to be

next to me was even better. The floor was cold, so I hurried under the covers and shivered until my body heat warmed up my spot.

I was almost asleep when he joined me. His hand ran along my hip, over my stomach, and curled around my waist. With a small jerk, he pulled my back to his chest.

"I missed you," he whispered into my hair. Something in his voice bothered me again.

I turned to see his face. "Why do I feel like you're going to tell me you're leaving soon?"

When he didn't answer, I turned back around and let the unspeakable battle fight itself out in my head.

I couldn't help but feel like I was his release when he needed to get rid of some stress or demons.

One a.m.

Two a.m.

Three a.m.

The numbers ticked by, but I was too nervous to close my eyes in case he left. Around three thirty, I couldn't take it anymore. I slid out of bed, wrapped my silk robe around myself, and headed to the living room.

Carefully, I climbed up on the window seat. It was my favorite spot. I could lie back and pretend everything was fine, and there was nothing but me and the stars to hear my thoughts.

Raindrops swirled around in different patterns, and a hint of frost was in the air, which left a white dusting along the edge of each window pane.

I pulled my blanket up to my chin and settled in further. My mother's voice found me.

"If your body naturally smiles when you see the

person you're with, that's a good sign."

What happened if you lived two different lives? How did that work?

I kicked the blanket off. It was no use; sleep wasn't going to come. I changed before scribbling a note.

> *Went into work. See you when I do.*
> *~Mia*

I stared at it and wondered if it was too much of a jab. I didn't mean it to be. Tossing it in the trash, I tried again.

> *Went to work. Talk to you later.*
> *~Mia*

With a glance over my shoulder to make sure he was still asleep, I headed for the hospital.

CHAPTER SIX

"What are you doing here?" Molly asked as she ran past the ER waiting room where I had settled with a good book.

"Couldn't sleep."

"You are the only one I know who comes to an emergency room to calm down." She laughed before she went on her way.

Around ten, I went to visit Kenny, who was a lot worse today. He could barely lift his head, and his eyes seemed distant.

"Hey, honey." I squeezed his right arm to let him know it was me. "What are you watching today?"

He didn't answer, so I went over and opened the blinds.

"It's raining, our favorite kind of weather."

Again nothing.

"Are you cold?" I sighed. When I started to move, I hit his left arm, and his hand shot forward and wrapped around my neck.

"Don't touch me!" he screamed, crushing me harder. "No more meds!" His eyes were cold, and I could tell he was lost in his other world.

I tried to suck in some air, but nothing could get through. The more I fought, the tighter his grip grew.

My hand raced around and finally found the emergency button on my pager. I pushed it hard.

"Ahh," Kenny screamed again, "leave me be!"

The door burst open, and Vikki bolted toward us.

"Security!" she yelled down the hall. "I need help now!"

Spots clouded my vision as his never-ending hold gradually took my life away.

"Kenny! Let go!" Vikki pretty much had to break his arm to get him to release me.

I fell backward off the bed and hit the floor. Wheezing, I gasped and coughed as the air flooded back into my lungs.

Dr. Evans came in and raced to my side. "Mia, what happened?"

Vikki had Kenny in a hold until another nurse sedated him.

"He had her around the neck," Vikki called out.

After he helped me to my feet and out of the room, Dr. Evans sat me on a chair and squatted down in front of me.

"I'm fine," I wheezed, but the tears threatened to come. He reached for my hand, but I stood on shaky legs. "I just need a moment."

"Mia."

"Please."

Each step felt like lead, and my stomach turned as I reached for the door handle of an empty room. I curled up in a ball on the end of the bed. Every breath was painful, my heart raced, and my feelings were so out of whack I didn't know where to start processing it all. One, two, three, four…I tried to calm myself, but it was no use. The reality of Kenny's condition could no longer be denied, and my heart broke for him.

I went with what my body wanted, which was to break down. The sobs hit hard; they were mostly silent but shook my core as they surfaced.

My head was buried against my knees as I tried to block the world out. I gave in and let all the pain rush in.

"Where is she?" I barely heard the shouting through my own personal struggle.

The door opened and a set of warm hands fell on top of mine.

"Shit," Mark cursed as he lifted me and held me in his arms. He wrapped around my body, holding me tight. "It's okay, Mia, I'm here."

I sobbed harder, sobbed for the fact that Kenny was almost gone, sobbed because I wanted my mother to be here with me to support him, and sobbed because Mark walked in and out of my life when I only wanted him to stay with me.

After a while, I felt so tired and sore. Mark never moved or complained—he was simply *there*.

"Can I see your neck?"

I unfolded from the safety net he had me in and saw his worried face.

He brushed my hair away. His thumbs dried my cheeks then gently tipped my head back.

"Ouch, Mia. Kenny is still pretty strong."

I closed my eyes and let more tears slip out. I

heard him move.

"Let's get you looked at." He helped me to my feet and onto the bed. I felt like a rock, drained of everything. I just wanted to sleep.

Mark moved to the door and flagged someone down. Vikki came in first.

"Oh, girl," she covered her mouth at my appearance, "you are damn lucky you pushed the emergency button. Does it hurt?"

I nodded, but I didn't speak. I really didn't know what to say.

Mark stood by my side and rubbed my back gently. Vikki glanced at him.

"I don't know how long he had her like that." Her voice cracked like she really cared what had happened to me. "God, Mark, I couldn't get him to let go. I actually had to fracture his arm."

"Jesus Christ," he muttered, "I'm glad you were there."

She put her hand on mine. "Mia, you should take a few days off."

"I agree," Dr. Evans said from the doorway. "Your shift doesn't even start yet. What were you doing at the hospital?"

I shrugged. The pain that pulsed through my neck left me with no desire to speak.

"Well, let's check you out."

Mark stayed by my side the entire time. He never said much, just flinched when I did.

Thankfully, there wasn't too much damage beyond some intense bruising. I was told to take a week off. I wasn't happy about it, but I didn't make the decisions. The chief did.

They also made a new rule that I wasn't allowed to be alone with Kenny anymore. That was the worst part. I knew Kenny didn't have much time left.

After I was given some pain meds, they tried to send me home.

I stopped Evans before he left. "I want to see Kenny first."

"No."

I glanced at Mark, who struggled to keep his feelings back. I jumped off the table and walked with unsteady knees. "He didn't mean it. You know he slips between two worlds."

"Go home, Mia." Dr. Evans sighed when he saw I wasn't about to back down. "You can see him tomorrow, but not today."

"Fine," I whispered just as Mark took my hand. Evans looked over my shoulder, his mouth tight with annoyance.

"Let's go home." Mark urged me forward and out into the hallway.

He opened an umbrella and helped me over the puddles until we got to his car.

"You warm enough?" He turned the hot air in my direction and pressed the button for the heated seat.

"Yeah," I croaked. I was exhausted.

Once home, I stripped out of my wet scrubs and into some yoga pants and a tank. I liked to be comfy when I was home.

Mark fiddled around in the kitchen while I made a cozy nest on the overstuffed sectional couch.

I went straight to my DVR and brought up *True*

Detective. I was obsessed with that show. The darker, the better.

Mark set a tray in front of me with chicken soup and warm bread. "You need to eat something with those pain meds in your stomach."

"Thanks." I was pleasantly surprised he did that for me. He returned a moment later with his own tray and settled in next to me. I stared at him, confused.

He sipped his water. "What?"

"You're staying?"

"Yeah." He dipped his bread into his soup.

"But I thought last night you said you had to leave."

"I did. I have a trip."

There was that sinking feeling again. "So then when do you leave?"

Mark set his bowl down and brushed the crumbs from his fingers. He leaned back and laid his arm along the back of the couch. "I opted not to go."

I shook my head, not following.

"First time ever." He grinned.

"Why?" It sounded stupid, but I needed him to say it.

He turned a bit more to face me, his fingers brushing my hair out of my face. "A while back, Savannah had a real hard time with Cole leaving when she found out she was pregnant." I nodded. "He knew it and stayed. Cole never missed an assignment. I've seen him take out men with his bare hands while sick with pneumonia. We are trained to fight through everything," he paused, "everything but this."

"But what?"

He smiled, one that made my stomach leap into my throat. "You." When I didn't say anything, he went on. "I knew Cole was in love. We all saw it. I couldn't believe he skipped the trip, skipped the chance to take out some bad guys. However, when I woke this morning and saw you had left, I decided to go to the hospital to say goodbye. When the nurse told me what had happened, nothing mattered after that except you. I texted Cole, and you want to know what his response was?"

"What?" barely slipped past my lips.

"He said, *'All right.'*" He snickered. "Guess it was more obvious than I thought."

"What was?"

"Mia…" His finger ran along my jaw and across my bottom lip. "I've had girlfriends before, but not like you. I normally like my space, my alone time, see my girlfriend on the weekends or one night a week or whenever. But with you, you're all I think about. My last trip was," he cleared his throat, "hard. The only thing I wanted was to hold you and sleep next to you. I've fallen fast, Mia, and frankly, it scares the shit out of me. I think I might even have lost my sense of humor!"

I smiled at his attempt at humor in such a serious moment. Moving my blanket aside, I shifted to straddle his lap. I put my hands on either side of his face and gazed into his chocolate brown eyes.

"I left so you didn't have to be first," I admitted in a whisper. "I know this is how it is going to be with us, but I hated the feeling last time it happened so badly that…"

His eyes closed while his chest rose and fell.

"It's okay, Mark, because now that I know I'm not alone in how I feel..." His eyes opened. "It won't hurt as much."

"Are you saying you *like*-like me?" He grinned playfully.

"Yes," I leaned forward, "I *like*-like you." I kissed his lips softly while his hands ran along my thighs. "How long do I get to keep you?"

"A week." He kissed me again before guiding me to the couch. "You need to rest." He caught me eyeing his excitement and shook his finger at me. "Rest."

With a much lighter chest than before, I rested my head on his lap and fell asleep with his fingers stroking my hair.

***

The next two days, I mostly slept off the pain and enjoyed his company. Mark hung out, cooked, cleaned, and helped out with Butters. I had to admit sleep and general lazing about felt wonderful. It had been a long time since I had allowed myself to simply rest.

A loud crack of thunder woke me. I jolted forward just as a lightning flash filled the entire apartment.

"Mark?" I called out when I realized I was in bed alone. "Ouch." My throat was still really sore.

The windows vibrated each time the thunder erupted. The storm was right above us, and it was intense. *Click, click.* The button on my lamp wouldn't turn on. Damn, the power was out too.

Slipping my robe on, I stepped out into the living room, but it was empty. The wind scraped a branch along the glass, making the night feel eerie. A moment later, I was startled by the door as it opened and in walked Mark and Butters, soaking wet.

"Hey." He let Butters off the lead before he came over. "How long have you been up?"

"Just a few minutes."

"Sorry, Butters needed to do some business, and boy, that fellow knows his stuff!" He hung his jacket over the back of the chair. "Come on, let's get you back to bed."

Once we settled in, he turned to face me with a pillow hugged to his chest. The candlelight flickered over his face.

"Tell me something else about you," I mumbled and moved my cold toes to his warm calf. "Where did you grow up?"

He tucked my hair behind my ear. "I grew up in California. My father was a screen writer, and he wrote for *Love Boat*."

"Really?" How interesting.

"No, not really," he said, laughing.

"Mark!" I shoved his shoulder.

"Fine. My family traveled a lot because of my mother's job."

I nodded, wanting him to go on.

"She was a lesbian stripper."

I flopped on my back as he laughed harder. "Forget it."

"No, no, no." He rolled me onto my side. He took a long breath while his eyes closed. "I'm not good with emotion when it comes to myself."

"Could have fooled me." I gave him an annoyed look.

"Oh, I see someone else enjoys a little sarcasm."

"When it's needed," I shot back.

"Okay," he shook his head, "my father left when I was born. I was raised by my mother until I was seven, and then Cole's nanny took me in."

"For real?"

He grinned at my words. "Yes, for real."

"Go on, then."

"I didn't have a very easy start to my life, Mia. It wasn't pretty. My mother drank and smoked a lot of pot. She would go days without feeding me. There was this old lady who lived in the trailer next to us, and she was pretty nice. Anyway, her husband worked for Hubba Bubba. She used to give me a pack a week for a treat."

"Oh, that explains it."

He gave me shrug, but I could tell it meant something. "I learned I could trick my hungry stomach into thinking it was full with that gum." *How sad.* "Mom soon figured out people liked me, so she'd send me out to ask for food. That's how I met the Logans and Abigail."

"Abigail worked for them, then?"

"Yes, she became Cole's nanny six months before I came to their door. She took pity on me and started feeding me a few times a week. She even gave me some of Cole's clothes to wear."

"How was Cole about all this?"

"Cole? He was…well, Cole. He became my best friend after he saw me get jumped one day after school. Turns out we were both pretty good at fighting. Soon after, I started heading there after school during the week. My mother barely noticed. As long as I brought food home a few days here and there, she'd leave me be."

"Any siblings?"

"Ah, yeah a brother. He is seven years older."

"Are you close?"

"No."

"That's too bad."

"No, it's not."

I moved to steal more of his warmth. "Where was he when you were growing up?"

"If he wasn't beating on me, he was gambling in some back alley. He still gets himself in shit because of it. He's addicted."

"Oh, I'm sorry."

"It is what it is." He shrugged. "Manuel is dangerous."

"Do you see him much anymore?"

He licked his lips. "Unfortunately, yes."

I wanted to ask more, but I decided against it. I didn't need to push too much on a topic that was obviously touchy.

"Where's your mom now?"

"What about you?" He dodged my question.

Oh, boy.

"Umm, born and raised, well, all over the U.S."

"Military family?" I nodded. "That explains why you used my rank so much." I smiled because I didn't even realize I had.

"One brother, but he's not around right now, and I'm not overly close with my parents anymore.

They weren't exactly happy that I 'settled for' nursing school. I wanted to be a nurse in the Army, but my father forbid it. He says it's no place for a woman." I shrugged. "I think he's scared at what I might see. To be honest, I was terrified to join. I just wanted him to stop caring whether I became a doctor or not. It only backfired on him. He just never understood I wanted to be a nurse."

He kissed each one of my fingers. "So what brought you to North Dakota?"

"Kenny," I whispered.

"Who is he to you?"

I blinked back the pain that came with this topic. A clap of thunder boomed, and I grabbed Mark's arm.

"Scarier than it really is." He kissed my head and tucked me in closer. The rain beat against the windows, the sound swirling around the room. "Reminds me of a storm a few years back," he began. "Cole and I were in a trench in Mexico. We had to watch this house that was holding our target. It started pouring around six at night, and we were literally in a pool of mud after about an hour. The storm was so intense we could barely hear one another, even when we were side by side. Couldn't even hear the sound of our bullets. We sat there for nine hours before we could make our move."

I gently kissed his chest. I knew he wasn't allowed to share things, yet he was. It made me feel special, but also a bit guilty.

"Was your target okay?"

He paused a beat. "Yeah, that one was."

"I'm sorry your last trip was so awful."

I felt him swallow hard. "That one will stay with me for a while."

Butters jumped up and lay across our feet.

Mark hugged me. "This is nice."

"At the risk of pushing you too far, can I ask one more question?"

His sigh wasn't lost on me. "Okay."

I shifted and pulled back the blanket. He let me run my fingers run along the deep gash.

"What—"

His face fell, and this time he didn't hide it. "My mother had a lot of boyfriends. I was five when the first guy tried to make a move on me."

I stilled.

"I had found a hunting knife in the woods one time, and I kept it by my nightstand for protection. You know that saying, if you have a gun in your house, you're more likely to get shot yourself? Well, I fought him off the first time, but the second time he came back, he decided to inflict pain instead. With my defense against him."

"Did any of them ever…" I couldn't even finish the sentence.

"No," he his tone was clipped, though he sounded a million miles away. "When they'd come over, I'd find somewhere else to be. Let's just say Abigail did more than just save me from my mother."

I rested my head on his chest and held him tightly. "I'm so sorry, Mark."

After some time, he wrapped his hand in mine. "Me too."

***

Mark

"Get up and get moving." Manuel kicked my side. My eyes opened, and I squinted at him above me, his arms folded. "Go get food."

"I'm tired," I complained, struggling to get to my feet. My dirty mattress on the floor was wearing down, which made my back sore.

"Did I ask how you were? You have five minutes to get out before Mom wakes and sees you're still here."

My boots were still wet from being out in the snow last night. This sucked. My jacket was barely a windbreaker and not meant for the snow that was coming down fast. With my hands in my pockets, I looked over at my mother passed out in her normal spot.

The snowdrifts were up to my knees. Ice formed around my ankles, but I didn't mind. It only fueled me to keep moving from door to door.

My muscles burned, my fingertips were numb, and my ears pulsed with a deep ache.

I didn't have to guess who was in the black SUV as the window descended.

"Marcus?" Abigail called out as she leaned over Cole's body. "What are you doing out on a night like this, honey?"

I shrugged, embarrassed she caught me out here again.

Her face fell. "Hop in. A storm is coming."

Abigail dropped me off at home later with fresh

clothes, boots, a pot full of hot soup, and rolls.

The snow came down harder, blinding my route back to our trailer. Finally, after serval minutes, I tugged on the handle, but it was locked.

"Momma?" I knocked on the door. "Are you in there?"

Nothing.

"Manuel!" I called out. "I have food, but the door is locked."

Nothing.

I set the pot down and removed my mittens. "Momma! Manuel!" I cleared the snow away and peeked through the glass. Mom wasn't on the couch, and Manuel's door was closed.

Wading through the snow, I worked my way over to the back and crawled up onto the propane tank.

Inching forward, I looked in Manuel's room. Sure enough, he was passed out on his bed with a joint stuck between two fingers.

I knocked loudly, but he didn't budge. "Manuel!"

With a push, I jumped into a pile of snow and worked my way back to the front. Where was Mom?

The wind picked up, blowing everything around me. I grabbed the hot pot and went under the trailer.

With my body curled close to the now warm steel, I weathered the storm. I had never been colder or more alone than in that moment. How could you forget about your own son and leave him out in a snowstorm?

***

My hand brushed over the cold sheets until I found her. With a hook of my arm, I slid her over to me. She stirred but didn't wake.

Another hour of sleep felt good, and I woke to her still next to me. I tugged the blankets off as if this was the first time I laid eyes on her. Her skin was fair, with only a few freckles along the base of her neck. Her back was to me, and I watched as the morning light cast over her curves.

I loved that she slept naked; it gave me time to study her.

With my hands placed at the small of her back, I dragged them up her spine and over her shoulders. She moaned as I started massaging her muscles.

"Ohh," she purred, "you're never leaving."

I chuckled and worked my thumbs in circles. "How sore are you?"

She shrugged, and I let the topic be. "You talk in your sleep." She stretched her neck so I could inch up further.

"Oh, yeah?"

"Something about being alone."

My hands stopped. She turned to see my face. I propped up on one arm and looked down at her.

Her eyes softened. "I'm sorry."

I shook the dark feeling back, but I knew she saw it. She brushed her hand over my morning stubble.

"You're not alone, Mark." Her voice was low, and I could tell she made sure she treaded carefully. "You have your family—Cole, Abigail, and Savannah."

"And?"

Her lips turned up on one side. "And me."

"Do I?"

Her smile faded as she studied me. "Yeah, you do."

I leaned down and caught her lips. "Good." Her lips were warm as I deepened the kiss. "Have I ever told you my secret?"

Her eyes lit up.

"I've never told anyone this."

"Okay."

I moved her so she was flat on her back and gazed down at her sleepy eyes. I waited a beat before I ripped the covers off her.

"Mark!" she shouted, coiling into a tiny ball. "You're so mean!" She batted me away as I blew cold air on her. "You're going to pay for this!"

"Bring it, doll!" I called out as she stomped off to the shower. "You're so sexy when you're mad."

She flipped me the bird as she shut the door. Of course, this made me laugh even harder.

I headed to the kitchen to make some coffee. Butters wove in between my legs, his big blue eyes begging me to take him out for a pee. The shower was still running, so I grabbed the lead and hurried out to the elevator.

"Come on, man, there's a perfectly good tree right there." I pointed to the frosty trunk. "Lift and release." The temperature had dropped from yesterday, and I was thankful I brought my heavy sweater. "Do your business so we can leave." Butters had his nose stuck on something under the park bench. "Countdown is on, little man."

When he still didn't listen, I went over to see what he was after. I bent down just as his tongue went out to lick the yellow liquid.

"Wow." I lifted him around the waist so he wouldn't touch it. "What the hell?" I stuck the spot with my finger and smelled it. "Shit." There was no reason for antifreeze to be in this private building's little park. I quickly grabbed the hose and diluted it the best I could. Butters finally went to the bathroom and we went back inside.

"Butters sucker you in for a walk?" Mia asked with her back to me. Her purple panties and braless tank made me stare.

She yelped when I ran my cold hands across her belly.

"Mark!" She tried to get away, but it wasn't gonna happen.

"When you wear this," my hand moved up under her warm breast, "I am not responsible for my actions." I stiffened and stared at what she held in front of her. "Where did you get those?"

"Oh," she bent to open the oven, "my new neighbor-slash-manager brought them by. They look good, don't they?"

"I don't want any."

She turned to face me. "Why?"

My mouth went dry when I saw the chocolate macaroons. They were the same ones my mother used to make, the same ones she "accidentally" laced with pot on my birthday.

"Not hungry."

She made a face. "Why are you lying?"

I cleared my throat as I leaned back against the counter. "Brings back some nasty memories."

"Okay." She picked up the tray and dumped the

whole container in the trash. "No more bad memories."

I took her hand and brought her to stand in front of me. "Thank you."

"You hungry?" She raised an eyebrow knowingly.

"Starved."

"Good." She laughed as she headed for her dresser. "Because after last night's workout, I need some carbs."

"Stock up, honey," I warned.

We walked to a mom and pop shop down the road, where a small table in front of the window was free. I noticed Mia left her scarf on after she removed her coat.

"Good morning," the waitress greeted us. "Can I offer you coffee or juice?"

"Both," we answered at the same time.

With a quick glance out the window, I had to ask. "Tell me something, does anyone work on their cars near the park at your building?"

"No, not that I've ever seen."

"Hmm." I thanked the waitress for the coffee. "When I went out this morning, Butters found antifreeze under the bench by the tree."

Her head shot up from her menu. "Did he drink any?"

"No, I stopped him before he did."

"Jesus." She flipped her hair out of her face. "That doesn't make any sense. There's no way to get a car in there, anyway."

"That was my thought. I'll speak to your landlord later."

"Okay." She nodded then looked outside. "Winter is coming in fast." I noticed her hand went to her neck.

"You going to visit Kenny today?"

Her eyes moved to mine. "Not sure yet."

"You sure go above and beyond for your patients, Mia." She didn't say anything. "Dr. Evans doesn't have time? What is wrong with the boy, anyway? We didn't get to that last night."

Her neck muscles strained as she covered her mouth. I took her hand to let her know she could talk to me about it.

"He has CJD."

"Oh, shit." I had heard of it. I rubbed my forehead with my free hand. Creutzfeldt-Jakob Disease would be a horrible way to go. It was mad cow disease for humans, making the brain look like a sponge when the nerves started to die.

"But CJD mostly occurs in older people."

"Hereditary. Turned out his grandfather tested positive for the genetic mutation. Kenny's case is extreme. They said they've never seen it in someone so young and have it attack so fast."

"Jesus."

"He's had it for five months, and his hallucinations hit hard." She stared out the window as she spoke. "His mother, Kiley, was my best friend. She died a year and a half ago from a head injury. Kenny's father never stuck around, and her parents never wanted anything to do with him." She paused to pick up her napkin and wiped the corner of her eye. "I was all she had, and she made me promise to look after him. She was the best friend I had in the world." Her throat contracted. "And I can't keep my promise to her."

"Hey," I held her hand tighter, "you couldn't have stopped him getting that disease."

She nodded, but I could see her guilt weighed her down.

"Doesn't make it easier, though."

"No, it doesn't." I shook my head at the waitress when she made eye contact with me. "So, that's why he calls you Mom?"

"He's seeing *her*. We looked a lot alike. We were best friends since we were six, and we spent a lot of time at each other's houses. I loved her like a sister. I couldn't let her down. If it brings her son any small bit of happiness, until the end, I will put my life on hold for him."

"Why isn't he somewhere he can get proper care?"

She gave me a sad smile. "I don't have custody of him. Her brother does. All Edison sees is a cash cow from the state. Whenever Kenny gets really bad, he just dumps him at the hospital. Once he's stable, he takes him home again, but I doubt he gives a damn about him. He doesn't even visit."

"Is that why you moved here?"

She let out a long breath and nodded. "Yeah, when I found out where Edison lived, and there was a position open nearby, I took it to keep an eye on Kenny."

"What do your parents think of the whole situation?"

She turned her cup in her hands. "They've known Kenny since he was baby, and they know what has happened to him, but they think I'm wasting my life worrying about him." Her chin quivered before she cupped her mouth. "He's just a boy who lost his mother and was robbed of a life. How do you let that go? How can you just walk away? If it was me in that position, I wouldn't want people to give up on me. I know there's still a part of him that knows what's going on." She saw the expression I hadn't realized was showing. "What?"

"Sorry." I kissed her hand before I let her go. "You're just a really good person."

"I'd trade that in for Kenny to have his life back."

"I know." I signaled the waitress to bring our check.

That evening, after a long walk, we swapped more stories and enjoyed dinner at a hole-in-the-wall restaurant.

It was dark, and the wind swirled the freshly fallen snow into a glitter storm. With Mia's hand in mine, we walked down the street toward her apartment. The day had been fun, but I could tell she was tired now. She finally took her painkillers when I pointed out it was hurting her when she spoke. She joked about the fact there was pocket fluff on the pills when I handed them to her, but she accepted them and managed to swallow them.

When I saw the gate was still open and the street was clear, I tugged her arm to follow.

"Where are we going, Mark?"

"Over here." I let her enter the park first. It was empty except for a man with his dog, and they were leaving. I stopped when we were a few feet inside the woods. "Look up."

She leaned her head back and saw the frosted treetops sparkle under the light of the moon.

"Wow." She grinned. "It's beautiful."

Wrapping my arms around her waist and holding her close, I bent down and whispered, "Close your eyes."

"Okay." She wiggled against me.

My lips touched her cold cheek. "Do you hear that?"

Her head twitched slightly. "No."

"Exactly," I sighed. "It's perfect."

Her arms covered mine, and we stood there enjoying a rare moment when nothing mattered but the two of us.

I rested my cheek against her hair and started to hum my one of my favorite Christmas carols, one Abigail used to sing to Cole and me when we were tucked in bed. "Oh, Holy Night." Mia turned in my arms, tucked one arm inside my jacket, and held my hand with the other. She started to sway to the music, her head falling to my chest with a happy sigh.

Right here, right now, this was why I fought so hard to keep the darkness out. I would not let my past jade me.

With a step back, I raised her hand and gave her a spin, and then I dipped her low. I pulled her back up with ease, but stopped to give her a kiss.

***

"Do you like the safe house?" Mia asked in a

sleepy voice. We'd been in bed for an hour by now, and this was the first time we'd actually stopped touching each other.

I tucked the pillow against my chest to look at her.

"I do. It's been my home for so long now it's hard to think of living anywhere else." My stomach fell when I saw her face. I reached over and ran my finger along her brow.

"What's wrong?" Her gaze dropped to my chest. "Hey."

She began to speak but then stopped herself and moved to sit up. She pulled the white sheet over her chest. "We've known each other for, what, roughly three months now?" I nodded, curious to see where this was going, but she didn't say anything else.

"What?"

Her mouth opened and closed. "Nothing."

"Tell me." I tried to push her, but she clammed up. Instead of pushing, I tucked her under my chin and we both fell asleep.

***

My cell rang around eleven o'clock the next night. Mia had fallen asleep after we watched a movie. Once I saw the name, I hurried to the hallway and answered.

"How did you get this number?"

Manuel laughed humorlessly. "You'd be surprised what I can find out."

I didn't bite. "What do you want?"

"Meet me at the carwash down the street."

"Wait," my skin prickled, "you're here?"

"Ten minutes, little bro." He hung up.

I gave Cole a quick call and filled him in. He said to be careful, but to go in case he showed up at her apartment.

Shit, shit, shit!

I draped a blanket over her small shoulders and wrote a quick note saying I'd be right back.

It was freezing outside. A thin layer of frost was already over my windshield. Slipping my gloves on, I decided to walk since it was only two blocks.

I tried not to think about how or why he was here. I was just glad he wanted me to meet him somewhere away from Mia.

Once at the carwash, I stayed under the light so he could find me. The place was dead, just some young kid with earphones watching the cash register.

"Mark." His voice came from somewhere at the side of the lot. I nearly jumped when he emerged from the shadows. "You came."

"Did I have a choice?"

He shrugged. "Look, I need cash now."

"And?"

He stepped toward me. "They're going to kill me."

"You made your bed, now sleep in it."

"You would let your own brother get murdered for the sake of a few bucks?"

"No." I stood straighter so I could prove I wasn't the little boy I once was. "Don't put your mistakes on me."

"You have a few of those, don't you, little

brother?"

I raised my fist, but stopped myself. "I was seven, Manuel, in a bad place, with no help from any of you. What happened was an accident, that was all."

"You should have gone to jail."

"Trust me," I nearly shouted, "I am."

***

Mia

I woke to a foul smell, one that dragged me off the couch and to my trash can, wondering what the hell it was. I lifted the lid and peeked inside, but found nothing but wrappers and a banana peel. I searched under the table, in the laundry room, in my closet. I dropped to my knees and ran my arm under the couch. That's when I felt it, and I wrapped my fingers around something wet and hard.

"Oh, my God!" My stomach turned when I saw what I was holding—a bloody bone with some flesh wrapped around the tip. I gagged, ran it over to the waste bin, and tossed it inside. I washed my hands and tied the bag in a large knot.

"Damn you, Butters," I cursed as I slipped on my furry boots. I looked down at my tight yoga pants and oversized tank. "Whatever." I grabbed my keys and headed out into the hallway and to the trash chute around the corner.

"You have got to be kidding me!" I tugged on the handle, but it wouldn't move. My skin crawled at the thought of the bone buried under a pile of wrappers. The only thing separating us was a thin layer of plastic.

The heavy door shut behind me. I looked down the staircase and muttered about how much effort this was going to take.

I made it down one flight before a shadow above me caught my attention. Tipping my head back, I tried to see who it was. A blue light flashed out over the edge but shot back when I set the trash bag down.

"Hello?" My fingers wrapped around the rail, I leaned over to see upward. I hated this old building. Everything was creepy, right down to the smell. Like an old theater, musty, and the ever present hum from the fluorescent lights.

Well, whoever it was must have left. A door shut, proving my theory. The nasty trash bag dragged behind me as I worked my way down.

Just as I hit the bottom floor, the lights flicked off.

"Shit." I pulled out my cell phone and fumbled with the screen but finally turned on my flashlight. I was scanning the wall next to me when something hard hit my arm and sent my phone flying across the floor.

"Ahhhh," I screamed before a hand slapped over my mouth. I jerked and managed to free myself. I leaped in the direction of the stairs, and I got three steps before he grabbed my ankle and brought my feet out from under me. My arms flew to protect my head, but my wrists took most of the impact, sending intense pain up to my elbows. "Stop! Help, somebody, please!"

He tried to pin me with his body, but I bucked and kicked. Somehow I wiggled free and crawled to my phone. Just as I went to reach for it, he kicked my ribs, and I fell to my stomach with a cry. My adrenaline pushed me on, but the pain was so bad I was sure one of the ribs was broken. I couldn't see a thing. It was pitch black; he could be anywhere.

His jeans made a flex noise as he bent down to the floor. He brushed my wet hair out of my tears. I squeezed my eyes shut, terrified of what he would do next.

"Pity to hurt to such a pretty woman," he cooed as his fingers slid across my sore neck. "I see I'm not the only one."

"Please," I sobbed into the darkness.

He locked his hand around my chin, which froze my nerves in place. His lips pushed to mine. I tried to fight him, but he slammed my arms to the ground. When I felt his hand move to my pants, I checked out. I wasn't me anymore.

"Anyone down there?" someone yelled from the top floor. A flashlight moved about.

I tried to scream, but his hand covered my mouth.

"Tell your boyfriend to pay up." He moved away from me. "Apartment 5G," he stated before I heard his footsteps retreating. I rolled my head to follow his sound. He stepped in front of my phone light, and I saw black jeans above white Vans sneakers.

With the last of my strength, I slithered over to my phone, and clutching it with my trembling fingers, I called my last dialed number.

I sobbed when I heard his voicemail click in.

"You've reached Mark Lopez. Leave a message."

"Mark," I barely squeaked, "I—ah…" I dropped the phone from my ear and sobbed into my hands.

"Hello?" the guy yelled from the top again. "The power should be back on soon."

I hurried to my feet and raced up the stairs with my phone lighting the way. My side hurt, but nothing mattered. I wanted to be home inside my apartment with a lock. His flashlight found me, illuminating my entire body. "Hey, miss, are you okay?"

Hurry, hurry, hurry. The blood pounded through my head.

I flung myself through my apartment door, slammed it shut, and twisted the deadbolt. *Be calm. You're safe. He didn't rape you. You. Are. Okay.*

"Holy shit." My hand shook as I raised it to my forehead and squeezed my temples for relief. I sucked in a sharp breath. *This is crazy.* My shaky legs wobbled when I reached out for the counter. *I already got hurt once this month. Why has it happened twice?* A few more steps, and I found the corner and sank to my knees. *Is Mark really involved in this?* The weight of the situation crushed me.

With a sigh, I let myself break, and soon fell into a heavy sleep on the floor where I wanted to believe I was safe.

He gripped my hand, and I was ready for his next move. I dodged his kiss, but he still hit my cheek. "Tell him to pay up." His words rushed to my ear, like a siren.

I jolted awake, but cried out in pain. Fuck. My phone flashed at me, and I saw I had missed two voice messages and three texts from Mark. With blurry eyes, I opened the message icon.

Mark: *I didn't get the rest of your voice message. Are you all right?*

Ten minutes later.

Mark: *I'm really sorry, Mia, I had to meet a co-worker. I'll be back in the morning, okay?*

Three hours later.

Mark: *Having a hard time falling asleep when I haven't heard from you. Call me, please. When you can. Xo.*

The phone landed on my bed as I very carefully pulled on my dark grey zip-up hoodie and Chucks. Thank God they were worn in and I didn't have to tie them. My ribs were a huge new pain I couldn't even tap into yet.

I took my wallet and phone and headed to the hospital.

Deep breath. I inched to my right to glance around the corner then pulled back. *Come on.* Again, I leaned forward and found Vikki Taylor speaking with Molly. *Fuck.* I tapped my finger against my leg and counted to ten.

"Mia? Is that you?"

Hello, Alvin.

181

"Hey." I gave a small wave.

"Are you okay?" He looked around then stepped toward me.

"Not really." I flinched when I attempted to stand straighter. He glanced over my shoulder, and I cleared my throat. "You think you could help me out? You know, quietly?"

He stared at me a moment then nodded for me to follow.

"Flippin' hell, Mia, you can see the dent where he kicked you." He shook his head at my face. I was beyond pissed that he had verbally beaten the truth out of me. "I'd say size eleven boot."

"Sneaker," I corrected his sarcasm.

"Unfucking believable."

"Tell that to my side."

I could he see was worried, and I was thankful. It was nice to see it in someone I didn't know that well. "Are you okay?"

I looked down. "I honestly don't know."

He placed a somewhat awkward hand on my shoulder. "You want me to call Mark for you?"

"No," I gave him a weak smile, "I called him."

"Okay."

"Thank you…though."

He flashed a smile before his serious expression returned. "We need to report this."

My blood pressure dropped, along with my ability to breathe. "No!"

"Mia, you were assaulted in your building. God knows who that man was."

I was going to be sick. "You think I'd dress like this in public? To go to my work? No! I came here

182

hoping a friend would help me without any questions."

"Mia," his eyes widened in shock at my outburst, "I'm only looking out for you."

"I know." I slipped off the table and tucked my jacket against my sore ribcage. "But what I need from you is your friendship." I hurried out and down the hallway.

Before the elevator doors even opened, I could hear the yelling from the bottom floor.

"This is outrageous!"

My stomach sank right as the doors opened. I stepped out and found Mark pacing the ER waiting room like he was about to erupt.

"Mark." The receptionist nodded in my direction.

His gaze snapped over to me, and his face fell and he seemed to shake off a twitch. In three strides he was in front of me. He started to touch me but stopped himself.

"Que se joda mi vida! Odio que estoy siendo perseguido por una sombra codicioso." He shook his head at my blank look. I had no idea what he just said.

I opened my mouth to speak, but closed it as he stepped toward me and kissed my cheek softly.

"Sorry." He closed his eyes. "Happens when I get that angry. Can I take you home?"

I nodded and took the hand he offered.

Once inside the elevator, he wrapped his arm around my hip but stayed very quiet. He acted the same way until we were almost home.

"Mia, I need to know what happened."

I sighed and pulled down my hoodie. "I went to take the trash out, and when I was at the bottom—"

"Bottom?"

"Yes, the bottom floor has the trash cans."

"What happened to the trash chute?"

"It wouldn't open."

He squinted at the road. "Okay."

"Anyway, I had to walk to the bottom floor."

"Why not take the elevator?" he interrupted.

"Am I a witness to something, here, Mark? What's with the questions?"

He closed his eyes briefly. "Sorry."

"I skipped the elevator because there were new neighbors moving in and tying up the elevator the whole day, keeping it blocked on the top floor while they loaded and unloaded. Once inside the stairwell, I saw someone, but could only see a bit of a jacket. I thought they had left, and maybe they did, but then he was just there." I felt myself slip, but I got it together.

"What did he do?" His grip tightened around the wheel.

"He tried to force himself on me, twice." I swallowed hard. "Gave my ribs a good beating." I moved to find a comfortable position. "He told me to tell *you*..." He looked over at me with a strange expression.

"Tell me what? Mia?"

"To tell you that you need to pay up."

He didn't blink, twitch, or flinch. He just looked back at the road and smoothly pulled over onto the shoulder.

"What did he look like?"

"I don't know—"

"How do you not know?"

"The power went out right before he—" I cleared my throat. "All I know is he wore jeans and white Vans sneakers."

"Accent? Smells? Feel anything different?"

"I-I don't know. I wasn't really taking notes as he drove his foot into my ribs or when he tried to rape me." A sob lodged in my throat and cut my voice off.

Mark closed his eyes and placed his hand on mine.

"Do you know who it was, Mark?"

"I have an idea." His voice changed as he pulled out his phone and held his it to his ear. "Lopez, ML536. I need a secure line to Colonel Logan."

He kept his eyes straight ahead.

"Cole." His voice broke through all my attempts to stay calm. "Order me a scotch, neat. I think I have dinner plans that might run long."

What the hell is going on?

"Never been more sure," he said, his eyes creasing as he listened. "Thanks."

He tucked his phone into the side pocket of his military style pants.

"What are you doing?"

He took my hand, brought it to his mouth, and kissed my knuckles. "Protecting you."

CHAPTER SEVEN

Mark

"Pack anything, Mia, just hurry." She stood at the end of her bed and watched me fill her duffle bag.

"I think you're overreacting." I shook my head and grabbed a handful of panties and pushed them to the bottom corner.

"Trust me, I'm not," I muttered.

"I need to work. What about Kenny?"

"Kenny doesn't even know you." As soon as I said it, I froze. Oh, my fuck. Did I really just say that? I turned to find her glossy eyes glued to the floor. Yeah, I did.

"Oh, Mia, I didn't mean that." I tried to pull her to me, but she jerked her arm back with a wince of pain. I dropped my head. *Such an asshole.*

She walked across the living room, to the kitchen, and opened the front door.

My fists went to my forehead. I wanted to haul her over my shoulder and race to the safe house, but

I couldn't.

I moved to stand in front of her and I whispered, "Please come with me."

"I've known you for three months. I've known Kenny for sixteen years. Don't make me pick, because I'll chose him."

"But he hurt you."

"So did you, with all this—" she waved her hand in a circle, "—situation." She closed her eyes briefly.

I wanted to say *ouch*, because she was right. I did. I understood what she meant.

Her hand rattled the doorknob. "I think you should go."

"Are we breaking up?" My hand went to hers. I needed to be grounded.

"No," her eyes moved to mine, "I think I just need a breather. Things are happening too fast between us, and it's all a bit intense."

Welcome to my life.

I slipped my hand into my pocket. I felt strange standing in the hallway while her hurt heart pulled away from mine.

"Jesus, Mia, I'm nervous! You were just attacked. I'm not sure how to protect you if you won't let me in."

"I'll call you later." Her face paled as she shut the steel door.

***

"You said what, exactly?" Savannah had been trying hard to understand what happened with Mia and me for the past three days. I'd remained quiet, but now I had a terrible feeling in the pit of my stomach, and it was screwing with my emotions. So I finally gave in, hoping I'd feel a tiny bit better. I was wrong. "You really said that about Kenny?"

"Yeah, 'cause Cole hasn't fucked up before?" I tossed back. She had trapped me in the living room.

She braced her hands on her hips. "Yeah, he has."

"Why you deflecting onto me?" Cole hissed from the chair around a mouthful of cookie. I didn't even know he was there.

"Sorry, man."

"Don't point fingers, Mark. Grow a set and man up," she scolded.

I glanced at Keith, who had decided to join us. "The lady's right."

"Ahh." I jammed my fists against either side of my head. I couldn't take any more fingers running through my hair. "Okay, I screwed up, but can we please focus on what is important? I think it was Manuel who attacked her."

Cole brushed his fingers clean. "Well, why don't we go and speak with him, then?"

"I've been trying to get hold of him, but he's not answering his phone."

Cole pulled out his radio. "John, track Manuel Lopez' phone. I need a location."

"10-4."

"We still have John watching her. She just goes to the hospital and then back to her place. She is lying pretty low. Only goes out with the dog and back in," Cole assured me.

"But you need to call her, Mark." Savannah handed me my cell phone. "Just check in on her, at least."

I found her name in my call log and hit dial. A line of sweat broke across my shoulders as it rang.

"Hi, you've reached Mia Harper." Her cheerful voice hit me hard.

"Hey, hon, I just..." I let out a long sigh when I saw Savannah's expression. "I just wanted to check in and see how you are." She flicked her hand at me to keep talking. "I miss you, Mia, a lot."

Savannah looked less than impressed.

"What?"

"Now what?"

I looked at Cole for help, but he pretended to play on his phone. I glanced at Keith for anything.

He shrugged as he popped a cookie in his mouth. "I would have chipped her, but that's just me."

Savannah tossed a pillow at him, and he caught it, laughing.

"When is your next assignment?" Savi asked Cole, who looked up when she spoke.

"This Friday."

"Okay, then." She looked at me.

"What?"

"Men." With a sigh, she dropped her arms and hit her legs with a thud. "Go get her. Win her back, fight for what you love." I blinked at her. "Mark," she moved in front of me, "Cole fought for me, and look where we are now." She gave me her famous sweet smile that let you feel how much she cared. "I want you to have what I have. I'm happy, and you should be too. I want my happy, cookie stealing, brother-in-law back."

"But she said she wanted space, and—"

"It's been three days. Have you spoken to her at all?"

"Yeah," I sank into a chair, "I reached out when I arrived at the house. Once after that, but only texting, never on the phone."

"Go, get her, then. What's the worst that can happen—?"

"She could reject me!"

"So," her tone made me look over at her, "don't let her. Prove you two are right for one another. Convince her it was just your fear that something would happen to her that made you act like such an idiot!"

"This is all very *Gone with the Wind* for me," Keith muttered as he stood, but Savannah whirled around and pointed in his direction. "Don't go far, Keith. You're next."

"Me?"

"Yes, you!"

"Run, man." Cole laughed as he held Savannah's chin and gave her a long kiss. "God, I love you!" He grinned. "I have work to do. Mark, go get Mia, but I need you Friday."

I nodded, knowing I couldn't miss another assignment. Truthfully, I didn't want to. Keith slipped out the moment Savannah was under Cole's spell. One kiss from Cole, and she was done.

I wasn't far behind but decided to take a detour into the kitchen where I snagged a couple of cookies. I had just made it to the top of the stairs when I heard her voice.

"Marcus Carter Lopez." Abigail stood in her bedroom doorway. "What's this I hear about you letting Mia go?"

"I didn't—"

"No excuses, son." She stepped forward and gave me a hug then turned me toward the door. "I'll let the chopper know you'll be ready in thirty."

Well, I guess that's that.

The whole way back to North Dakota, I kept in contact with Cole. Manuel's phone said he was still in North Dakota, but he wasn't answering. Odd, considering he was so hard up for cash.

***

When I got to the hospital, it was crazy. Apparently, a city bus hit some black ice and ended up in a river. Two dead at the scene, and nine more with serious injuries. The cab driver had filled me in on the way. The noise was incredible.

"Hey!" a man yelled as Alvin went to check the cut on his shoulder. A small pole had been driven into his muscle. "Don't touch me. I'm not a homo."

Alvin held his hands up. He looked beyond beat. I wondered if they all had had to pull double shifts because of this accident.

I hurried over just as the guy made another loud comment. I noticed the pole was at an odd angle and might be close to the guy's spine. I'd seen enough combat injuries to know it was in a bad place. "This guy better be heading to the OR, Alvin, that pole is pretty near the spine."

"Okay." Alvin didn't question he just ran off.

"Pervert!" the guy commented again, looking at the departing Alvin. "I'm not into men!"

I shook my head and leaned over to warn him to shut up when the smell of booze hit me. His beard was full of puke, and his breath stank.

"Lucky for you, I'm not either," I muttered. I checked no one was looking, and carefully felt along his neck.

"Too many men were put together wrong. They have dicks and want tits."

Wow.

"You know, pal, statistics show men who are homophobic are actually hiding from their own truth."

His face flinched, but he shut up for a moment. I looked down and noticed his bloody knuckles.

"You running your mouth on the bus, buddy?"

He gave me a dirty look but didn't deny it.

I did notice two police officers were hanging out by the door. I scanned the room and picked up on a young man with a pink polo sporting a fat lip and black eye. The pieces of the puzzle immediately dropped into place.

Just as I was about to leave, one of the officers was at my side with cuffs.

"Mr. Tarp, we need to cuff you to the bed until we have all the details of what happened on that bus."

"The hell you are!" The man attempted to move but screamed out in pain. The officer cuffed the man and stayed by his bed as I left.

Piece of trash.

I finally made it upstairs to her floor. A frazzled

Nurse Taylor was handling two phones, talking on one and texting on the other.

"What can I help you with today?" She didn't look up as I stood at the counter.

"Busy downstairs."

Her head snapped up, but her normal smile wasn't there. "Hey, Mark, bad timing, hon."

"What's wrong?"

She looked around and was about to say more, but cursed when the phone rang. "Third door on your right." She pointed behind me.

I didn't stick around to ask. I just followed her directions…to a door that read **'Chapel.'**

Pushing the heavy door open, I stepped into a dark room where candles pulsed to the hum of the central air.

A huge wooden cross tipped forward from the base. The backlight made the shadow even larger.

I wasn't overly religious, but I did believe our energy had to go somewhere. I didn't believe we were meant to live only this life. I thought when this life was up, we just pressed restart and did it again as someone or something else. I didn't like to dig too deep into the how and why of it. I found my peace in other ways.

A sniff off to the left indicated where she was. Mia sat looking so tiny and staring up at the ceiling.

She jumped when she saw me. She dried her cheeks and let out a long breath.

"Hi," she whispered as I moved closer. "What are you doing here?"

"I needed to see you."

Her eyes filled with fresh tears as she nodded

sadly. Then she let out a silent sob, her shoulders shaking.

"Oh, hon." I grabbed her shoulders and pulled her to me. She sobbed into my shirt. I lowered to the bench and brought her with me. "I'm here." I rubbed her back, keeping my rhythm while she poured out her pain. The chapel was quiet and cool and peaceful.

"He's gone," she said softly.

Kenny. I silently thanked Savi for the timing so I was able to be here for her right now.

"Oh, Mia, I'm so sorry about Kenny. I was such an idiot before. I know how much you loved him. I know how much you hurt. You know that, right?" I kissed her head.

"I know. I'm sorry too, and so sad, and so tired." She leaned forward and stared up at the cross. "I can honestly say I'm not sure what to do now. I feel numb inside."

"It's the shock." I cleared my throat and pulled advice from my own history. "It's hard to see the path you'll take this far ahead. It's hard to believe the pain will pass, but it will, slowly, over time. You'll find your direction."

She looked up at me as a tear slipped down her cheek. "The moment anyone stepped in between me and Kenny I put up a wall. I've been fighting to be with him for so long, against everyone's advice." She closed her eyes as more tears leaked out. "I'm sorry I pushed you away."

I hated to see her hurting. "When does your shift end?"

She checked her watch. "Two hours ago."

I stood and offered her a hand, and she let me help her up. I started to give her a kiss but stopped right above her lips.

"Is this what you want?" I needed her to know I would not push her.

She slid her hand around my neck and gently pulled me to her. The kiss was slow and soft. I moved my body closer and wrapped my arm around her back, needing to feel her.

She pulled back and rested her forehead on my chest. "Can you take me home?"

My hand found hers, and she slipped her fingers between mine and held on.

We managed to get out of the hospital before anyone spotted her, although Alvin did mouth a 'Thank you' to me when he saw us leaving, which was nice.

Once we were in the car, Mia leaned her head against the door and closed her eyes. Poor thing was exhausted.

"When was the last time you had a good night's sleep?" I asked, turning the hot air on her.

She yawned. "Four days ago."

I cursed under my breath and waved to the security guard who raised the gate as we left the property and headed for her apartment.

Mia wrapped her body around me as we waited inside the elevator.

"You hungry?" My lips brushed her ear. She shook her head.

My phone rang, and I saw it was Cole.

"Lopez." I gave Mia a sleepy look when she gazed up at me.

"His phone says North Dakota, but his sergeant said he was in New York yesterday. We'll keep digging. Meanwhile, what's your plan?"

"Not sure yet."

"You're with Mia."

"Yes."

"Okay, call me with the details. I'll pull John back in."

"Copy that."

I opened the door to let her go inside first. An odd feeling hit me as I scanned the apartment. Something was off.

"Is the heat in the building turned off?" I asked and moved over to her thermostat. It read 50° F.

"Not that I'm aware of." She wrapped a blanket over her shoulders. "It's freezing in here."

I didn't want to scare her, so I quietly moved to her bed behind the partition and found her fire escape window was wedged open. I followed the wet puddles to her dresser then to her closet. This must have been how they got in to plant the bone to lure her out of her apartment before. With a look over my shoulder, I saw Mia fill the kettle. With a defensive stance I tugged open the door and flipped on the light.

"Hey, Mia, can you come here, please?"

Her footsteps got louder then stopped when she could see the mess her closet was in.

"Oh, my God." She looked at me, wide-eyed.

I turned to face her scared expression. "Did you have cash hidden up there? Or anything of any value?"

"Ahh," she shook her head, "no cash. I have a

196

loose baseboard for that." She stepped into the walk-in closet and felt around until she found a red little box. "Just this, my father's watch."

I stepped back out and noticed her jewelry, crystal vase, and camera were still there.

"I don't think this was a robbery." I went back to the window and closed it easily. "I think this was a message."

"What?" Her voice matched her body language.

"They left everything, left the window open when they could have closed it, and purposely left footprints. Mia, you're not safe here. Will you please come with me this time? Please?"

Her wide eyes looked around her place as it all sank in. "Okay."

"Okay?" I questioned and hoped I was right in my feeling.

"Okay, I'll go wherever with you."

In two strides, I was in front of her. I wrapped my arms around her body and held on tightly.

We packed, checked in with her neighbor, and headed downstairs to my car. Just as we stepped into the lobby, a guy approached us.

"Hi, Mia." He smiled and came a bit closer to her than I liked. "Are you off on a trip?"

Mia glanced at me. "Mark, this is the new building manager, Chris."

I offered my hand but he didn't take it. *Okay...*

"Yes," I answered for her and purposely wrapped my arm around her and kissed her cheek. "A much needed vacation."

"Nice," he muttered then opened the door for us. "Have fun and stay safe."

"Thanks." She waved as we headed out to my car. I did notice he watched from the lobby.

I explained to Mia on the way to the chopper a bit about what to expect up ahead. Most people would be intimidated about being taken to an unknown destination, but she smiled her trust at me. My heart swelled, and if I hadn't been so worried, I would have stopped the car and hugged her. A short time later, I pulled the car over and reached behind her seat and placed a contract on her lap.

"I am sorry for this part, Mia, but—"

"It's okay." She took the contract and started to read. Once she was finished, she signed it and handed it back. "I understand, Mark, and it is okay. I don't mind signing."

I smiled at her and gave her a peck on the side of the head. Then I tucked the paperwork in my bag and moved the car forward and around an old building. "Well, hon," I grinned at her, "hope you're not afraid of heights."

"Why?" She looked around then her hand flew to her stomach when she saw the chopper. "Please tell me you have an Ativan in your bag!"

"How about a stiff drink?" I opened my door, grabbed her bags, and moved around the car to her door. "I'll let you hold my hand."

"You always hold my hand." She smiled but took my hand in a death grip.

"You help ground me." I shrugged. I didn't care how I sounded; it was the truth. I tugged her in the direction of the chopper. Its blades, true to its name, were chopping the air into tiny bits.

Her gaze locked onto the pilot's seat as we took

off. I felt bad for her. I had never experienced the kind of fear that seemed to cripple some people. Fear of flying, fear of heights, fear of the dark, none of it ever fazed me, and I was damn glad of it.

Once in the air and on our way, I reached over and unattached the death grip her fingers had on the front of her seat and gave it what I hoped was a comforting squeeze.

"You okay?" My voiced crackled over the speakers.

"Ask me again when my feet are on solid ground." She grimaced but went back to her deep breathing.

I leaned over, tilted her chin so she'd look at me, and kissed her softly.

"You deal with gunshot wounds, collapsed lungs, and car wrecks, but heights make you freeze." I laughed.

"Everyone has a fear, Mark," her eyes narrowed in on mine, "even you."

With a smirk, I nodded. "I got you."

"I know," she said, but her tight smile and white face said otherwise.

I grinned at her. "You know I can tell when you're lying, right?"

CHAPTER EIGHT

Mia

My fingers clawed at the five-point harness that, for the life of me, I could not release. I tugged, yanked, and shook the damn thing, but nothing happened. Mark, of course, slipped out of his with ease. He smiled at my fumbling, kissed me, and commented that he rather enjoyed me when I was pissed. I was about to head butt him when he batted my hands away and finally released me from the beast.

Once I was free, I threw myself into his arms and let him lift me to the sweet earth.

His hands went to my elbows as I got my still shaking legs firmed up under me.

"Next time, I think I'll drive," I muttered as he laughed. His mood seemed to lighten since we touched down on his stomping grounds. Which was good, because it just sank in that I was about to meet his family.

"Come, let me show you my home." He beamed

with obvious pride. He introduced me to Dell, who smiled at me and winked as he took our bags and followed us down a slippery path. I stopped when we came to a clearing.

"Wow." I gawked at the specular view of a massive cabin in front of a lake, wedged in between the mountains. I knew this place would be nice but this…this was something else.

"I know, hey!"

I'd never seen him so bubbly.

"Oh, my word!" An older lady with the kindest smile was making a beeline for us. Her hands were up in the air before she even reached us, ready for a hug. "Would you look at you!"

"Mia, this little lady," he hugged her hard then tucked her under his chin, "is the light of my life and the woman who raised me, Abigail."

"Mark, put me down, boy, and let me see her!" she admonished him, laughing. I could see the love that surrounded them. I liked her already.

"Oh, I've heard a lot about you." I smiled and welcomed the hug she wrapped me in.

"We are so pleased you chose to come, Mia. Are you hungry, or maybe you'd like a drink?"

"A drink! Please!" My body definitely needed help to relax. "I think I died a thousand deaths inside that hunk of steel on the way here." I shuddered, looking back over my shoulder at the thing. "Please tell me we can drive home."

Abigail laughed as she linked arms with me and walked me to the house. She waited until Mark spoke with Dell, who stood politely waiting next to my bags. "I rode that horrible contraption once, and they never got me in it again."

"Oh, Abby! She's here!" A woman who looked just like Abigail came toward us, smiling a welcome.

"This is my sister June. She lives here as well."

"Nice to meet you, June."

"Oh, Marcus, she's a doll." June winked then she and her sister walked me into the living room.

"Wow." I couldn't hold back my reaction. This place just kept going.

Somehow I finished one glass of red wine and was on my second, I thought, and trying to take everything in. June was one slippery woman with the bottle.

Savannah popped down earlier to give me a hug and to welcome me, but had to attend to their daughter. Several men came and went, and each one stopped and was introduced. They all seemed nice, but their names had not stuck. Only one guy stood out—Keith. I remembered him because he seemed to be a bit on edge and kept glancing at his phone. He must have been waiting for someone. I fleetingly wondered if he had girlfriend troubles. *I wonder if Keith is his first name or last?* When Abigail called him out, he just shook his head and dismissed the question.

"Come on." Mark motioned for me to follow. He led me downstairs and began to give me a tour. I was amazed by all the rooms, particularly the entertainment room, the offices, and Savannah's piano room. I got a kick out of the Jolly Jumper next to the bench. Olivia was a very lucky baby. This place would be a trip to grow up in. So many little rooms and cubbyholes. I could only imagine what else there was here that they couldn't even show me.

We climbed the stairs to the main floor again. "So we have the kitchen over there," he continued, pointing to a huge kitchen that overlooked the lake. "Dining room, living room. Then down that way," he pointed toward a long hallway, "is Cole's office at the end. The house shrink normally holds his sessions in the office next to his." He took my hand, nearly pulling my arm off in his excitement as we climbed more stairs. "These are our bedrooms up here. All team Blackstone lives up here, as well as the main staff and a few others who have moved up in their ranks since they got here. So Abby, June, Cole, and there's a few open rooms for when we have guests. The rest of the men live in the other wing of the house."

My head was spinning. There was a lot to take in, and Mark's enthusiasm made him talk so fast I knew I'd never remember it all. I followed as he started down the hallway.

"This is Mike's room. He's really scary looking, but he's a giant—"

"Oh, I'm not all that scary," a deep voice boomed behind me. I nearly leaped onto Mark's back. "Sorry," he said with a grin. I had to tilt my head back to get a good look at his appearance.

"Nice tats," I blurted out, mentally smacking myself but deciding to brave it through. His hands where covered in red and black swirls. I stepped forward to get a better look at his sleeve. Black and silver warriors were fighting while one man on top of a rock stood and watched. Interesting. I bet there was a story behind those...wait, now. "Ahh." I pointed to a small troll doll tattoo nearly hidden down by his wrist.

"Long story." He smiled, but a fleeting expression showed something I couldn't pinpoint.

Mark laughed behind me. "Trust me he's a vault on that topic."

"Lopez, blow me a bubble." Mike shook his head. "Welcome to the house, Mia."

"Thanks." I waved as he disappeared into his room.

"My room...umm, I mean *our* room is down here." As we were about to go into the room, a strange bell-type sound came over an intercom. "Dinner," he said in answer to my puzzled look. "House is too big to yell."

I had never seen so much food in my life. Two huge chickens sat on either end of the table, with every possible side dish in between. Large bowls of mashed potatoes, carrots, green beans, broccoli, and turnips were handed about. The cranberry sauce was made fresh and served with something called bread sauce. It looked pretty strange but tasted amazing. Abigail explained it was a British tradition she grew up with, and the meal simply wasn't complete without it.

There came a flurry of activity as Savannah entered carrying an adorable little girl who had to be Olivia, along with an older couple I knew must be related to Cole. The man was an older version of him. They apologized for being late as they took their seats.

"You must be Mia." The older woman offered her hand. It was freezing, so I guessed they'd just arrived. "I'm Sue, Cole's mother, and this is his father Daniel."

Daniel and Sue, Daniel and Sue, I repeated to myself, trying to keep everyone's name straight.

"This," Savannah held up her daughter, who had an itty-bitty pink tutu over her tiny round belly, "is Olivia."

"It's lovely to meet you all." I rose and shook the Logans' hands and waved to the cute bubble blower.

Cole took the baby as soon as Savannah sat. He placed her on his thigh and ate with one hand. Dad of the year, right there.

I watched in awe of everyone. Their family bond was just as large as this house. The men were funny and joked around a lot. Mark had my jaw dropping with the amount of food he inhaled.

Dell leaned over and whispered, "He'll still have room for dessert too."

My gaze went to his. "No way!"

"Five bucks he'll go for—" Dell leaned behind me to look at the dessert table, "—a quarter of the apple crisp, three chocolate chip cookies, and Abigail will get him and Keith a glass of milk."

I sneaked a peek at Keith, who still had a mountain of food to get through. Mark was polishing off a chicken leg but still had lots on his plate. There was no way they could possibly squeeze in dessert.

"You're on." I shook his hand under the table.

"So, Mia," Daniel said, stealing my attention

away, "how do you enjoy working at North Dakota Hospital?"

"It's a good job." I stopped there because Kenny's face popped up. I did notice he gave me a strange look but didn't push it any more.

"I hope my boys behave when they're there," Sue commented as she delicately speared a green bean and placed it in her mouth. "That hospital has been good to us over the years."

"Well, yes." I caught Mark grinning at me. "Although this one has all the nurses under his spell."

Daniel laughed. "I can see that."

"Mia, what do you like to do for fun?" Savannah stirred the baby food and touched it to her lips before she gave the baby some.

"Ahh," I nearly laughed, "I'm not really one for playing sports. I seem to have two left feet. I love to read, though."

"Oh, yeah?"

"Yes, mostly mysteries." I failed to mention my love of dirty books, as that wouldn't exactly be dinner table conversation.

"That's lovely." June swirled her wine around her glass. "We have two libraries in this house. I'm sure Mark or Savannah will gladly give you a tour."

"I'd like that, thanks."

Dell bumped my arm as Mark turned in his chair and picked up a fresh plate. Sure enough, he took exactly what Dell said he would. Mark even served a plate for Keith.

"Abby," Keith smiled at her, "would you mind?"

"Of course, sweetie." She jumped up and

returned with two large glasses of milk.

I tried to contain my laughter, but it was no use. I pulled some singles from my back pocket and tossed five of them next to Dell's plate.

"What is that?" Mark's curiosity was piqued.

"Hot date later," I joked before realizing it might have been an inappropriate comment, considering I had given Dell *stripper ones*. But before I could correct myself, Daniel started to laugh—he really, really laughed. He had to put his fork down to cover his mouth. Didn't take long before the whole table broke out.

"Oh, you're gonna fit in really well here." Mike proclaimed, his big voice booming over everyone.

***

Relaxing after dinner, I found myself watching Savannah and Cole. Talk about two people who were meant for one another. He obviously worshiped her, and she couldn't go even a few moments without touching him. Then there was little Olivia, who had the entire house under her spell. Who could blame them? She was the sweetest little girl, with enormous black eyes. She seemed so happy and full of smiles all the time.

"Would you mind if I held her?" I warmed my hands before I took her. They'd changed her into a fuzzy purple Onesie, and she had little baby Uggs on her tiny feet. "Well, hello there, sweetheart." I bounced her gently on my hip. She seemed to like this and smiled her drooly smile up at me. With a dive toward me, her fingers grabbed my necklace, which she immediately put in her mouth.

"Sorry," Savannah said with a chuckle. "She loves jewelry, and she puts absolutely everything in her mouth." She pulled out her own necklace with a snowflake dangling from it and held it up. "I've had to replace this chain about three times now."

"I don't mind," I said in a pseudo-baby voice and rested my forehead to hers. "You're so cute I could eat you up in one bite."

"She is pretty yummy." Mark took a seat on the couch and sipped something dark in a crystal glass.

"No." I turned the baby out of his view. "You cost me five dollars with your predictability."

"Am I that predictable?"

"Yes," Savannah answered, "you and Keith. But only when it comes to your tummies."

Mark thought for a moment. "I *do* love food."

Cole laughed but then groaned as a huge cat jumped up and sat on his lap. It did two circles before it wedged itself between him and Savannah and very crudely flopped its legs open.

"Wow, he certainly makes an entrance." I laughed.

"This is Scoot," Cole rubbed the cat's tummy, "second in command. He keeps the men in line, or at least that's what he believes."

"Not too shy, is he?" I nodded toward his legs.

"Hey, man," Mark said to the cat, "let 'em hang out."

Olivia started to wiggle for her dad, so I handed her back to Cole. She went for the cat's ear. I cringed at the thought of what he would do, but to my surprise, he just lay there and took it. Her father certainly didn't seem worried, so I relaxed.

I cuddled in next to Mark and listened to everyone talk. I could see myself becoming attached to this place. Such a warm vibe with lots of people, but room to be alone.

By ten, Mark noticed how tired I had become and was only too happy to stand and say goodnight for us and guide us up the stairs to his room.

I stood inside the door, taking it all in. His sleigh bed had grey sheets with a dark blue duvet over top. Six pillows and a throw rested perfectly in place. The rest of the room matched the color scheme, and it flowed into the bathroom. Everything was so big and grand. No detail was left undone, right down to the grey curtains held in place by cast iron hooks that matched the chandelier in the center of the room.

Mark gave me a hug and a pat on the butt to push me gently into the room.

"Hon, this is our room now, okay? I need to go talk to Cole for a few minutes, so you get settled in. I won't be long, I promise." He kissed the top of my head before he left.

My bags were on top of a bench. I got out my toiletries and headed into the bathroom and tried to decide, bath or shower? Shower. I was afraid I might fall asleep in the warmth of the tub.

Four different knobs stared back at me, then there was the control panel. *Good Lord!* Finally, after almost scalding myself, I figured out how to turn it on and get the right temperature and stepped gingerly into the marble rectangle.

I smiled when I saw that there were shampoo and

lady products all ready for me. It was strange, but Savannah had warned me earlier tonight not to feel awkward with what was provided for me. It was just part of the routine of the house, considering the type of work they did.

My finger ran along the path of gold that threaded through the solid slab of marble. The hot water beat down on me as steam filled the shower, surrounding me with the warmth my body so badly craved. Squeezing the lovely floral scented shampoo into my hand, I lathered my long hair from scalp to tips. A brass handle stirred my curiosity, and I decided to give it a careful twist, ready to jump out if need be. The water beat a completely different rhythm on my lower back and shoulders. The lights dimmed, and the faint smell of lavender found me. Oh my, this was perfect! *Sorry, Mark, but these power jets kneading the tension from my muscles might become your competition.*

Only problem with letting your mind wander was unexpected and sometimes unwanted thoughts intruded. I finished, towel dried, and braided my hair. With a quick swipe of the towel across the mirror, I stared back at my reflection.

"Tell him!" my subconscious advised.

I can't! I squeezed my eyes shut. *What if he's not all right with it?*

"You had a chance, and every day that goes by will only make it worse!" it yelled at me and caused my head to ache.

Stop.

I flipped off the light and headed into the bedroom.

The bed was big—*really* big. I tucked my arm around my head and burrowed down in the puffy blanket. I grinned into my pillow as Mark's scent surrounded me in instant comfort.

Mark said he'd be back soon, but it didn't take long for my eyes to close.

"Tell your boyfriend to pay up!"

My eyes popped open. The clock flashed blue numbers at me—3 a.m. Mark hadn't come to bed yet? I began to feel odd being here. Silly thoughts started to flood my brain. Did I make the right choice? Should I have gone back home? I decided to get up and go downstairs.

I pulled a long sweater on over my shorts and tank top and peeked outside the door. I pulled the elastic free and let my messy hair fall in front of my face. I flicked it back and stepped onto the cold wooden floor, moving down the stairs and into the living room.

Silent lightning filled the room. I stepped to the window, watching the streaks of power as they dove toward the lake.

With my blanket in hand, I unlocked the patio door and breathed in the fresh storm air. The humidity was heavy, and the promise of some thundershowers was enough for me to tuck into a ball and enjoy the show.

A low rumble crept up the mountain, a little closer each time it came. My thoughts started to scramble and mix with some dark ones.

Kenny's lifeless body flashed in front of me,

211

which made the hold on my heart squeeze tighter. It wasn't fair; he was so young. I spent so much time reassuring him he was going to be okay that I almost believed it myself. The mind is a dangerous tool sometimes. My only peace was that he was now with his mother.

I pulled up the blanket as a cold breeze from the open patio door moved my hair around. A loud clap of thunder sent my mind racing in another direction.

The voice of the man in the basement who stole my courage from me came next. My fingers curled around my knees. I needed an anchor. Mark had asked so many times if I was okay. I didn't tell him, but I wasn't. That was why I didn't communicate all that much with him when he was gone. My attacker left me with a taste of fear in my mouth every time the lights went out. I became anxious whenever the trash bin was full, and even right before the elevator doors closed. He was faceless. Nothing but a shadow. I had only that one glimpse of him. I could have run into him at the market and not even known it.

"Pretty amazing, huh?" Savannah's voice broke through my thoughts. She had a teacup in her hand. "I love a good storm, myself. I often wandered down here when I first arrived to watch the weather." She pointed to the chair next to me. "May I?"

"Of course."

She curled up and let out a sleepy sigh. "I love my baby girl, but the child doesn't sleep unless she's on top of me." She laughed softly. "Cole wakes at a snap of a twig, but his daughter could crawl all over him and he wouldn't budge." She eyed me carefully as she spoke. "So I drape her over him and sneak out for some me time."

"Smart," I said, chuckling.

She touched my arm. "A little overwhelmed?"

The storm interrupted my reply with a huge downpour of rain. Savannah laughed with pure enjoyment over what many would curse. I loved that. It was how I felt. Rain was like a shower for my soul; it allowed me to reboot. Perhaps because it often meant a day inside wrapped up with a good book. Either way, I loved it, and apparently Savannah did too.

I opened my blanket and spread it over her lap. Her smile made me feel at home.

"I guess I really should shut the door?"

"No, leave it. It's wonderful." She scooted around to face me.

"So let me give you the scoop on this place."

I turned to look at her. "Please do."

"The aunts."

"Abigail and June?"

"Yes. They're the sweetest, most loving women you'll ever find, next to Sue. Cole's mother is amazing. Dr. Roberts is Abigail's boyfriend, and they are so cute together. But don't bring it up to Mark. He's a bit sensitive on the topic." She couldn't hide her grin. "Paul and John are really cool, and Mike, he has tattoos all over and looks scary, but he's a huge teddy bear."

"I've actually met Mike. He does seem really nice. Though not someone I'd like to meet in a back alley." She shook her head, smiling. "What about

Keith? What's his deal?"

"Ha! Keith is like the big bad wolf in fluffy pajamas with the ass flap hanging down. He acts scary, but he's harmless. We're really close. He walked me down the aisle." She stopped and thought. "Why did you ask?"

"He just seemed a bit on edge since I've been here, and he checks his phone a lot."

"Yeah, I've noticed that too." She seemed to get lost in thought, so I moved on.

"What about Mark?"

"Mark is the funny one. No matter how shitty your day has been, he'll make you laugh in a way that makes you feel good afterward, *not* just during. He's protective of our family, and I think for the longest time didn't date because he didn't want to leave Abigail or Cole." Her shoulders rose and fell. "That's what Cole told me."

"That's a strong bond to have." My throat tightened. I hated that Mark had a horrible family at first.

"It is. He does love to gamble, though. Don't ever play poker with him." My stomach sank. I didn't like the sound of that at all. My mind immediately flew to his brother's addiction and to my attack. "He doesn't lose," she continued. "I don't get it. Cole says he has a horseshoe stuck up his…" She looked over at me and shut her mouth. Then I saw her make the connection. "Oh, no. Mia, he's not like his brother at all. This is different." When she saw the surprised look on my face, she patted my arm and smiled. "Cole tells me a lot. I hope that's okay?"

"Yeah, it's okay." I was barely listening when I answered her.

"Mark and Manuel are polar opposites, Mia." Savannah's hand rested reassuringly on my arm again, and her expression was sincere. "Mark won two grand when all the guys bet on when Olivia would be born. You know what he did with the money?" I shook my head. "He started an investment account for her for college. Mark may have had an awful family, but he's nothing like they are."

"Thank you for saying that." I did believe her.

The sky lit up and poured down more rain. The lake twisted and churned with the mix of rain and wind.

I needed to focus on something else.

"What about Cole? Any tips?"

Her face softened and her eyes lit up. "What to say about the Colonel? His bark is bigger than his bite. However, don't ever break the house rules. He has a one strike policy."

"Good to know." I had heard bits of this before, so it rang true.

"He's really kind and warm. It just takes a while to break down his walls." She looked at me. "Are you okay with what happened to you?"

I glanced back at the water and let that foreign feeling seep back in. "Ahh…" I tucked my hair behind my ear. "Not entirely sure yet."

"I get that."

"I'm pretty good at blocking things out, and after Mark and I had our…" I paused to sigh and point to my head. "Well, I just pushed it all aside for now.

I'll deal with it when I can."

"Spoken like someone who has a lot to shed." She touched my arm again and drew my attention to her. "Please know that Dr. Roberts is a wonderful man who helped me a lot. He's often around if you ever needed some advice or someone else to talk to. You can always see him."

I nodded. "Thanks." I paused, considered, and decided to ask. "Savi?"

"Yeah?"

"Do you miss your family? Mark filled me in."

Her face twisted for a moment before it relaxed. "Family isn't about blood, Mia. It's about who you surround yourself with, who makes you feel loved and safe. I never had that from my father. I thought I had it with my best friend, Lynn, but that proved to be wrong." She blinked a few times then rubbed her arms. I could see this was a hard topic for her, so I didn't push further. "I do miss my mother, though, very much." She stood and wrapped her robe around her. "I'll leave you be, or would you like to walk up to your room with me?"

"I'll take a few more minutes, then I'll head up."

"Have a good night, Mia."

"You too."

***

Mark

Cole and I had been trying to hunt down Manuel all night. We finally got hold of his phone records and saw the last cell tower that picked up his signal was in North Dakota, just four streets over from Mia's apartment. What the hell was he doing there? Manuel had been unstable for as long as I could remember, but to hurt someone like Mia…I just couldn't believe he would go that far.

We decided when we returned from our next assignment we would find him and confront him. This shit had gone way too far.

It wasn't until after five a.m. that I crawled in next to Mia and pulled her close to my chest. She was as cold as normal and immediately molded to me as I shared my heat.

"Where were you?" She wiggled closer.

"Sorry, I didn't mean to be that long." I kissed the back of her neck. "Lots going on."

She rolled over and squinted up at me. "Everything all right?"

"Not sure yet. Come here, my little icicle, and let me melt off some of that sweetness," I joked, tickling her. I kissed her nose then her lips, but she pushed my shoulder back so she could look at me.

"Don't joke with me right now, Mark. Is this how it is? Late nights and few answers?" She softened her words with one swift, hard kiss.

I closed my eyes and wished I were in love with a different profession. "Sometimes, maybe, yes." She gave me a look as if to say *don't you dare lie.* "Yeah, a lot of times this is how it will be."

She gave me a slight nod before she moved to her side again. With a sigh, I rolled back into position and held her tightly. My stomach twisted and I decided to think before I spoke too quickly. Mia was becoming my rock, my anchor, my confidante. I loved the way she made me feel; even her smile made the dark turn to grey. The mere idea of my brother's hands on her made my heart rate jump. Wow, I'd fallen hard. I glanced at the clock and saw it was late or early, depending how you looked at it.

I wasn't sure what my next few days would be like, so I decided to give her as much as I could.

"I was left alone a lot when I lived with my mother," I whispered, releasing my haunted past into the chilly air. Her body began to relax as I spoke. "More than any child should be. My brother Manuel was horrible. If he wasn't high, he was ordering me around or forcing me to go out to find food. It was an excuse to get rid of me half the time. He much preferred I was gone than to have to deal with me." Wincing at the memories that unfolded in front of me, I continued, wanting to share my biggest burden.

"I stayed out all day over at Abby's house. The Logans were having a game day because of the snow storm. They were so warm and inviting that I lost track of time and didn't come home until it was nearly dark." Mia turned to face me, her hand wedged between her cheek and the pillow. Her big eyes held onto mine, her gaze encouraging me to go on.

"You know when your gut tells you something isn't right? The way your skin prickles and your mouth goes dry? Well, when I opened my front door that day, the feeling that washed over me was like that. I dropped my book bag and pulled out a piece of my Hubba Bubba to calm myself. I remember I poured a small glass of Kool-Aid from a jug that was on the counter and sat on the stool and waited for the punishment I knew had to come, but nothing happened. I called out for my mother. She didn't answer, but I thought I heard an odd noise from her bedroom."

Mia's fingers traced one of my scars across my shoulder. Her touch was soothing. "Was it Manuel?" she asked as she watched her hand skate about.

"I don't know."

She looked up, confused.

"One minute I was standing in the doorway, and the next I was in the hospital."

"What?"

"I guess I blacked out."

"Why?"

My vision tilted momentarily. "Because I...I killed my mother."

Her body tensed, and she barely even blinked as it sank in. I wanted to plow on and tell her everything, but first I needed to know if she was okay.

"Mia?"

"How old where you?" Her voice was low.

"Seven years and three months."

Her skin paled and her tongue ran along her lips. "Just a boy." She seemed to think. "Okay, so you were at the hospital..."

I didn't miss a beat. I wanted to show I would no longer hide things from her.

"There was a psychologist sitting in a silly light pink chair, writing on a pad when I came to. I was so confused and disoriented, and my head hurt a lot. The bright light made me blink, which got the lady to look over."

Mia's full attention was on me.

"I asked what I was doing there, and she told me I had a breakdown. I asked where my mother was, and she gave me a strange look. I asked where Manuel was, and she told me he was in the waiting room. She pulled up a chair and fixed her glasses to sit up further on her nose." Every detail was so vivid. "She asked me what I remembered. Where I was that day. What my mother was like toward us. The entire experience was odd. No one would answer anything until I got upset. Finally, Manuel was allowed to see me. He looked awful, his shirt was dirty, and his hair was a mess, like he hadn't slept in days. He told me I needed to keep my mouth shut, that I'd done something really bad, and if I said anything, they'd take me away and I'd never see the Logans again. I didn't even know he knew about the Logans."

Mia moved to sit crossed-legged. She pulled the blanket around her middle, tossed her hair off to one side, and waited for me to continue. It was hard not to stare at her. The faint light from the bathroom cast a soft glow on half her face.

"He told me then what happened, that I stabbed her. Some kind of a mental breakdown. I have no memory, and nothing is left over from it. All I knew was she was dead, and I did it." I swallowed hard and cleared my throat. "Manuel coached me on what to say to the police. They came in afterward. I was too scared, and I didn't know any better, so I went along with it. The police bought every word, and no one was charged."

"Where was Manuel during all this?"

I placed my hand on her knee, loving that she wanted to know all the facts. It meant she hadn't fully judged me yet.

"Manuel had a side job for one of our neighbors, outside maintenance stuff. So he had a solid alibi."

"So then what?"

"Abigail got wind of what happened and showed up at the hospital. Cole's father stacked up his lawyers and had me released to her care. The police came back only once to ask more questions. My prints were all over the handle, but that didn't mean much since we could have touched it at some point. I never spoke to them, as Abigail kept me upstairs. Cole's father dealt with them."

"What happened to your brother?"

"I didn't see him a lot after that. Except when he needed something from me. He drank and got into drugs for a few years, then around twenty-one, I guess, he started at the casinos. He had always gambled, but got into it big time after that. Didn't take long for them to catch on that he was counting cards and they blacklisted him. He started playing underground poker, at really scary places. His debts started to climb, and so did his need for his little brother. I've been bailing him out for the past nine years. He joined the police force at thirty, and how they let him in is beyond me. He's trouble, and he doesn't care who he brings down with him."

Mia nodded, but I could tell she was a million miles away.

I took her hand to get her attention. "I have to live every day with the fact I killed my mother. Truth be told, I hated her. She was a drunk, brought home random men, made me beg for food, and even made me sleep out in the snow when she forgot about me." I felt my tongue thicken. "I know what I did was unspeakable, and it screws with me that I can't remember, but I swear I'm not a monster, Mia—"

She leaned forward and cupped my face. "You are not a monster, Mark." She sealed her lips over mine before she pulled back. "You were just a child, in a bad situation. She's gone. Let it go. Free yourself from this darkness."

So many emotions ran through me, but my heart took over. I grabbed her waist, and in a blink, she was under me and my lips were on hers. I pushed her shirt up and over her head, and her panties were off just as quick.

My fingers felt gravitated toward her heat and dipped inside to feel her arousal. She was hot and wet, and her slickness coated my fingers. Her chin tilted back and a smile raced across her lips.

Her back arched, her breasts pushing into my chest. Skin to skin. "Deeper."

I eased three fingers deep inside, eliciting a moan from her. With all that was driving through me, I couldn't last. I lined up, and as soon as my fingers were out I slid my erection inside. She sucked in a deep breath and stilled.

"Okay?" I brushed the hair out of her face.

"Yeah," she panted and flexed until I was fully in. I waited for her body to adjust to the invasion before I started to move my hips.

Jesus.

She felt so good, but then a sudden realization came over me.

"I don't have a condom on."

"I'm on the pill, and we get tested yearly." I knew she knew we had to as well. The Army—but mostly Cole—was strict with our health.

She wiggled for me to keep moving. I stretched out and put my weight on my forearms. She hooked her leg over my hip and reached above to the headboard. The curve of her body snapped me back into the now. My hand slid up the length of her side, under her breast, and around her neck.

She was so beautiful. She stole the air from my lungs when I watched her face. Her warm breath shot in little bursts across my arm as she built herself up.

"How can someone feel this good?" I muttered as I eased out. We rocked together, holding tight to each other, eyes locked. Her eyes glazed over and she rode out her orgasm until it peaked along with mine. Then we slept.

***

"You can't tell anyone what really happened, Mark," Manuel warned me for the tenth time. "Just stick with your story."

I swung my book bag over my shoulder. I wanted to get started on the walk to Abigail's house.

Manuel ran up beside me. "If you fuck this up, you'll go to jail. You'll be known as the kid who killed his own mother."

I stopped to look at him. "I didn't kill her, Manuel!" I swallowed back the pain. "I mean, I don't remember doing it." He studied me for a moment then put both his hands on my shoulders.

"I saw you do it."

I shook my head. "How? You weren't even there."

"I was, and I saw you stab our mother like the ruthless animal you are."

"Why didn't you stop me?" I felt betrayed and sick.

"There wasn't enough time. Look at your hands."

I looked down to find my fingernails had bloodstains under them. "Ahh!" I cried and wiped them on my pants, but more blood welled up from under my nails, dripping onto the snow. "I'm sorry, I'm sorry!" I raced to a snowbank, dropped to my knees, and started to scrub my hands clean. "I'm so sorry, Mom! I didn't mean it!"

***

I woke with a jolt, my chest heaving painfully from the nightmare. I took in my surroundings and realized I was home. My hands were clean, but my stomachache lingered. Mia was gone. I glanced at the clock and saw it was nine thirty. I rubbed my tired eyes and forced myself up.

After a long shower, I made my way downstairs and saw Mia and Savannah outside talking, while Savi pulled Liv around on a wooden sleigh. You could hardly see her little face under her snowsuit hood. I watched from the living room window with a coffee in hand.

"She seems lovely, dear." Sue smiled as she raised her mug to her mouth. "Cole said he was trying to find her a position at the house so she can stay until we get this thing cleared up."

I shrugged. "I hope so, and there's always the medical center in town. That's assuming she wants to leave her life in North Dakota."

"She seems to be fitting in just fine." Sue nodded at the girls. Savannah bent down to scoop up a bit of new fallen snow and made a snowball. "Oh no," Sue said with a laugh.

I watched with curiosity. Savannah could get away with murder. She had all the men in the house under her spell because she was an amazing person with a huge heart. She leaned in and whispered something to Mia.

"Keith or Mike?" Sue asked as the guys rounded the corner.

"Mike."

"You think?"

"Yeah, she owes him one. Mike got her the other day."

Sure enough, Savannah turned and chucked the snowball at Mike, nailing him in the stomach. Then, to my surprise, Mia tossed her arm back and hit Keith in the chest. Sue burst out laughing as both men stood in shock.

Mike glanced at Keith, who wore his murderous look, then pointed a finger at the girls.

"Run!" Sue laughed.

Mia grabbed Liv and ran after Savi, heading for the stables. The men hurried around the house, no doubt to cut them off. We could hear Liv's shrieks of joy from the house as her little head bobbed around in Mia's arms.

"Go have some fun, dear." Sue kissed my cheek and took the mug out of my hand. "Take your brother with you. He's been holed up in his office all morning."

I grinned. "I have an idea."

"Cole." I stuck my head in his office door. He was at his desk reading a file. I knew it was the one that came in yesterday about the men who slaughtered that house full of people.

"Yeah?" He didn't look up.

"We head out tomorrow, right?"

He raised his head. "Yes."

"Come on."

"Where?" He rolled his head back to release some tension.

"It's Savannah."

His face fell and he hurried around his desk. "Is she okay?"

I may get my ass kicked for this.

"Yeah, she just needs your help."

I followed him down the hallway and out to the door, where he stopped on the front doorstep.

"Now!" Savannah screamed, and four snowballs flew from all directions. The air lit up with tiny sparkles of snow glistening in the sunlight. Cole turned to me, then back to his wife, who already had another snowball ready to go. Keith and Mike came up next to Mia, looking mighty pleased with themselves.

"Really?" Cole brushed the snow out of his hair before he stepped purposefully down the stairs.

Savannah grinned and tossed the ball into the air and caught it. "Looks like my aim is getting better." She pointed down at Olivia tucked into her sleigh in front of her. Her kitty mittens dangled and her furry boots peeked out from her snow pants. "Be nice. You wouldn't want to scare your baby daughter, now, would you?"

"Lopez." Cole nodded at me as I zipped down and scooped the little snow kitten before Savannah could use her as a shield.

"You see, sweet face, Mommy is using you as defense. Shame on her." I kissed her cool, wet cheek.

"This was your idea!" Savannah chucked a snowball at my feet. "Keith?" She looked at him for help.

"I have no idea what you're talking about, Savi." Keith reached out and held onto Olivia's hand. "Mommy is trying to get us all in trouble, isn't she?"

"Oh," she held up her hand, "it's on."

Cole bent down and hauled Savi over his shoulder. He slapped her ass, which made her giggle. She was used to him manhandling her.

"Mia!" she called out as Cole walked her to the house.

"Sorry, Savi," Mia moved in behind me with a laugh, "but he scares me a little."

"Wait," I stopped Cole, "let's go into town and have some fun before we go." I stopped talking, aware Savannah didn't need the sad reminder that we were going.

Cole set Savannah on her feet and wrapped his arm around her shoulders loosely. "What do you think?"

She grinned and her eyes sparkled. Oh, I knew that look. She'd make this happen. I tossed Olivia up in the air and flew her around like an airplane. A tiny line of drool shot down like a line on a fishing pole and landed in my mouth.

"Oh, pla!" I shifted her on my hip as I spat on the ground. "How can something so cute be so nasty?" I wiped my mouth dry. "Well, I can tell you had pineapple this morning."

"And breast milk," Savi chimed in with a raised eyebrow, clearly loving this moment. I guessed it was my karma. "Pla, pla, pla!"

I ran my hand in front of me. "Line. You're crossing it." She laughed as I handed Olivia off. "Here, go to Uncle Keith."

"Okay." Cole turned to us. "Let's go into town, maybe a movie and dinner at Zack's."

"Actually," Savannah placed a hand on his chest, "I have another idea."

***

"Oh, my." Mia gripped the boards. "Don't I need a helmet and knee pads?"

I laughed and took her shaky hands in mine. "Just let me guide you." She nodded but didn't move. "You have to trust me. Come with me, my little icicle."

Her head moved up to look at me straight in the eye. "I do."

Fighting the grin that shot across my face, I urged her forward. She shook and wobbled as I skated backward, but soon she got the hang of it and became steadier.

Mike, Keith, Paul, and John were off on the other end of the rink playing a hockey game. Abigail held Olivia in her arms as she whisked her around the ice. Her silent open-mouthed laugh had all of us in fits. Savannah was chasing Cole, who whipped by us like a pro. His hand trailed along the ice when he dipped down low and curled around her, dropping her into his arms.

"Show-off." Mia giggled with her death grip on my hands.

"You wanna try on your own?"

"Don't…let…go!"

I squeezed her hands. "I won't, not until you're ready."

"What if…" She paused.

"What, Mia?"

She looked up at me, her green eyes showing her vulnerability. "What if I'm never ready for you to let me go?"

I stopped moving, unsure I heard her correctly.

"I'm sorry, I didn't—I mean—"

"Mia, don't." I slid closer. "Don't say something like that and take it back."

She glanced down, but I raised her chin to look at me. My other hand slid around her neck. "Is this fear about me leaving? Or do you really like me?"

"Would it be okay to say both?"

I smiled my understanding. "Yeah, it is."

"I really like you, Mark." She started to move but lost her balance and fell into me. I caught her in my arms and held her tightly.

"I really like you too, Mia." Our lips met, and I didn't hold back, and neither did she. I knew we more than *liked* each other, but I could tell she was nervous to say it, and that was okay for now. Besides, she made me feel like a high school kid again, when just liking someone was a big deal. You didn't always have to fall in love right away. I felt love took time, and it was fun to feel it grow inside you. A constant bubble of warmth that expanded every day.

"Hey, no kissing during the game!" Keith yelled out, and I flipped him off.

"Ahhhhhh." My feet went everywhere and then straight up in the air, and my arms pinwheeled. I desperately reached for Mia, and we went down hard together. "Ouch! My butt hurts," I cried dramatically. "Can you feel if I hurt anything there, Mia?"

"Mark, you did that on purpose!" She laughed, her eyes bright. She hit me on the head with her mitten.

"What? No way!" I tightened my grip on her. "Tonight you can check out my bottom to see the bruises." I kissed her, happily listening to her delighted laughter.

Afterward we changed out of our skates and made our way outdoors to the frosty air.

"Seriously?" Paul groaned at the two horse-drawn carriages waiting for us outside. "This will be humiliating."

"Don't be insecure with your manhood, Paul." Savannah patted the horses and let Olivia sit on one of their backs for a minute. "It doesn't always have to be about the boys."

"Yeah," Keith chimed in. He climbed up and took a seat next to John before propping his arm along the back of the cushions. "It's romantic."

"So," Savi said, ignoring them, "Paul and John, you ride together, and Mark and Mia will ride with us."

"What about Abby?" Mia asked me, puzzled.

"She'll drive the baby home—"

"Ha, not yet. We have a date with the doctor." Abby, who was now holding Olivia, passed her to John while I cleared my throat free of the comment about how he'd better be good to her. She stepped back and laughed at the three of them in the carriage. "Three men and a baby."

"Savi…" John shot her a look, but all she did was smile and wave for me to join them.

"Be a good girl for your uncles, honey," she called over her shoulder.

Abby jumped in the SUV and went ahead to the restaurant.

Mia cuddled up close as the horse started to move. The wind was quite cold, so I could only imagine she was freezing.

"There're blankets in the trunk under you," the driver with the top hat called out. I pulled a heavy knit deep green blanket free and covered Mia before handing one to Savi.

"Thank you," Mia called out and was granted a

tip of the man's hat.

We took a few side streets before we turned onto a path that brought us over a light stone bridge. The driver stopped as Mia snapped a few photos.

"Wow," she said, beaming, "this place is like a fairy tale." The dusting of snow sparkled under the glow of the street lamps. The lake wasn't completely frozen yet, so the movement under the ice flickered. Twinkle lights threaded through the weeping trees danced in the quickening breeze. I couldn't think of a more romantic spot in the city. However, the groans from the carriage behind us soon stole the moment from me.

"Come on!" John called out in the night, making us all stop and turn around. "No one can make that kind of smell!"

"Oh," Keith made a gagging sound, "it's all up her back!"

"I'm calling a taxi," Paul announced.

"Please keep moving," Savannah called to the driver then looked at me before she lost her composure. We all laughed and barely stopped until we arrived at Zack's.

"Take your child, take her smelly load, I'm out," Keith huffed, holding Olivia like she might bite him. "I'm officially off uncle duty until she's clean again."

Cole turned to Savannah, who shot him *a don't even think of it* look.

I smacked his shoulder as I breezed on by with Mia. For once, I was thankful I wasn't holding that little crapper. Last time Savannah decided it was time for me to learn how to change her diaper. It wouldn't be happening again anytime soon.

"Oh!" Zack spotted us the moment we stepped inside his busy restaurant. "How wonderful to see all of you."

Mia stepped forward, and I introduced her to Zack. "It's a pleasure to meet you, Zack. I've heard great things about your place."

Zack wrapped his arm around her shoulders. "Please come, you must try this new wine I brought in from Spain. You like wine?"

"Yes."

"Perfect."

I followed behind with a dorky grin, enjoying how she seemed at ease with all the important people in my life. I only hoped I did with hers.

"Well, hello, there," Jake, the bartender and Savannah's best friend, greeted us as we stepped up to the bar. "Zack want you to try the new wine we just got?"

"I believe so." She leaned over the counter. "I'm Mia. Nice to meet you."

Jake opened a new bottle, stuck a decanter in the top, and poured her a generous portion. "It goes great with the salmon." He winked before he had to move onto a new customer.

She swirled the wine around then took a sip. "Oaky, with a hint of cranberries?"

Zack glanced at me before he nodded. "Well done. Come, let's get you guys something to eat."

***

Mia

"Good morning." I patted the fat cat's head as I headed for the coffee maker, thinking it smelled like the coffee had been spiked with a dash of cinnamon.

With my coffee in hand, I headed outside and down toward the water. A red wooden chair sat at the boathouse. I carefully carried it down and placed it on the end of the dock.

With my legs tucked up on one side, I leaned back and let nature gradually wake me up. I closed my eyes and focused on the chilly breeze that brushed by my cheek and flickered against the moist parts of my lips. The tips of my hair fluttered while I inhaled a deep breath of fresh air. Perfect.

"I love this time of day."

I nearly dropped my coffee. "Hi, Daniel."

"Do you mind if I join you?"

"Not at all," I was pleased he didn't seem to notice my startled expression. He pulled up another seat and settled in next to me.

We sat and watched a hawk swoop down and effortlessly pluck a fish out of the water. What was even more spectacular was the reflection of the bird over the smooth water as it breezed by us.

"I spent last night trying to place your face." Daniel gave me a side-glance. "You look just like him."

My stomach drew into a tiny ball, and I blinked a few times, not sure what to say.

"I'll take it Mark doesn't know."

I shook my head.

He took a long sip from his travel mug. "Mark is

all about honestly, Mia. If I may suggest, you should tell him soon."

"Will it be a deal breaker?" I whispered.

Daniel squinted as he looked over the water, the grooves around his eyes deepening. "The trust will be the deal breaker, sweetheart. It doesn't matter who you're related to."

I nodded. He was right. It wasn't a big deal, but Mark had shared so much with me that it almost felt like it might be too late.

"It's not," he said as if he read my mind. He stood and looked over my shoulder. "I always knew he had a daughter," he gave me a warm smile, "and I knew he wanted to keep you away from all of this."

"Yeah," I muttered into my mug.

"He's seen a lot, Mia, things that can change your outlook on life. Hard to push those thoughts away." His free hand slipped into his pocket. "Well, I'll leave you to enjoy this beautiful morning."

***

"Are you sure?" I stood in front of Savannah in an outfit she loaned me. The dark blue skirt clung to my hips, and the black silk blouse fit like a dream.

"Mia, you look beautiful. Mark will be all over you tonight." She grinned. "I'm actually looking forward to seeing the show."

"Umm…" I turned back to the mirror and slipped a pair of dangly earrings through my ears. We were having drinks before the guys left in the morning. Apparently, this was a tradition in the house. I stepped back and took in my appearance, but then the idea of the guys leaving tomorrow sank in.

"It's hard, Mia, I won't lie." She moved to stand next to me. "We just need to keep busy and not think about it too much."

I nodded and shook the nervousness from my hands. The reality that he was leaving was bad enough, but made worse by the fact I had overheard Paul talking about the weapons they'd need.

"You look hot, so go grab his attention and give him a reason to come home safe."

I stopped at the bottom of the stairs and waited for Savannah to go in first. Cole immediately found her and locked his gaze onto hers. She went to his side and gave him an ass-grab. He grinned and kissed her passionately. Their love was intense and made me ache for Mark.

"You headin' in, little lady, or just looking?" Keith grinned at me. He didn't seem as intense as before. "Come on." He offered his arm. "You can't waste that outfit out here."

"Guess I feel a little out of place."

"Really? You seem to fit in fine."

"Thank you, Keith."

John bumped Mark's arm and he looked in my direction. His gaze dragged down my body before his famous smile filled his lips and made my body dizzily head in his direction.

"Wow." He leaned down and kissed my cheek gently and hovered there for moment. "You look amazing. My little icicle is pretty hot tonight! Though I do love your scrubs and Chucks."

"Thank you, and noted." I tilted my chin and rubbed my cheek across his.

"You're blushing," he teased.

"You fill my head with all kinds of thoughts, and some are not to be shared."

He laughed. "Do I?" He slipped his hand around my waist and pulled me to him.

I took a step back as Paul joined us and almost tripped when I ran into someone. Mark grabbed my side so I wouldn't fall. Daniel's pointed expression caught my attention as I regained my footing.

"Oh, I'm sorry…" I started, then turned and froze.

"Mia?"

Oh, shit! No…

CHAPTER NINE

"What the hell are *you* doing here?"

Mark looked at me, then at Frank—my father. "You two know each other?"

"Do *you* two know each other?" he asked Mark.

Oh, fuck, this is bad!

"Yes, Mia is my girlfriend." Mark pulled me closer.

My father reached over and tugged me to his side. "Yeah? Well, she's *my* daughter."

There were audible gasps around the room.

Mark's face dropped. So much ran across his face, from shock to puzzlement, but they all ended with hurt.

He shook his head, stepped back, then turned and walked away. I started to go after him, but my father caught my arm.

"We need to speak. Now, Mia."

I looked at Savannah for help, but she was too busy dealing with Cole, who looked like he might flip his shit any moment.

"Mia," my father ordered from the hallway.

"Move, now."

With a deep breath, I followed him outside, grabbing my jacket on the way. I did hear Daniel call out to Cole.

The air was cold, and a few flurries fell. I wrapped my jacket around me and leaned against the wooden rail. My father lit a cigar and sat in one of the chairs with his ankle resting on his knee.

"What the hell are you doing here?" His voice rubbed me the wrong way.

"I'm a thirty-year-old woman, Dad. I'm here because I'm dating Mark."

"The hell you are."

I squeezed my hands together in frustration. I was so tired of my father trying to run my life.

I shrugged, lost for words at this point.

"Mia, listen to me for once in your life! The kind of work Mark and guys like him do involves horrible things, things no one wants to know about. Damn it, tomorrow he's going on a mission that involves hunting down the savages who killed seventy people. Many of them were children. Do you want to have to deal with the fallout from that kind of work? What kind of life will you have? Is that what you want for yourself?"

The blood drained down to my toes, leaving me lightheaded.

He went on. "He may not come home from one of these missions. You know what happened to Cole? He was taken and held in captivity. The video they sent of him being beheaded caused Savannah to miscarry their first child. Did you know that?" He leaned forward and rested his elbows on his thighs.

"Do you really want that kind of life? The constant fear, the wondering, never knowing what is really happening to him every day?" He was relentless, his words shocking.

I stared at a floorboard, not sure what to say.

"How in the hell did Cole even allow you to come here?"

I felt the need to protect the house. "I was attacked at my apartment."

"In Minnesota?"

"North Dakota," I corrected, not caring at this point. "Mark got worried after my apartment was broken into after that, so he and Cole worked out a deal. I signed the NDA and came here to be safe until they find out who's behind it."

Now it was his turn to look shocked. "What? Tell me more about this. Any leads?" His tone was mixed with concern and anger.

"You should talk to them." I had no interest in giving more information than I needed to.

He shook his head before he stood. "Lies cause nothing but hurt, baby girl." He turned and pointed over his shoulder at the house. "Get your stuff. We're leaving."

"No." I knew I needed to stand my ground. My father was not going to take control of my life. I was finished with his bullying tactics.

"This house is built on truth, and you broke rule number one by lying to Mark about who you are. If you don't leave with me, Cole will send you packing anyway. Save yourself the embarrassment and get your stuff so we can leave tonight."

After my many conversations with Savannah

about the house rules, I knew he was right, and that made it worse.

I pushed off the rail and headed inside, but not before I heard him mutter, "Once again, I'll try to clean up your mess."

I whirled on him, furious. "I only started lying when you wouldn't let me live my life my own way. I moved to North Dakota for Kenny. Who, in case you didn't know, passed away. I even missed his funeral because I came here. I've never measured up enough in your eyes, Dad, so please," I wiped my face free of tears, "let me clean up my own messes." With that, I headed inside.

I raced up the stairs and heard shouting. *Shit.* I slipped into Mark's room and tossed my bags on the bed. I hadn't been here long enough to completely unpack, so it didn't take long.

"Why didn't you tell me?" Mark asked from the doorway. He looked as though he was drunk. Wow, this wasn't the Mark I knew.

"Tell you I'm the boss's daughter? Because you wouldn't have been yourself with me." I zipped my last bag.

"It really explains so much." He almost chuckled. Yes, he was defiantly tipsy. How long was I talking to my father? "You did say you came from a military family."

"I didn't mean to keep it from you, Mark. I wanted to tell you so many times, but I didn't know how."

"Please, save me the 'I wanted to' speech. It's a cop-out."

"Maybe it is." I picked up my bags and stood in

front of him. "Frank isn't the easiest man to like, and I just wanted you to know me before you knew the rest."

"*Do* I know you?"

Ouch.

I knew better than to answer that one, so instead I waited for him to move. He did but only a little.

"So you're leaving?"

"You want me to stay?" A glimmer of hope showed itself.

"No...I don't know." He madly rubbed his head as he sank into a chair against the wall. "You really hurt me, Mia."

I bit my tongue. I didn't want to cry. It wasn't my right to. "I know."

"I shared more with you than anyone. You were my person."

Wow. I swallowed back the sob that wanted to erupt from my heart.

"You broke my trust, Mia, and that's unforgiveable."

I started to take a step forward, but he lowered his head, rooting me in place. I stood there for a few moments, not sure whether to go to him or not. I went with my gut.

Three shaking steps forward, and I gently rested my hands on his slumped shoulders. He didn't look up, but he didn't flinch either. I tried to moisten my dry mouth before I found the courage to speak.

"I'm so sorry, Mark. You do know me. I'm your little icicle, the one who," a heavy breath passed my lips, "loves you so very much. I think we just need to step back and—"

"You need to leave." He leaned back and removed my hands from his shoulders. He stood and towered over me. He wouldn't make eye contact, but I saw a tear slip before he wiped it away. "You need to leave, Mia."

I nearly crumbled at his words. I dug my teeth into my bottom lip to stop the cry, but it wasn't working. I was about to break.

He opened the door and waited. As I gathered my bags, he moved out into the hallway, back against the wall. I walked past the only man I'd ever fallen in love with.

"Goodbye, Mark."

He gave me a quick nod while his eyes stayed glued to the floor.

I turned slowly and walked down the stairs. I jumped when I saw Abigail in the hallway with tears in her eyes. She unexpectedly held her arms open. I didn't think; I just walked right in, wishing it was my mother.

"I'm so sorry, Abby," I sobbed into her shoulder. "I never meant to hurt anyone."

"I know, honey." She stroked my hair with one hand. "I know. Marcus has never let anyone in like he has with you, and he's hurting. He'll be better tomorrow morning. Come, let's get you into a spare bedroom."

"No," my dad hissed behind us, "I'm taking my daughter home. Seems we have a few things to discuss."

"Frank," Abigail pleaded, "at least let her and Mark mend their fences before you take her."

"Seems your boy asked her to leave. She's not

wanted here."

As much as I wanted to remind everyone we were grown adults, for the first time in my life I felt a hint of warmth coming from my father.

He marched over and took my bags. "Let's go."

"Call me." Abigail kissed my cheek. "Keep in contact, please, honey."

I nodded and followed him down the stairs. I looked over my shoulder one last time before I left. Savannah caught my eye and blew me a quick kiss before Cole called her to his side. I was thankful he didn't see me. I was at my worst, so the fewer around, the better.

Once inside the dreaded chopper, I held on for dear life. As we rose, my heart sank. I was too tired to fight it, so I welcomed my punishment and let the pain and the fear hit me like an avalanche.

Dad instructed the pilot to take us to the North Dakota airport. We were going to his home. I didn't even care if the damn machine crashed on the way.

***

Mark

Location: Mexico
Coordinates: Classified

The steady sound of the chopper blades made my mind wander back to a week ago when I lay curled around Mia. I had never felt more complete than that moment when I told her the painful truth of my past. Instead of running, she made love to me. It was the first time in my life I had ever let go of the past and could actually see myself with a future. Where had it all gone?

This was take two of this trip. The first mission was aborted halfway there. I almost drove myself crazy. I was so badly in need of some distraction. I hadn't been able to get Mia off my mind, and it didn't help that Savannah and Abigail were always right there to remind me of her. I missed her so much, but I was still confused and hurt over her lie, and I couldn't get past it. I knew I'd lost trust in her, and I questioned my inability to come to terms with it. I simply couldn't get my head around her pretense.

My mind came back to the mission. Thankfully, we were finally able to get confirmation on the location of their rendezvous spot. We were able to mark their traffic and find a pattern, allowing us to pinpoint it. I was itching for relief. I needed action.

Keith bumped my foot and tossed me a Red Bull, giving me a long look before he went back to watching out the window. Keith and I had never been as close as Cole and I, but I had a lot of respect for him. He was a great soldier, a true friend, and had my back with no questions asked. Though, lately, he seemed to be struggling with something personal. He wouldn't share, and I thought he even told Cole only as much as he needed to know.

Cole caught my attention and gave me a signal, asking if my head was there. I nodded and looked away.

Around it went in my head again…How could she not have told me? With everything I shared with her, she failed to mention her father was my boss. I'd never had a problem with Frank, but I wouldn't go out of my way to spend time with the man. Clearly, he kept his personal life private. So much, in fact, we never even knew his daughter's name, only that he had one.

I leaned forward and rubbed my face. This was so screwed up. Savannah gave me shit the next morning. She had heard what I said to Mia and was surprised at how cold I was to her. Yes, the happy Mark did have a breaking point, and Mia had found it. I wasn't ready to internally rehash that conversation.

First, I needed to get through this mission. Cole had worked his contacts and found out the group that originally took out the house full of illegals was killed by a small branch of the cartels called the *Reyes Mortales*. In English, they were called Dark Pride. They were relatively new, which made this mission a bit more intense, since we didn't know much about them. Our intel said they were little more than savages, even more so than the rest of the cartels, and that was saying something.

"ETA ten minutes, men," Cole croaked over the radio.

John added extra ammo to his vest, while Paul checked his rifle clip. Cole pulled out a photo of Savannah and gave it a kiss before tucking it inside the pocket in the chopper. It killed him not to take her picture, but after last time, he learned his lesson. Keith, on the other hand, sat perfectly still, staring at the wall. He would be our sniper this mission. He had the best aim and was the most patient. I pretended not to notice Cole wanted me in the action this time around. He knew I needed it.

With two fingers, I pulled a piece of cherry Hubba Bubba free and popped it in my mouth. The flavor ran along my taste buds and shot through me with a wave of excitement.

We'd barely hit the ground before we jumped to our feet inside a dust cloud. Moving swiftly toward our cover, we spread out and would check in with each other after the sun went down.

Forty minutes of straight running, and thirty to make our shelter, went down well with me, but the four hours of watching made me antsy.

The sun finally went down, which was nice, since my head was pounding. I never got headaches, but I had a real bitch of one.

"Here." Cole handed me a packet.

Crushed Excedrin with a light dusting of Benadryl. Cole swore by it. Ripping the plastic, I emptied it in my mouth and let it dissolve under my tongue.

"Take twenty," he ordered, shifting so I could rest against the tree trunk. Surprisingly, my eyes felt heavy, and I was out.

***

"Mark," Manuel whispered from somewhere. My PJs were twisted around me. I must have had another nightmare.

"Manuel?" I called out, unable to see him.

"I saw what you did to Mom. I know you killed her."

"I-I don't remember doing it," I cried as the pain ripped through my chest. "I don't remember."

I heard his footsteps move toward me. "You killed her, and I'm the only one who knows. Now you have to do what I say, or I'll tell."

"You would tell?"

I moved the sheet off and the coldness of my room surrounded me.

"You were a bad little boy, Mark. I want you to kill her."

"Who?"

"The girl you love. Mia."

***

Zip! Zip! Zip!

"Lopez!" Cole's sharp voice cut through my dream. I scrambled to catch up, and he tossed me night goggles that I slipped on quickly to see the lines of green from the bullets.

Without hesitation, I lifted my gun and opened fire. Twenty-one bullets later, and the assholes were down.

"Let's just hope they didn't call it in," Cole huffed as he opened a protein bar. He offered me one, but I shook my head. "Really?" His mouth hung open.

"Your powder concoction took my hunger away."

He still looked shocked. "Head better?"

"Much, thanks." I settled into the dugout, opened my canteen, and downed more than half of it.

I watched as he munched away. Just before he

finished it, I snatched the last bite and popped it in my mouth.

I grinned while he flipped me off. Who was I kidding? My belly could never be denied.

What I liked about Cole was he knew when to push me and when not to. So we sat in silence until the morning, when we woke to the sound of gunfire echoing off the mountains.

"Confirm!" Cole barked into the radio.

Immediately, the team checked in that it wasn't us.

"Raven One, this is Beta Seven." Keith's voice was quiet but steady. "We have company."

"I need confirmation it's our target."

"Copy that, Raven One. Stand by for confirmation."

We quickly gathered our things and erased our tracks from our hideout. On our way down the mountain, we stopped to camouflage our faces. The more we blended, the better. Besides, I might have had a Hispanic last name, but I was only a quarter. My near-white skin was a dead giveaway, and we didn't need to stand out any more than we already did.

"There." Cole pointed to the tree line, where we ducked down and scanned the area.

My radio wasn't sitting right on my neck. I thought the mix of sweat and paint was messing with the Velcro. I clicked it a few times and got it to settle back in place.

"Beta Seven has confirmation that targets are in sight. I repeat, targets are in sight. Fifty-six due east."

With my eye to the scope, I followed his directions and got sight of the targets.

"Copy that, Beta Seven," Cole answered. "Move in on my command."

"Copy that, move on command," John whispered from a distance away. I watched as he and Paul inched closer to the clearing. They blended perfectly, but because I knew where they were, I could see them.

"Heads up." I squinted at a man about take a piss just off to the right of them. "You have company at your three o'clock."

"Copy that," John answered just as Paul stepped from the bushes, stabbed the man in the neck, lowered him to the ground, then pulled him back into the shrubs as if he hadn't even been there at all.

Cole gave me the signal, and we booked it to the side of the house. Inching our way toward the front, we stopped when we heard the screen door shut. Cole removed his mirror and tilted it around the corner. Two fingers went up and then gave a silent count down. On one, we both jumped the men, covered their mouths, and snapped their necks—a silent kill. Rolling their bodies under the house, we glanced through the screen door and saw six more men drinking and smoking, too busy to pay much attention to what was happening outside. I nodded at the crate full of AK-47s. Ammunition was spread out everywhere.

As I stepped forward, I kicked something soft with my boot. I swooped down and came eye to nose with a small orange kitten. It had the audacity to hiss and strike at my nose with its tiny paw. After a quick rub of apology on the top of its head, I swiped the fluffy little body under the edge of the foundation. This was no place for an animal.

Shouting came from inside, and we jumped to the ground and out of sight. The door opened, and two muddy boots stood in front of us. The kitten wound itself around one of the guy's feet, only to be kicked to the side, tumbling over the ground with a squeak. I started to move, but Cole stopped me.

He gave me the sign to focus on our task. With a nod, I got my head back in the game. He was right, of course; it was just reflex.

The boots turned and went back inside.

"Raven One, you may have company in ten." Keith sounded like he was on the move.

"10-4." Cole nodded and gave the orders to the other men to move in.

Just as I was about to head inside, I caught sight of the kitten again taking advantage of the opportunity to get inside. I scooped it up and tucked it into one of my big flapped pockets.

With my gun drawn, my eye to the scope, we moved in, shooting anything that moved. We cleared the kitchen, two bedrooms, a bathroom, and the living room before we stopped at the bottom of the stairs. Six bodies were laid out, and blood covered the floors. I was immune to this type of bloodshed after years of chasing shits like this who killed the innocent for their own entertainment and profit. I found the one I was looking for, the guy who had kicked the cat. I wanted to pop another in his head, but he wheezed, so I left him to drown painfully in his own blood. Hatred burned through me.

Cole whistled at me to follow upstairs.

I hated stairs. No matter if you were coming or going, there were always blind spots and no way to shield yourself from oncoming fire.

Cole went ahead of me, and I gripped my gun tighter with each step. My finger was snug around the trigger, and I kept turning my body to watch ahead as well as our rear as we went up. Sweat dripped down my spine and soaked the waistband of my pants.

As soon as Cole flinched, I locked onto what he saw, and we fired. Two men fell heavily, and one came tumbling down on us. Cole managed to move, but I was firing when he hit me and knocked the gun out of my hands. He got tangled in my strap and landed on top of it.

"Fuck," I cursed and ran back down the stairs after it. John was in the other room, watching from the corner. He needed to keep an eye out for any unexpected company.

Paul raced up to join Cole as I tried to free my gun.

Two tugs later the strap finally released from the man's leg. A sound made me look up in time to see the guy with the muddy boots run out the back door.

"Oh, hell, no!" I jumped over the dead body, through the kitchen, and out the screen door.

With my fingers to my neck, I pushed the button. "Subject on the move." I waited, but got nothing. The trees were thicker as I pushed further into the woods. "Beta Seven, do you copy?" Nothing. I jiggled the wires, but it only made a strange clicking noise. "Fuck!"

I ripped it off my neck and let it dangle over my shoulder. I was gaining ground on him, and he was slowing, so it was only a matter of time.

The ground dropped, and the man disappeared momentarily. I raced forward, feet pounding, while my heartbeat matched their pace.

Stop, my gut screamed at me. All my training told me to stop. I couldn't see what was coming; I could be running full speed into a bullet.

My heels dug in and I came to a halt. Dropping to my knees, I inched up over a rock to get a peek and saw the coast was clear.

I heard gunshots back at the house and looked over my shoulder. I closed my eyes and relied on my hearing to find him. Filtering out all the natural noises, I honed in on the sound of snapping wood. I jumped to my feet and raced off to my left. It didn't take me long to get a good visual on him. His dark red shirt stood out against the muted tones of the forest. Picking up speed, I gained some distance. He darted right, and then it dawned on me what we were coming up to. I branched off and hoped to cut him off. My feet were light as I swiftly jumped and dodged boulders and pits. Just another two feet before…

I jolted to a stop and raised my gun at the man who had one pointed at me.

His mouth was moving, muttering something. Wait…

"Amen," he whispered in English before he stuck the gun in his mouth and fired. His eyes popped open before he tilted backward and fell.

I hurried to the ledge and watched as his body bounced and spun down the mountain. I waited until he landed before I left. *One down, a billion to go.*

The run back gave me time to process what happened, but it also allowed me time to think of Mia. I hated the pain that came with her name. Would I ever be able to forgive her? Would I really be able to live without her?

I slowed and pulled my radio over my shoulder to see if I could find what was wrong with it. One of the wires had wiggled lose. Kneeling, I carefully rewired my radio.

With it back in place, I turned in on, and I heard, "Man down! I repeat, man down!" Keith's voice sliced through my brain. The woods became a blur as I raced back to the house. I hardly remembered my feet touching the ground, I was so focused on the team. As soon as I got to the clearing, I saw the men all huddled around a stretcher.

"Lopez!" Cole shouted when he caught sight of me. "Hurry!"

I didn't think as I grabbed a handle and ran with them toward the chopper that was touching down in a field across the road.

"Go! Go! Go!" Cole screamed at the pilot. Within minutes, we were in the air en route to the hospital.

"What the hell happened?" I looked at Keith, who was trying to pack the golf ball sized hole in Paul's chest as he talked calmly to him. Cole was yelling into a radio to prep the medical team for our arrival, and John, looking grim, was forcing an IV into his arm.

"Sniper."

Fuck!

"Paul, buddy, you're gonna be okay." I leaned over so he could see me, but he didn't so much as blink. I remained calm—that's what we were taught to do—but I could feel the severity of the situation sneaking up on me, and I knew Keith felt it too.

"Hey," John grabbed his hand from the other side and squeezed it hard, "don't you go anywhere, you hear me?"

Nothing.

"We've been through too much, Paul. Move your eyes and look at me, dammit!"

Nothing.

I glanced at Keith, who gave me a nod. My fingers inched down to his wrist, and I closed my eyes as my heart sank.

When I opened them again, both men were staring at me, and the hope started to drain out of the chopper.

"No." I propped myself up on my knees and started to press on his chest. Blood oozed around us, and my pant legs started to feel damp. "Shit!" I was thrown into the seats, where a buckle from a belt slammed into my forehead as the chopper took a dip to the side.

"Shots fired!" the pilot announced over our headsets. Cole got into position behind a gun and started to shower the horizon with bullets.

Everything went fuzzy as I tried to raise my head. A tug backward, and I found myself looking into Cole's face. He yelled something, but there was no sound. He repeated it, and I blinked as I read his lips.

"You all right?"

I nodded and let him help me to my knees. My stomach turned, but I managed to fight back the nausea.

That was when reality slapped me back.

Paul.

CHAPTER TEN

Mia

My mother held my hand as my father stared at me from the other end of the table. We had been arguing for five days, and I was tired of it. Between the loss of Kenny and my breakup with Mark, I was finished and knew I had to make some major decisions about my life.

I had made some calls and was transferring to Boston Memorial. I submitted my two weeks' notice last week and only had to get through six more shifts before I was done. A change was needed, and if I stayed in North Dakota, I had to deal with too many painful memories.

"I think I may need to have a talk with Logan over this mess," my father muttered. "First Savannah, now you. It's like a goddamn frat party over there."

"There are over thirty men who work there, Dad. Thirty men who love what they do because they believe in it, but they also need a life. What Cole did

257

was allow Mark to be happy."

"He allowed a civilian into a safe house when she didn't need to be there."

"Cole handled it professionally. I signed the NDA before I knew anything. I only knew what I knew because of you." I squared my shoulders. "I know the Blackstone motto, know each of their ranks, and know a bit about their families because of you."

"You are my daughter." His tone was clipped.

"And Mark was my boyfriend."

"It's different."

I leaned forward. "Really? Different, like how you let Mom in on your assignments before you were married?"

"Be careful, Mia," he warned.

"Or what, Dad? You'll punish me? Send me to my room? In case you forgot, I'm thirty, live on my own, and work a job I love. A job you've never been proud of me for. Do you have any idea how much that bothers me?"

His face dropped. I'd never spoken to him like that. We'd always kept our feelings to ourselves. Well, not anymore.

"I am proud of you, Mia, I just wanted more for you, and I don't want you in my world."

"Why? What is so bad about being in the military world?"

"It's dangerous, and you'll always be wondering if this time he won't be coming home. It's no life."

"But, Dad, it's up to me to decide if I want that, not you."

My mother spoke up. "She has a point, Frank."

Dad shook his head then left the table. The fact he didn't argue more wasn't lost on me.

Mom waited until he was gone before she changed her tone. "Your father has a contact that will be watching your building for the next while." She handed me a folded piece of paper. "Here is his number. He said for you to call at any time."

I gladly took it. Without Mark in my life, all the scary things seemed worse than before.

***

"Mia." Dr. Evans opened his office door and welcomed me. I unfolded from the chair and walked in. "Thank you for coming."

He looked worried as he gingerly picked up the copy of the email I had sent to Human Resources and scanned it. "Can I ask why you're leaving?"

"I came here because of Kenny, and now that he's—" I cleared my throat. "I'm not needed here anymore."

"I disagree. You're very good at what you do. Please don't leave because of that. This hospital needs someone like you."

"Thank you for everything, Dr. Evans, but I have rounds to do, and I have already used up my lunch break."

"Please, Mia, just think about staying."

I closed my eyes and pushed to my feet. My mind had been made up. "I need to go."

With that, I closed the door and let out a long, heavy sigh. It was for the best. I wasn't one for staying long in places anyway.

I stopped at my locker and grabbed an apple. My blood sugar was running low since I barely ate anything. As I rounded the nurse's station, Vikki yelled at me from the emergency doors.

"Mia!" She waved me over just as a whole sea of people came rushing in.

The entire Blackstone team was there. They looked as if they had come back from a war.

"Male, Henry Paul, age thirty-three, gunshot wound to the chest. Unresponsive for nearly forty-five minutes."

"I got it." Molly started barking out orders before they rushed Paul to the OR.

Cole's heavy hand landed on my shoulder. He nodded toward Mark, who was covered in blood. He looked a bit pale, and the cut above his eyes appeared pretty deep. I watched as he stepped outside into the freezing night air.

"I'll go get a nurse." I was about to turn when Cole stopped me.

"It should be you." His voice was flat. "He needs you right now."

"Yeah." I nodded as I carefully approached my ex.

The white long-sleeved shirt I wore under my dark blue scrubs might as well have been paper, it was so thin. I pulled my hair free from its band so it would act like a blanket over my shoulders.

Mark was on a bench, face in his hands, while his leg bounced. His uniform was all black, and borderline intimidating. His hands were dirty with mud, and his face had streaks of blood that disappeared into his shirt.

"Mark?" I could barely find my voice. I was so scared he was going to tell me to leave. He slowly lifted his head, and his eyes were haunted. I hated that the first time we saw one another again was because one of his team members was clinging to life. "Can I check your," I pointed to my brow, "cut?"

"I'm fine." He turned to stare at the cars passing by.

I folded my arms and gave him a look. "Please, Mark, I need to check your cut."

"You're going to freeze, Mia. Go back inside."

My emotions were all over the place, so instead of leaving to sort them out, I took a deep breath and moved to sit next to him, wincing at how cold the bench was.

"What are you doing?" He was pissed.

"Sitting."

"Mia," he warned.

"Mark, I can be just as stubborn, you know."

He leaned back and let out a long breath. I tucked my bare hands between my legs and tried to keep my shivering to a low vibration.

Something wiggled in his pocket. I pulled back, startled, and a furry head popped out of the flap.

Mark reached down and gave him a soft pat before the kitty dove back down into the warmth.

That was random…

"You're going to get sick," he finally said.

"I'll live." I had to fight the urge to move closer. With a deep breath I decided now would be better than never. "I never meant to hurt you, Mark. I'm so sorry I did."

He stood and gestured for me to follow. "Let's do this."

I led him to an empty bed and closed the curtains so we'd have some privacy. I didn't say anything as I cleaned his cut, froze the area around it, and started to stitch his wound. He just stared over my shoulder. What I wouldn't do to know what was going on inside his head.

I turned my back to him as I tossed out the bloody bandages. "All done." Before I could say anything else, he was on his feet and gathering his things.

"Thanks." He opened the curtain and left.

"Welcome." I watched as the curtain swung closed behind him.

I decided to sleep in the on-call room in case I was needed. I was so tired of analyzing what happened earlier that when I hit the pillow I was out cold.

My alarm failed to go off, and another nurse had to wake me up so she could sleep. I showered and changed and headed out to the ER floor as fast as humanly possible. It was pretty quiet, with only a few people scattered around the waiting room.

"Mia," Vikki waved me over, "they left."

My stomach sank. "What do you mean?"

"They all left about three hours ago."

"Oh." I nodded. Well, then…any hope I had for us flickered out.

She put her hand on mine. "We should talk."

***

Mark

Everything inside felt numb as my feet dragged in the soil. Each step took effort; each breath was painful. Every heartbeat chipped away at the dam that was holding me together.

Keith was on the other side, stone-faced like me, and we all kept our eyes forward.

Snowflakes prickled my exposed skin. It was the only sign I was still alive.

Cole awkwardly cleared his throat before he commanded us to move inside.

I hated this part, all eyes on us, but at least it was only a small gathering.

My grip on the handle was tight, and my white gloves flexed over my knuckles as I stepped into the church. Savannah was up front playing "Amazing Grace."

After we rested the black coffin on the stand, we turned and saluted one of our brothers.

I removed my glove and placed my hand to the cold wood. "Until we meet again," I whispered, "watch over us."

Cole placed his hand next to mine and waited a beat before removing it.

The service was…hard. I was happy it was over, and even happier when we returned home and all went our separate ways for the night.

After a stiff drink, I lay in bed and allowed myself to fall asleep.

***

263

Two Weeks Later

The house was finally getting back to some sense of normalcy. Savannah kept busy decorating for Christmas. June kept an eye on John, who had some pretty low dips over his best friend's death. They had served together in the Army before they joined Shadows, and they had a lot of history. Keith remained the same. His phone seemed to ring less, and I wasn't sure if that was a good thing or not.

A loud crash made me jump, and I turned to find Olivia had dropped a big bowl over her head. Clementines rolled all over the place.

"Mark, could you take her to Abby, please?" Savannah had tape in her mouth while she strung lights inside the window.

"Sure thing." I stopped when I saw what she was covered in. "Oh, hell, no." My hands shot up. "I don't do sparkles."

Savi huffed, but I could see I was her entertainment right now. "Now, Uncle Mark, can you really tell me that you won't pick up your little sidekick?"

I looked down at the silver-speckled, dark-eyed baby who had jammed a set of her father's keys in her mouth. She grinned and reached for me, so I picked her up.

"Where's Keith?"

"Nope," he called out from somewhere else.

"Livy, we've spoken about sparkles before. I thought we had an understanding, here." I reached over and pulled the blanket free. She giggled as I rolled her up like a burrito and carried her to Abby.

***

I took a seat across from Cole.

"You good?" He raised an eyebrow at me across from his desk.

"How many times are you going to ask me that?"

"As many times as it takes for you to admit you miss her."

We'd been over this topic at least nine times.

I began to speak, but he held up a finger. "I ran into Frank yesterday in town."

"And?"

He studied me for a moment. "Mia got into a car accident last night."

"What?" I jumped to my feet as my heart raced. "Jesus, I have to—"

He leaned back with a smirk. He fucking lied! "That was fucked up, Cole. Shit!" I moved to the bar and poured a double brandy.

"Yeah, but I needed to know where your head really was on the subject." He let out a long sigh. "That feeling you have, the one that eats at you until you see her face or until you're near her and can inhale her scent, the scent you need to ground you, won't go away easily, if ever. Trust me." His face became serious. "A part of you will go mad, and the other will hurt so much you'd do anything to make it go away. You love her."

"I know," I finally admitted to myself and to him. While I had been able to release some of the pent-up pain, what was left still hung heavy around me.

"Mark, I've been where you are. You need to fix

this before you get killed in the field simply because your head isn't in the game." We both flinched at his comment, but we moved past it—we had to. But we wouldn't forget.

"Yeah, I know." I stared at the floor. He was right. Fuck me, he was right. "I need to go."

"No!"

We turned to find Savannah in the doorway.

"I'm sorry," her hands waved in the air, "but as much as this bro-mance was sweet to eavesdrop on, you two really need a female wakeup call."

"Baby," Cole tried to cut in, but Savannah gave him a look, and he backed down. I loved that about them. They knew when the other needed to speak.

"Mia got hurt twice since you came into her life. You lashed out on a topic she held dear to her heart the first time, and the second, you let her go without trying to work through it." I opened my mouth to argue, but she stopped me. "It's my advice, and you may not take it, but you'll hear me out because I'm helping you get her back. You need to put this whole Manuel thing behind you before you even think about having Mia back in your life."

The leather on Cole's chair squeaked as he turned to face me. "I agree."

"Now, pull that hurt stick out of that cute little ass and make shit happen." Savannah might have been small and pretty, but she knew how to give it to you straight.

"You think my ass is cute?" I winked as Cole rolled his eyes. I did use humor to help me cope. "Okay, you're right."

"Oh, I know." She blew Cole a kiss and shut the

door behind her.

"And if I get her back?"

"We'll work it out." Cole gave me a nod before he motioned to the chair in front of him. "Can we talk about Manuel now?"

CHAPTER ELEVEN

Under Cole's advisement, I had a session with Dr. Roberts about the missing pieces of my memory.

I respected the doctor, I really did, but I had a hard time with the fact he was dating Abby.

He asked a lot of questions as I lay with my head on a pillow, staring up at the ceiling fan. Without really thinking, I let him in and showed him around the maze of jumbled memories, some more clear than others.

Mostly, I noticed my brother was always there in the distance. He never said or did anything, but stood and watched as I gave the doc a tour of my past. He was like a picture on a wall you've seen a thousand times, but unless you were thinking about it, you didn't pay attention to it. That was Manuel inside my head.

"I'm going to count back from three," Doc's voice was low and calm, "and when I do, you will wake fully rested and alert. Three, two, one, wake up, Mark."

I blinked and noticed the time on his watch. Somehow I misplaced the last forty minutes of our session.

"What happened?"

"I hypnotized you."

All the doors inside my head slammed shut. "You what? Why?"

"You asked me to."

"I did?" *Really?*

"Give your brain a moment to process it, then you'll remember." He removed his glasses and used the loose part of his dress shirt to clean them. "You have a marvelous way of blocking things out, Mark. I've never seen someone still try to control the situation when they are the one being hypnotized. However, you seemed to be distracted by something. Do you recall what that was?"

Rubbing my head, I tried to pull back the memory. "My brother. He was watching us move about my thoughts. When we'd move into one room, he'd follow, just watching."

"Hmm." Doc put his glasses back in place, his expression turning thoughtful. "It's pretty obvious to me that you have blocked out a major part of what happened that day. Your brain is trying to tell you Manuel is involved."

My phone rang and I pulled it free from my jean pocket.

Cole: Pack your bags, found Manuel. Be ready in thirty.

Mark: 10-4.

"Sorry, Doc." I was headed for the door when he spoke up.

"Mark, I know we've been off on the wrong foot since I started dating Abigail. I want you to know I really care for her."

I felt nervous. "I hope I didn't say anything—"

"You didn't, I just wanted to clear the air."

"Okay." I respected that. "Thanks."

"Oh, and Mark…" I stopped at the door. "Call Mia. She is the cause of your headaches."

I gave him a small smile. "I plan to."

"Good." He went back to his notes, and I left feeling surprisingly better than I did going in.

I hurried down the hallway and up the stairs to pack.

Twenty minutes later, Cole gave me a rundown as we raced to the chopper. Keith decided to come along, while John stayed behind. Cole wasn't sure what we were walking into, and he wanted him to stay put but be ready in case we needed him later. Plus, we knew he wasn't really ready for fieldwork yet.

We landed in North Dakota and set up surveillance in a hotel with a bird's eye view of an old warehouse that was presently used as a butcher shop.

I pulled the invitation free from the white envelope that was sent to Frank anonymously. It was for an underground poker tournament. Rumor had it the jackpot was up to seventy-five thousand. It was pretty clear Manuel planned to make an appearance, so we made sure I was going to be there too. My finger ran over the number five; that was the room I'd be in.

"Check one, two, alpha, beta, delta." Cole waited for me to give the signal that I could hear him. I gave him a thumbs up from across the dirty hotel room.

"This place is a fucking—" Keith slammed his hand down over a spider, "—dump."

Cole bent and rested his eye to the lip of the scope. I shrugged a sweater over my head and made sure my mic was hidden through the heavy yarn. I couldn't help but glance at my phone. What I wouldn't do to hear her voice just once, to ground me.

Cole and Keith seemed to be preoccupied with the preparation, so I snatched my phone and slipped into the bathroom.

"Oh, fuck." I retracted my hand from the sink where a beetle crawled out of the drain. I flipped a cup over top of it, scooped it up, and dropped it out on the windowsill. My thumb scrolled through my contacts and stopped at her name. I brought the phone to my ear and let out a long breath. Of course it went straight to voicemail.

"You've reached Mia. Leave a message."

I glanced in the mirror and went with my gut. "Hey, it's me, Mark. I…um…I'm just about to go find my brother at this underground poker thing." I paused and wondered why the hell I was telling her this. "Look, I miss you, Mia. I know I've messed up with us, pushed you away when really I wanted to hold you. I just needed you to know." My mouth went dry and my hands turned cold. "I—"

"Press one to keep the message, or press two to

rerecord."

Fuck. I lowered the phone. My head did the same.

"I love you."

"Shake it and leave, dude." Keith pounded on the door. "You're up."

With thirty grand in my pocket, I walked down the back alley and knocked three times, adding another quick knock at the end.

The door opened, and a huge Latino man looked me up and down before he asked if I was carrying.

"No." I lifted my shirt to show I was clean.

"Money?"

"Yeah." I didn't offer to show him, though.

"Fifth door on your right."

I moved inside the dark room and made sure my shoulder scanned the perimeter since Cole was recording all of this.

Thick smoke burned my lungs as I descended deeper into the warehouse. They definitely made sure you got the *underground* feel with this place. Hardly any lighting and more guns than the cartels carried.

When I stood in front of door number five, I wondered if I should knock. I decided against it and walked in playing the fool instead of the cautious one.

Five men were at a table playing cards, while another two talked in the corner.

The men playing cards rose quickly when I entered, as did their guns.

I looked at them with fake surprise. "You're pointing guns at me?"

"Weapon on the table, and who the fuck are you?" one barked out.

"Well, I'm not carrying, but you already know that since no one could get by the sumo out there. Second, I was invited." I reached in my jacket but held my other hand up to show I didn't mean any harm. I tossed the invitation at the guy's feet.

He reached down and examined it.

"Cash?"

"Yeah." I patted the liner of my jacket.

He stared at me for a moment then nodded toward the table. "Buy in is ten thousand."

"Lovely. Welcome to the game." I snickered to show I wasn't nervous. I took the open seat between a skinny guy who I guessed would cheat by the way he was eyeing my jacket, and another who might die of a heart attack by the time he finished his fries and gravy. *Lucky me.*

The door opened again, and in walked Dell. Before I could even process him, Cole started prattling in my ear. Dell froze when he saw me, but he regained his composure as he gave a slight nod toward the bar off in the corner. I waited a few beats before I cleared my throat.

"Before I buy in, you got any bourbon?" I pointed to the bar, only to get a grunt from the fat man. "So that's a yes?" I stared at him. "Okay." I moved out of my chair and to the bar, where Dell chucked a lime into his rum and Coke.

"What the fuck, Dell?" I hissed before I ordered. Dell hadn't even been with Shadows for a year, and now he was here in this fucking warehouse. Great. One more person to watch over.

273

"That was going to be my question," he mumbled as he checked the time.

"You come here often?" I glanced at the table where the skinny guy eyed me.

"The past six years, I have been. Look, you can't tell anyone. Logan would forbid it."

"Fuck, yeah, I do!" Cole cursed in my ear.

"Not helping," I muttered to Cole. I shifted so they couldn't see my face. "You happen to know a New York cop named Manuel Lopez?"

Dell stopped, his glass at his lips, and peered at me over the rim. "Yes, we're good friends. He's a good guy. Wh—" The light went on inside his head. "Holy shit, is he any relation to you?"

"My brother." I looked around the room.

"Holy shit, I didn't even know you had a brother!"

"Yeah, well, he's only my brother through blood. Look, Dell, you've just walked into the middle of a shit storm. We don't know each other, and if Manuel shows—"

"He'll be here. He invited me."

"When he does and when shit goes down, I don't want to see you."

"Copy that."

"You guys planning a date, or do you want to play cards?" a man asked, annoyed.

"Be careful of that one." Dell downed his drink and took his spot at the table.

Two games in, I purposely lost, not wanting to show my habits. It wasn't until the third game that I won back what I lost. Dell was uncomfortable, his hand rubbing over his brow more often than not. I'd played with him enough times to know he played better than this. I could tell he was rattled by me being there.

Just as I piled my winnings in front of me, the door opened, and it took all I had not to lose my composure.

"Sorry I'm late, Noah." Manuel removed his jacket and handed it to the guy I spoke with earlier. Holy shit. Noah, as in Noah Beck? I couldn't believe it. Noah was Manuel's best friend growing up. I hadn't recognized him.

Fuck me, I hated that guy!

Manuel sat down at the table and looked directly at me. "So you got my invite."

"I did." I wasn't sure if we were brothers at that point, or if I should be playing along.

"Abort," Cole muttered in my ear.

"No," I hissed when Mia's face popped in front of me. This needed to end tonight.

Manuel smirked right before he nodded at Noah. "Left ear and chest."

Noah came over and ripped off the tiny earpiece and crushed it with his boot. He did the same with the wire. All I had left was a camera, no audio.

"You a cop?" The skinny guy shuffled the cards as he puffed away on a cigarette.

"Special ops," Manuel chimed in again. "The all-American boy."

"Right, and he's a cop, so what am I doing here?" Oddly enough, I wasn't nervous. All I saw was red. This was the showdown we needed.

"You," Noah moved into my direct line of sight, "are going to win what your brother owes us."

"And if I don't?"

Manuel made a strange face, one I didn't recognize. Noah snapped his fingers at Mr. Heart Attack Guy next to me. He slid a phone over so I could see the photo that was on its small screen. It was of Mia reading a book outside the ER. Then the screen flipped to another picture of her talking to Molly by the nurse's station.

No, no, no! I glanced over at Manuel, who watched me carefully.

"We have someone watching your pretty lady at the hospital. You wouldn't want anything to happen to her, would you?"

I remained calm on the outside. Gathering my strength, I compressed all my fear and tucked it in the center of my stomach and flicked my gaze over to Manuel. I cleared my throat. "You can tell them to leave her alone." I let my eyes burn into Noah's. "Okay, let's play."

"Excellent." Manuel grinned at Noah. "Let's light this shit up."

Noah opened a different door off to the side and greeted some new players as they entered.

"Welcome, welcome." He clapped in excitement. "I hope you brought enough cash for me to win." The men chuckled at his lame joke.

Seven new men joined the table. They were served a drink and were told the rules before the skinny guy dealt the cards.

With my head down, I played, and not once did I engage more than I had to. I did only what was needed and continued.

Three games in and two hours later, I won

seventy-three thousand dollars. I didn't blink at the cash that was piling up in front of me. The rage inside was enough to keep me focused.

I tapped the table over and over. None of them realized I was letting Cole know to stand down. I made sure my fingers were in view of the tiny camera on my sweater. Nothing could fuck this up. I needed to wash my hands clean of this situation once and for all.

At eighty grand, I tossed my cards down. "I'm done."

"Ah, no, you're not." Noah pulled his gun from his pants. "Your brother's debt is two hundred thousand."

I glanced at my brother, wondering how we could be so different and why his *best friend* was holding a gun to my head.

"Not my problem." I shrugged.

"Mark," Manuel warned, but this time I didn't care. "Don't fuck with these guys."

Dell shifted and rubbed his nose, which was a sign to not push them.

Noah nodded at the guy next to me, who shoved his phone in my face again.

There was Mia, walking out of a patient's room. *Oh, God, please don't let her get hurt because of me again*. I knew I had to call their bluff.

Bluff. That was what this was. It had to be. They had to know I'd never play if they hurt her. "Like I said, I'm done."

Noah thought for a moment as Manuel started to panic.

"Fucking shoot the bitch!" Manuel yelled and

tossed his drink on the table. "He cares, Noah, you just have to push him." He stood and waved his arms. "Take him in the other room and let him play with the high rollers. Mark could beat the dealer at his own game. Stop with this practice. It's time to play for real. You see he's unbeatable."

Noah looked at the two of us before he pointed his gun at Manuel and calmly shot him in the knee.

Holy shit!

Manuel screamed as he fell to the floor. Five of the men picked up their cash and headed out the door. The other two moved to the wall, but watched. The fat guy next to me suddenly pushed the table off to the side and left me in a chair facing Manuel and Noah. The skinny guy pointed a gun at me, though it was almost comical because the weight of the gun seemed to be too much for him to hold steady.

Dell stood in the corner, ready to intervene if necessary. I shook my head for him to stand down. This was my fight.

"I'm a little confused, here." I laced my fingers together. "Aren't you two old friends?"

Noah scratched his head with the tip of his 40 cal. His greasy hair stuck in place. "We were, until your brother lost two hundred thousand of my money in one sitting."

I turned my eyes to Manuel, who rolled around on the floor, hugging his bloody leg.

"He needs to pay up." Noah stared down at him.

Again I held up my hand so Cole would see to stand down. However, I wasn't sure how long he'd let me do this solo.

Noah grabbed Manuel by the hair and raised him to his knees. His cheeks puffed in and out as the pain increased. Saliva sprayed out as he cried, trying to cover his wound with his hand.

"Mark!" His eyes pleaded with me, but all I could hear was his comment about Mia. S*hoot the bitch.*

"Should've known better than to trust a cop," Noah hissed as he turned toward Manuel. "Any last words before you pay your debt?"

I cleared my throat. "I have one."

Noah looked at me, surprised and no doubt wondering why I wasn't trying to stop this. He motioned for me to go on.

I let the darkness consume me. I gave in to the horrible thoughts I had tried so hard to push away. With my heart pounding like a drum in my chest, I kneeled down to my brother's level.

Some said the eyes were the window to your soul. I said they were the window to the truth. Something always bothered me about the day our mother was killed. Manuel said my prints were on the knife.

"These might be the last few moments we ever have together, *brother*." The word stuck on my tongue. "If you want to go out with any kind of honor, tell me the truth." I swallowed back the pain this topic brought me. "Did I really kill our mother?"

The twitch of his mouth brought all my senses to attention. "You are such an idiot. You had no idea what it was like living in that house." His words were like ice—no emotion, only emptiness. "All you had to do was get food, keep your mouth shut, and go to school. I was the one who had to deal with *them*."

"Them, who?"

"All Mom's boyfriends." His eyes opened and closed with pain, and his face and neck were covered in a thick layer of sweat. "Some wanted more than just Mom." His fists flexed. "They wanted me too. I fought, but it didn't stop them."

"You weren't the only one." I raised my sweater and showed him the deep scar. "I didn't know they were after you too."

"Of course you didn't, you were always running off to your *other* family."

"Because of you! You made me leave, even if it was a fucking storm, just to find you food, or siphon gas from cars so *you* could get more pot." I jabbed a finger at his chest. "Trust me, Manuel, I've had my fair share of pain. We were just kids. Mom should have taken better care of us."

I looked up at Noah. He was listening to our exchange with interest. No one moved as they stood back and watched, fascinated as our little drama played out around them.

"Mom was a waste of space, so *I* took care of her." My brother's words pulled me back.

Sweat broke out across my chest. "*You* killed her?" I was lost for words. Manuel was an asshole, but to commit murder was an entirely different thing.

"Yeah." He laughed then wiped his mouth dry. "*I* killed her."

My heart dropped into my stomach. "You

fucking killed our mom? But I—"

"I hated you," he coughed, "so fucking much. I still do." He dragged his body to the wall and propped himself up. "But what's worse than killing someone, huh, Mark? Going down for the murder of someone you love, even that shit of a mother of ours."

"I *didn't* love her." I tried to stand my ground while it crumbled beneath me.

"Oh, *Marky*," he flexed his neck, "yes, you did. You don't remember that day, do you?"

"You came home, poured yourself a drink of Kool-Aid." Manuel sneered. "Did it taste funny?"

The memory came then…

"Mom, I'm home!" I dropped my book bag at the door and listened. All was quiet. I poured myself a glass of cherry Kool-Aid from the jug sitting on the counter. It slid down my throat. There was a funny aftertaste that left a gritty film over my teeth. I guessed I should have stirred it. I pulled my spelling test free from my folder. I wanted to show her I got 100. Maybe she'd actually be sober and be proud of me.

When I went past the living room, I stopped as a strange smell caught my attention. Slowly, I turned my head and saw my mother on the couch with a knife sticking out of her stomach.

I froze. The blood attacked my senses and I started to get dizzy.

"Mom?" I called out, but she didn't move. My toes dragged along the shag carpet and got entwined in the loose threads. "Mama, are you

okay?" Everything wobbled and spun. I felt my head hit the carpet. A strange ringing noise traveled from ear to ear, bouncing around like a rubber ball inside a box.

A pair of boots stepped over me. Noah? His voice hissed at someone to hurry. Manuel bent down and shook me. I saw him, but I couldn't respond. My arms and legs were like they weren't connected.

"Nah, he's out," Noah assured him. "Their eyes don't always close."

"Fucking creepy." Manuel pulled the knife out of her stomach and wiped it clean with my blanket. Wilfred! I loved that blanket. It was my only friend when I was here. He protected me from all the evil in this house. Manuel wiped the handle then wrapped my fingers around it.

What was he doing?

He carefully jammed the knife back into her and tossed Wilfred next to me. I wanted to reach down and hold him to my face. His silky edges made me calm, but now he was full of blood—my mother's blood.

Manuel lowered himself to the floor and looked directly at me. "I've never hated someone as much as I've hated you. Now it's your turn to feel some pain."

His face changed as he pulled out his cell phone and made a dramatic call to 911.

I was crying on the inside, but I couldn't move. Pain ripped through me. It was all too much, and I let the hurt in, let it swallow me whole. I let my mind go and fell into a sea of darkness...

My vison came back into focus, and my eyes honed in on my brother, my own flesh and blood, knowing he had killed our mother.

So many questions came at me, but the only one that made it off my tongue was, "How?" I fought the rage. "How could you do such a thing? I was seven, just a kid. We share the same blood."

He shrugged like we were talking about the weather. "It was easy. They couldn't prove anything, and I knew the Logans would get you the best hotshot lawyer."

"Was it worth it? To have me blame myself my whole life for killing Mom?"

He smirked. "It was the icing on the cake. The bitch was gone, I got the trailer, and I had my all-American brother bail me out whenever I needed it. It was a win-win!"

Pop!

Half of Manuel's neck was splattered on the wall. Air lodged in my throat. Noah lowered his gun and watched as Manuel's body slumped to the ground.

"Now that the drama is over," Noah pulled a rag from his breast pocket and wiped his mouth, "we have a debt to settle, and you're still short."

I stood frozen. Oddly enough, there was no emotion running through me. I wasn't sad that Manuel was gone. It was a huge relief to know the truth. Truth has consequences, and I guessed this was his. Now there was Noah. I now knew he was part of my mother's murder. Here he was, telling me I had to pay off my brother's debt to him. This was too much.

As these thoughts swirled in my brain, Noah's gaze flicked around the room. "Did you know your mother had a tattoo on her pelvis?" He patted himself in that general area as I channeled all my pain into anger.

Son of a bitch.

"When Manuel told me of his plan to get you to pay back his debt to me, I couldn't help but play along. The best part for me was playing cat and mouse with your pretty lady friend."

The skin tightened around my knuckles, and I glanced at Dell, who looked just as angry. "She shook as I stood behind her in the dark. I could hear her breathing when she sensed me." Noah's eyes lit up. "You know that feeling, where the hair on your arms stands up, your heartbeat quickens, and your brain is almost too scared to process what's about to happen?" He smiled like he was visualizing it. "Then she felt me, and I couldn't help myself. I needed to have her."

Nothing registered as I hurled myself in his direction and slammed him to the wall. My forearm crushed into his windpipe as he tried to fight me off. The skinny guy yelped as Dell knocked him unconscious.

"On the ground!" Cole's booming voice ripped through my murderous rage. Shots started to fly, and I grabbed Noah's head and crushed it. I wasn't me anymore. All I saw was Mia under this asshole fighting to get free.

I sensed movement and looked up as the bartender pointed a shotgun in my direction, but right before he pulled the trigger, I twisted and let

Noah take the hit. His body jerked at the impact, and I stared into his eyes as the life drained out of them.

"Good luck on the other side."

Keith took out the bartender before he could get off any more shots.

I dropped Noah and glanced at my brother again, still feeling no remorse for his death.

"You all right?" Cole shouted as he elbowed a man who came running in to see what was going on. "We have to get out of here. We don't have much time."

Dell wavered and seemed to stumble. *Wait...oh shit...*

I raced to his side as he fell. I caught him and lowered him to the concrete floor.

"Dell?" Blood soaked through his jacket. I ripped it open and saw a quickly spreading dark stain on the right side of his chest. "No! No way, not again!"

Keith dropped to his knees, ripped off his vest and shirt, and started to pack the wound.

Cole turned and shouted, "We have to move—" His face dropped when he saw us. "Grab him and let's go."

"Shit." I grabbed Dell's arm, and Keith took the other, and we carried him out of the room between us. Cole cleared our path as we raced toward the front door. Shots from behind us told me we didn't have much time. "Fuck, Dell, use your feet."

Our training kept us moving. You forced the pain aside until you were safe. It was hard to do when it was one of your own.

Keith closed his eyes briefly when we stopped at a corner. He was placing his anger. He was better at it than I was.

"Move," Cole whispered over his shoulder, but he wouldn't look at us. We were all too terrified we were carrying another corpse.

"Lopez," Keith turned to look at me, "focus on Mia. Let's get out of here. That's it right now, nothing else."

I gave a quick nod and removed Dell's gun from his hip. We ran with Keith and Dell between us.

We were moments from the door, and the men behind us were catching up fast. Their footsteps were close, and it fueled us on. Keith was as strong as an ox and made Dell look like he weighed as much as a rag doll.

We passed some dead bodies piled on top of one another. I recognized this as Cole and Keith's work. We didn't want to go out the same way we came, so we had to take a detour out a side door.

As Cole burst through, we were greeted by a team of agents and an ambulance. Cole must have called them before they came to get us.

Keith ran over to the paramedics and placed Dell on a stretcher.

"Damn, dude!" Dell hissed. "Gentle."

Keith shook his head. "Couldn't have spoken up before?"

"Then you wouldn't have carried me." He laughed, but then coughed in pain.

Cole moved to stand over him. "When you get home, we need to talk."

"I know." He nodded before the paramedics

wheeled him off.

I asked a paramedic if I could use one of the trucks to make a quick call. The truck was warm and helped with calming my nerves. Mia's phone went straight to voicemail again. *Damn, where are you, Mia?* With a swipe through my contacts, I called the nurse's station at the hospital.

"North Dakota Hospital, this is Molly." Her cheery voice didn't match my mood.

"Hey, Molly, it's Mark—"

"Oh, my God, Mark! How are you? Why are you calling this line?"

I squeezed my eyes shut at her chatter. "I need to speak to Mia."

There was a long pause.

"She's not here, Mark. She took a job in Boston. Left a few days ago with Nurse Taylor. They went together. I just hung up from talking to her, and they seem to be settling in okay."

What? *Thank God!* So Noah was bluffing. Mia wasn't even in North Dakota. I sank down in the seat; my body felt like putty.

"Mark? Mark, are you still there? I'm sorry. You didn't know?"

"No, I didn't." I rubbed my sore neck. "Thanks, Molly."

***

Three Days Later

Savannah had planted a tree in the front yard in Paul's memory, since his family wanted to bury him back east. I thought it was great idea. It was like a part of him was still here. Cole had to help because the ground was mostly frozen, but she insisted on doing it now rather than in the spring. She said we needed a place to go to let the pain out.

"Meow," the kitten squeaked as she weaved through my legs in the kitchen. I bent down and picked up my tiny Mexican spitfire. She took a swipe at my nose and then shoved her paw into the milk on my Cheerios.

"Did Scoot put you up to this?" I glanced over at Scoot, whose ear was being tugged off by Olivia. He looked pissed, but I knew he didn't care. We were all suckers for that little monster.

Lowering the dish, I let Little Lady have the whole bowl.

"Well, hello, there." Dr. Roberts stopped at the island and scooped up Lady. "What's your nam—" Lady quickly batted his face and caught his cheek with her claws. "Wow, you are a feisty kitty."

I wanted to see what he was going to do. To my surprise, he smiled and examined the moody, sometimes downright nasty cat.

"Is she yours?" He peered over his shoulder.

"I rescued her, but she's not really mine." Lady swatted at his nose again and added a kitten-sized hiss. "She could use a good home."

"Lady, huh? Not quite the name I'd pick for such a feisty little devil. Poor thing. She just needs someone who understands her, don't you, sweetie? Perhaps you should come home with me, hey?" He set her down so she could go back to eating. But she attacked his shoelaces instead. I laughed. She was such a little shit. Maybe she was pissed I thought she was a boy at first. "Hey!" He tried to move, but she chased him, latching onto his ankle. "Ouch!" he yelped.

"She's all yours, Doc."

"Thanks," he muttered and tried to free himself.

"Good luck with that." I chuckled on the way out of the kitchen and headed down the hallway.

I had skipped the service the NYPD had for Manuel. I'd no interest in watching my brother be laid to rest. As far as I was concerned, the first seven years of my life never happened. He could rot in hell for eternity, for all I cared.

"Mark," Cole stood in the doorway, "Frank is downstairs and wants to have a word with you."

Shit. Guess it's time.

Taking two steps at a time, I hurried to the conference room. I knocked before I entered.

"Frank," I addressed him as I stood behind a tall leather chair. "I suppose you want a detailed summary of what went down."

"Yes, but it can wait." He chewed on the inside of his mouth while he thought. "Sorry about Paul. He was a good soldier and a good man. How are you holding up?"

I let out a long breath. "Hanging in there."

"Good." He nodded. "Look, Mark, I'm a man of a few words, so I'll cut to it. Mia and I have had a rough go for the past ten years. Since she moved to Boston a few days ago, we haven't heard a word from her." He stopped and rubbed his chin. He seemed like he was battling with himself. "Life's too short not to have the ones you love around you."

He looked over at me. "I realize now I was wrong in how I reacted when I saw her here and heard she was dating you. I've tried hard to keep Mia away from this world. It may be 2015, but the Army is not the place for someone as kindhearted as Mia. She's my baby, always will be." He cleared his throat. "I still see her with pigtails jumping into my arms and calling me her hero. Hurts a dad's ego when you see her looking at someone else that way."

This was a side of Frank I never expected to see.

"If it counts for anything, you have my blessing, Mark." He stood and offered me his hand. "You're a good man, and I know she cares a lot about you."

It took me a moment to catch up. He always was direct, and this time was no different.

"That, ah…that really means a lot, Frank." I shook his hand, completely blown away by his honesty.

"Right, well…" He started for the door. "She's working today, so…"

"Yeah, all right." I leaned against the table.

"I want that report by Monday."

"Will do."

Cole came in, but leaned back to make sure Frank was gone. "You get ripped a new one?"

"No," I was still in shock, but checked my watch, "I actually just got his blessing."

"What?" Savannah squealed behind Cole. "Oh, my God!" She clapped Livy's hands together. I smiled, and it felt nice. It'd been a while.

"Where did you come from?" Cole wrapped his arm around his wife's waist. He kissed her cheek then did the same to Livy.

"I'm everywhere." She winked, which lightened the mood. "So what's next?"

I shrugged. "Even if she did take me back, how could it work?"

Savannah beamed at me. "Actually, we've come up with a plan."

"Oh?"

"Yes, but first you need to go get her."

CHAPTER TWELVE

Mia

I hated it there. The staff wasn't nearly as friendly as North Dakota, and Dr. Rice was way too hands on for my liking. To make matters worse, he was at least a few years younger than I was.

I was happy to leave my old apartment, even though the new landlord, Chris, was nice, and he seemed genuinely sad to see me go. Not that I really knew the man at all. He was a funny fellow. I wasn't the happiest in that old building anyway since my friend moved out, and after the attack in the basement, it held too many bad memories.

My father and I were working on repairing our relationship. He did a background check on Chris, and he was harmless, just a bit creepy. Regardless, I was happy to be away from him. I never did find out who left the antifreeze in the courtyard, but if I were to guess, I would bet it was the man who attacked me. My father informed me the man was working with Mark's brother, but I didn't need to worry about him anymore. I pushed back the pain that followed whenever I thought of anything to do with Mark.

The only thing keeping me going was that Vikki Taylor transferred here with me, since her son was now going to school here.

With my legs curled under me, I opened my book and sipped my coffee while I tuned in and out of the craziness of the ER. The weathered pages of my novel made me happy. I loved this story. It was one I always fell back on whenever I needed to feel love. Jodi Ellen Malpas stole my heart with Jesse Ward. Who didn't like a great love story? Especially one you could read over and over and know this was one story that would always end the same way—with happiness. Wasn't that what everyone went through life searching for?

They said the moment you stopped looking for love, you'd find it. I thought that was crap. I was determined to stick to my books to find love. That way I knew I could cry, get the release I needed, and still close the cover and feel happy with the ending.

"What are you reading?" Dr. Rice studied the cover. "*This Man*? This man, what?" I rolled my eyes. *Men. They'll never understand the romance book world.*

"Something I can help you with?" I tucked my book in my bag and picked up my coffee as I stood.

"You looked lonely, so I thought I'd grant you my company." He raised his cocky arms. "I'll walk you back to your floor."

Gee, thanks. What is it with doctors always

hitting on you? I guess it's just that they don't get out of the hospital enough.

"So, Mia, you have any plans tonight?"

I'm wide open, I have no life. I have only one friend here. The last week, I've spent every night sobbing into my pillow over my ex. The worst part is I can't even smell him on it anymore! I hate it here, and would sell my soul to rewind my life about five months.

"Sorry, I have plans." *Lies, lies, lies.*

"Tomorrow?" He stopped me when I started to speak. "It wouldn't hurt for you to make some friends. Where have I heard that before?"

True.

"Mia," Vikki caught my attention as she pointed behind me, "the patient in room 2056 is asking for his pain meds. Could you please help me out and administer them for me?"

"Sure." I was happy for the out.

"Oh, Mia?" she called.

"Yes?"

"Drinks tonight at the wine bar, on Barrington Street."

I began to decline when her hands moved to her hips. "Sounds good." I supposed it couldn't hurt.

The rest of my shift crawled by at a snail's pace. My hands acted independently from my mind, which wandered back over things I couldn't change, only bringing me more heartache. After my shift, I changed, closed my locker, and headed outside. I decided to stop on the way home to buy a bottle of wine. I might need a bit of buzz to get through tonight.

My place was cold and empty when I returned home. My only joy was seeing Butters stretched out on the couch. "Well, at least you're comfy." I chuckled at him, and he barely moved except for his thumping tail. I was so thankful Ed was fine with me bringing Butters with me. I thought he was more thankful than I was; Ed wasn't really a dog person.

"Hi, buddy." I kissed his head. "Can you help me pick out something to wear?"

Three outfits later, I decided to go with something pretty versus sexy. I didn't know anyone, anyway, and didn't want to make the wrong impression. I ran my fingers over a purple long-sleeved lace dress. It stopped above the knee, and my boots stopped just below the knee. It seemed like a good choice. My hair hung long, and I curled it at the ends for an extra bounce. I looked all right on the outside. I only wished I felt all right inside.

Before I could open that wound, my buzzer rang to let me know the taxi was here. Weaving through my unopened boxes of crap, I hurried down the stairs and gave the cabbie the address. The sky was black, with angry clouds whipping by at a good pace. Must have been windy up there. It brought me comfort. I could relate to the weather tonight. It seemed to reflect what was brewing inside of me.

"Lower Deck, please." I leaned back and fought the heavy smell of the cologne the cabbie must have bathed in. Why did men wear it? Body soap smelled much better.

The bar was busy, but I found our table easily. Vikki was on the phone when I arrived. She waved me over to an open chair and handed me a beer.

"You look great." She glanced down at her sweater and laughed. "I lost my fashion flare at forty-five."

"I think you look lovely." I tapped her bottle to mine. My stomach nearly rolled when I saw Dr. Rice coming toward us.

"Huh!" she snorted. "You know, I saw him outside of the hospital one day and called him Mr. Rice, and he corrected me." She rolled her eyes. "I get it that you worked damn hard to use the title '*doctor,*' but you don't have to be a dick about it."

I laughed. She was right; that was a little dicky.

"Come on." She took my hand and led me out on the dancefloor, where we—and I meant only the two of us—danced to *Hey Baby* by Bruce Channel. *I think I may have fallen in love with this place. At least they have good taste in music.*

The song ended, but Vikki reached for my arm to hold me in place. "Go with your heart."

"What? What does that—?"

She pointed, and I started to move but jerked back in place. She nodded at Mark, and he returned it with a smile.

Music started to play softly. It took me a moment to recognize the voice singing the song. She sang in a bluesy, soulful voice, and from the first word, her tone made me want to weep.

Savannah sat behind the brown piano, her eyes closed, playing "Can't Help Falling In Love."

"What on earth…" I couldn't even think straight. Mark stepped forward, asking for my hand, and with a confused step forward, I accepted it. His warm hand instantly made me think of being at home. His free arm slipped around my back and held me close.

Where do I look? Am I too stiff? A thousand things ran through my mind, but most of all—why was he here? I went over things in my mind until his lips touched my ear. He let out a painful sigh, and that was it.

Everything just gave…nothing left to hold me up except his arms. My body sagged against his, my cheek pressed to his chest, and we swayed.

He started to sing about falling in love. His voice had a slight hitch to it, but there was a thread of confidence that made it incredibly powerful.

I knew he felt my hesitation. I started to pull away, but he held me in place. His lips moved to the shell of my ear. "You were the first girl I opened up to and told my secrets. After you, when I did wake up alone, I didn't mess up the sheets in the morning because I wasn't alone. I had you." He nuzzled my hair. "I understand now why you didn't tell me. You were right; I wouldn't have let my guard down with you. Which would have been a shame, because I wouldn't have fallen so *soul crushingly* hard for you."

I pressed off his chest and looked into those deep, dark eyes that dared me to doubt him. Even his jaw showed confidence, but I could see the vulnerability behind his smile.

"I'm sorry for what I said. I lashed out in anger, and there was still a part of me that was upset you picked Kenny over your own life, but that was because I cared a lot about you. Kenny wasn't the one in danger, but you were." He gave a slight

297

shrug. "Heart won over sensitivity."

I had to look away and take a minute. I spent the last how many nights thinking he hated me? That I was the last person on his mind. That I was only the afterthought of something unpleasant.

"I took care of my problem, but I lost a good friend along the way." I nodded. Nurse Taylor told me about Paul. I was so sad; I could only imagine what the house went through. "I can't lose you too, Mia."

I licked my lips. "I never meant to hurt you, Mark, but if it's worth anything, I felt the pain of my lie the moment after I told it, and that pain never left me."

"Don't. It's not worth it, because the bottom line is it showed me how much I am in love with you." He blinked like he hadn't realized what he had said. Then a lazy smile stole across his lips and up to the corners of his eyes. "I have a bit of a temper when it comes to you, but damn, Mia, I *am* so in love with you."

I threw off his rhythm when I dropped his hand and leaned up on my tippy-toes to press my lips to his. Both his arms wrapped around my back and held me close. His tongue curled around mine to deepen his kiss.

"I love you too, Mark."

***

Three Months Later

Mark

"Where is he going?" I sipped my coffee. Keith walked down to the dock after he received a phone call.

"I don't know." Daniel gave me a hopeful look.

I knew he thought Keith had a girl, and maybe that was it, but something still didn't feel right. It felt off.

Butters went running after him with a huge stick in his mouth. He jumped and barked until Keith chucked it down the sand that followed the lake, then went running after it.

Surprisingly, Scoot had accepted Butters in the house as a part-time visitor. Although not before they fought over the bed Savannah had given Scoot last Christmas. I ended up having to buy Butters his own bed, only to have Scoot want that one more than his own. Spoiled furball. At least they had finally declared a truce, and Butters patiently waited for Scoot to choose one bed before he would settle in the one not chosen.

Dell nodded as he headed toward his Jeep. He had one more month at the peak before he'd return to his normal post. I shivered at the thought of my last experience there. As much fun as it was having Savannah play paintball, I wouldn't be volunteering her for anything else.

Cole moved in my line of vision as he whistled to get Keith's attention. Keith quickly ended his call and jogged back up the lawn with Butters hard on his heels.

Cole closed the door behind him. "House meeting, three minutes, dining room table."

I shrugged at Daniel as we took a seat a few minutes later.

Once everyone gathered, Cole placed three boxes in front of us.

"I was going to give them out at Christmas, but I decided to wait." He slid a black, shiny box over to Keith and one to John. They each opened theirs and grinned at their new Blackstone watches. "Tracking devices inside are undetectable. After what went down with me, I think it's imperative we wear them."

"Thank you." Keith put his on immediately. I looked over at John, who was looking at the extra box—Paul's box.

"Now," Cole looked around the room, "no one wants to admit how much they're hurting right now, but the best thing we can do for Paul is to move forward. Moving forward doesn't mean we will ever forget." He glanced at me before he went on. "I have really thought about this, and I know his seat is still warm, but we have a lot of trips coming up, and we need our team to be full. So," he picked up the box, "the man who will be filling Paul's very large shoes is..." The sadness was mixed with a little excitement, something the house really needed right now. Cole leaned down and slid the box right into a hand covered in red and black swirls.

The room went silent as he picked it up and admired the box.

John leaned over the table and reached his hand

out for a shake. "Welcome to Blackstone, Mike."

"Thank you, John." Mike let out a long sigh before Daniel started to cheer and lifted the mood back up. He had a lot to live up to.

"Let's have a drink." Dell shifted his arm in his sling. "Lord knows I need one!"

As the place started to roar with happy laughter, I moved to the window where a set of headlights was moving across the frosty pattern.

Mike joined me, interested to see what I was looking at. I pointed to the door with my mug. "Here she comes."

I had convinced Mia to move to Montana. We found her an apartment three blocks from Daniel and Sue's, and one block from her new job at the Red Stone Medical Center. It was perfect. I got to see her whenever I wanted, and she seemed happy that she was able to spend time with her father more often. It was nice to see them getting along better.

Cole gave her clearance to the house, but we couldn't bend any more rules to have her live there. Everything worked out for the best. She and I agreed to take things one day at a time. After all, we hadn't even known each other for a year yet. She said she was looking forward to going out on date nights so she could check out my dance moves. Ladies loved my moves.

"Hey, you." She tugged her scarf free and hooked it over the wooden peg in the entryway. "How was your day?"

"Better now." I kissed her frozen nose and wrapped her in my warmth. She knew I loved her, though I hadn't said it since Boston. I just wanted to hold on to her with all my strength and never let go, no matter what life threw at us.

"Mmm," her chest vibrated against mine, "I needed this."

"Hungry?" She nodded but didn't let go. I didn't let go either.

"Oh, great!" Savannah broke our moment. "Mia, I have such a story for you!" She took Mia's hand and dragged her into the kitchen.

Mia looked over her shoulder and cast me a smile that nearly knocked me off my feet. Wow…I was so lucky.

After all I'd been through in life, I refused to look back, and I wouldn't hold back. I knew that no matter what, I had the perfect woman. One who helped me chase the demons from my past, and one who I knew would stand solidly with me in the future. I could truly hold my head high with honor. I knew, because I was finally free of any doubt that I was a good and honorable man.

The End

CONTINUE THE BLACKSTONE SERIES
WITH BOOK 2, ESCAPE. AVAILABLE
ON AMAZON.

ACKNOWLEDGEMENTS

Mary Drake
Erin Smith
Ana Armstrong
My Blackstone Girls Street Team

SUGGESTED READING ORDER

World One
(All books connect in World One)
Broken
Shattered
Mended
Honor
Escape
Trigger
Demons
Unleashed
Freedom
Omertà
Courage
Darkness Lurks
Darkness Follows
Darkness Falls

World Two
(Not connected to World One)
Behind My Words
All In
Quiet Wealth

ABOUT THE AUTHOR

Author J.L. Drake was born and raised in Nova Scotia, Canada, later moving to Southern California where she lives with her husband and two children.

When she's not writing she loves to spend time with her family, traveling or just enjoying a night at home. One thing you might notice in her books is her love for the four seasons. Growing up on the east coast of Canada the change in the seasons is in her blood and is often mentioned in her writing.

Her books can be found in different languages around the world.

You can connect with J.L. Drake on Facebook, Instagram, Twitter, BookBub, and Goodreads!

You can also check out her website at www.authorjldrake.com.

Join our Reader Group on Facebook and don't miss out on meeting our authors and entering epic giveaways!

Limitless Reading

Where reading a book
is your first step to becoming
limitless...

LIMITLESS PUBLISHING *Reader Group*

Join today! *"Where reading a book is your first step to becoming limitless..."*

https://www.facebook.com/groups/LimitlessReading/

Made in United States
Orlando, FL
01 August 2022